THE LEANING LAND

Also by Rex Burns, published by Walker and Company

Blood Line

THE LEANING LAND

A Gabe Wager Mystery

REX BURNS

WALKER AND COMPANY
NEW YORK

First published in the United States of America in 1997 by
Walker Publishing Company, Inc.

Published simultaneously in Canada by
Thomas Allen & Son Canada, Limited, Markham, Ontario

Library of Congress Cataloging-in-Publication Data
Burns, Rex.
The leaning land : a Gabe Wager mystery/Rex Burns.
p. cm.
ISBN 0-8027-3306-9
1. Wager, Gabriel (Fictitious character)—Fiction. 2. Police—Colorado—
Denver—Fiction. I. Title.
PS3552.U7325L43   1997
813'.54—dc21   97-3581
CIP

Printed in the United States of America
2 4 6 8 10 9 7 5 3 1

The Leaning Land

1

EARLY MARCH IN Denver is a time when the trees, on one cold and windy day, are still bare with winter, and on the next—though the wind is just as sharp—are suddenly swollen with buds and timid leaves. And everyone shakes their heads at the foolishness of the early bloomers because winter hasn't finished yet and more snow, the heavy, wet, limb-breaking kind, is bound to come.

That thought rode on the others that filled Gabe Wager's mind as he listened to Captain Melrose finish thumbing through the whispery pages of the homicide detective's official life.

"Any personal reasons why you can't leave Denver for a few days, Detective Wager?"

There weren't. No major reason, anyway. Elizabeth wouldn't be overjoyed about it, but she would understand. That was one of the benefits of going with somebody whose professional life demanded as much time as his own: A city-council person understood what it took to do the job.

"All right. Let's talk to the feds."

The captain went to the office door and opened it to lean out; the dark skirt of her uniform emphasized the chunky rear end that tilted toward Wager as she said something to someone. Then she led two men in. Both wore suits, both were in their late forties or early fifties, both had the assurance of people who told a lot of other people what to do. And both carefully sized up Wager.

"This is Detective Sergeant Wager, currently in Homicide. Chief Menzor, Department of Agriculture, who's with the U.S. Forest Service's enforcement section—and Chief Director Leicht, head of the Bureau of Land Management's enforcement operations."

Wager leaned across the small conference table to shake hands with the two feds.

The captain sat with her back to the large window that looked out over the leafless twigs of treetops. "What we talk about here is, of course, confidential." She waited until Wager nodded at the obvious and then turned her eyes to Chief Menzor.

The man's red, fleshy cheeks creased in a brief smile and he leaned forward slightly. "How long have you been in Homicide, Detective Wager?"

"Nine years."

That seemed to make the man happy. "And Captain Melrose tells me you have prior experience working with federal agencies?"

"Yes." Wager couldn't think of any experience that wouldn't be "prior," but he could think of the work piled on his desk. "Why not tell me just what it is you're after. Then I can tell you whether or not I have the background to handle it."

Menzor's eyebrows bounced just enough to imply that he wouldn't take that tone from one of his own people, then he smiled. "Fine with me. Julian?"

The other man, gazing at the tabletop, shrugged one shoulder.

"All right. What we're after is someone with strong investigative experience, especially in homicides, who can talk to locals on and off the Indian reservation. We want somebody who won't be an official representative of the federal government. To be frank, Detective Wager, the federal government has become the—ah—whipping boy for a lot of problems out there. Even our people have become targets. I've had to issue weapons to a number of park rangers in that region for their self-protection, and Julian here's had several of his BLM agents assaulted. One of them was murdered, recently."

"I thought the FBI and Indian police handled crimes on federal land and reservations."

"Yes, in general. And the FBI's been working that end of it on the Squaw Point Reservation, where Julian's BLM agent was killed. But there have been some other problems, too." He paused and looked away, as if reading a list of those problems in his mind. "Much of what we're concerned with has occurred on state land in the La Sal County sheriff's jurisdiction. But liaison there is—ah—spotty. What we need is somebody who seems neutral and who can act as liaison for us. Somebody who doesn't have close ties to any of the agencies involved but who's able to work with all of them, as well as gain the trust of the locals."

"Three federal agencies plus the county sheriff's office? That still sounds like FBI responsibility."

The other man, Leicht, finally spoke up. "Damn well should be. But it looks like the FBI doesn't want to do much anymore. Ruby Ridge—Waco—screwups like that have made those people walk mighty light in the area. They don't want any part of another shoot-out. So the FBI's policy now is to delegate enforcement responsibilities to other involved jurisdictions and limit themselves to technical support only." Leicht snorted. "They do have one investigator whose primary responsibility is the reservation. Anyway, the result is we've got a goddamn alphabet soup out there, and nobody comfortable working with the other agencies. And don't count on any help from the sheriff's office—not if he thinks you're working for BLM."

"He doesn't have much good to say about the park service, either. But at least he's not shooting at us."

"The sheriff's shooting at you?" Wager asked.

"The bastard would like to," said Leicht. "He's elected by

the ranchers out there, and since they don't get along with BLM, neither does he."

Menzor cleared his throat. "I'm not going to tell you that it's not—ah—dangerous out there, Detective Wager. At least three people have been murdered on government land since the beginning of the year, plus another suspicious death off federal land. We're beginning to wonder if the killings aren't tied together. No evidence that they are, but nothing saying they're not, either. That would be your principal assignment: Determine if the deaths are related, and—ah—sort of coordinate the efforts of the several agencies. Bring together what the several jurisdictions have learned about the cases. Frankly, it's a mess, and given the—ah—political realities, you'd be pretty much on your own among a lot of citizens who won't want to tell you much." He paused and glanced at Captain Melrose.

That was her cue. "What do you think, Detective Wager? Are you still interested?"

Wager nodded. "I am."

WAGER LATER TOLD Elizabeth as much as security allowed. She stared at him across the oversized platter with its little piles of artfully arranged green and orange vegetables, pilaf mounded into a seashell pattern, barbecued and lightly glazed chicken. "Two to four weeks?" Against the burst of laughter from a nearby table, her voice sounded faint.

"It came up all of a sudden—they told me about it this morning."

"When do you leave?"

"Tomorrow."

"Oh." Then, "Will you be able to call me?"

He nodded. "I can't say when. I won't find out what's involved until I get out there, but I'll be in touch." He added, "I'll

be working with the FBI and some other federal agencies."
She cut a small piece from the chicken.

"It won't take that long."

"You'll do a good job."

She was making some connection there, but he wasn't quite sure what it was. "What's the latest on the Downtown Development Committee?" It was a clumsy attempt to change the subject, but she accepted it.

"The Cultural and Entertainment Center's financial report finally came in. McGraw tried to hide as much as he could, but it still looks pretty bad."

Weldon McGraw chaired the city council's Downtown Development Committee. Liz was the vice-chair. She had once told Wager that her main job was to keep a lid on the number of sweetheart deals McGraw made on public-private enterprises. The Cultural and Entertainment Center was a good example of what could go wrong. Most of its funding had been provided by the taxpayers of the city and county of Denver through bonds underwritten by the building's projected value plus a percentage of the entry and concessions fees. An unpublicized clause in the contract promised the private investors an exemption from payments out of those fees if the center's profits fell below a certain level. Now, predictably, the entry and concessions income was falling short of the initial rosy estimates.

Wager scraped at his rice and tried to make a joke. "Old McGraw have anything to do with Denver International Airport?"

"No, but he's been making up for it ever since."

At last month's committee meeting, Liz had moved for an evaluation of the entertainment center's operations by the county assessor's office, but McGraw had ruled the motion out of order. So it looked like the city budget would have to absorb bond payments that should have come from the profits the private investors claimed they weren't making.

"And those same investors are talking now about developing

a riverfront entertainment area along the South Platte. Opening up restaurants and an aquarium, water sports, music venues, whatever."

"Paid for by the city?"

She nodded. "Another 'public-private partnership.' It's Ronald Pyne and his gang, again." A wry smile twisted the corner of her mouth. "He's calling it the Weldon F. McGraw River Park Project. If nothing else, you have to admire the man's gall."

There was nothing illegal in the name or the deal, if the city approved it. But it made Wager grateful that he was working Homicide. At least with murder, the fact, if not the degree, of guilt was a lot clearer than it was in city politics.

Liz suddenly asked, "Do you know Evelyn Litvak?"

"The state representative?" Wager shook his head. "Only by name. Why?"

"One of her committee assignments is state waterways, and I had a meeting with her the other day about Pyne's newest boondoggle. While we talked, the poor thing broke down crying."

Wager waited for Liz to tell him why.

"Her ex is suing for sole custody of their daughter. He claims Evelyn can't be a state representative and a parent, too."

"What's he, a house husband?"

"Rancher. Recently remarried. He and his new wife can offer the girl a more stable home life, he says. He also says he doesn't want his daughter going to school in Denver."

Depending on the school, the man might have a point. "How old is the girl?"

"Six. Evelyn says the hearing is scheduled for three weeks from now and she's absolutely distraught."

Liz didn't consider herself a feminist—at least that's what she repeated to Wager. But she did want equal and fair treatment for everyone—regardless of gender, race, ethnicity, religion, sexual orientation, and all the other terms of political identification. It was only fair, she argued, that human rights should be applicable to all humans, an attitude that, in Colorado state politics, marked her as a raving liberal. Wager didn't see why Liz or anyone else got all fired up over the idea; as far as he was concerned, the crooks he caught were equally guilty despite their gender, race, ethnicity, etc., etc. But he didn't quite understand why Liz was telling him about Evelyn Litvak. "Has she asked you for some kind of help?"

"No—she just needed to talk with someone and I happened to be there. But La Sal County is in her district. Didn't you say that's where you're going?"

He nodded. "Part of the Squaw Point Reservation's there. It goes along the line into eastern Utah, too."

"I thought so. It's where her husband's ranch is. It just made me think of her—and of how angry I got when she told me about it."

"What does her daughter want?"

"To stay with her mother. But the court may decide she's too young to have a considered opinion. Certainly Evelyn's worried about it. She says her husband is very vindictive and doesn't want their daughter as much as he wants to hurt Evelyn for daring to divorce him." Liz tilted her wineglass and looked at the pale yellow light filtered by its contents. "Now that he's remarried, he has a strong claim. He says he doesn't want his daughter to be another latchkey kid."

And her ex had everything to win and nothing to lose by trying. Wager's ex would have had no trouble claiming any children they might have had, either. But Wager, given the kind of life he led, would not have fought it. There would have been no point. He was just grateful that children had not suffered his marriage or his divorce. And, besides, Lorraine hated him enough by herself without having to hate him on behalf of any children, too. "Well, good luck to her. But I don't expect to be seeing any state representatives or their exes where I'm going."

"No," said Liz. "I suppose not."

2

BELOW, THE AIRPLANE'S tiny black shadow rippled across an earth that looked like treeless and rutted mud. In shades of red and yellow and gray, it was an alluvial expanse that spread out and away from the snow-covered clusters of mountain ranges and pine-shaded plateaus of west-central Colorado. Here and there dirt roads scratched straight lines through the thin covering of sagebrush and scattered piñon; the occasional ranch was a convergence of wavering cattle trails and splotches of bare, churned earth that surrounded water tanks and weathered roofs. The writhing beds of gulches and washes carved by seasonal streams were marked by tongues and ripples of dry sand; the larger canyons were abrupt crevices where, in the shadowed bottoms, pools winked with reflected sky.

It didn't look much different from the ground, except that the scattered mountaintops, hanging just above the flat horizons, were hazy with the blue and silver of distance, and you couldn't see the sudden chasms and gorges sliced by the occasional small river.

Despite the thin streak of heat waves that rippled at the rim of the wide earth, the late-morning air still had the bite of early spring and high altitude, and Wager was glad for his old denim jacket, taut across his shoulders. Joining the half-dozen other passengers, Wager had trailed across the tarmac to the flat-roofed airport with its stubby control tower at one end. From another door flanked by plate-glass windows, a second small line of passengers toted their hand luggage toward the idling airplane. When it took off on the return to Denver—with stops at Durango, Alamosa, and Trinidad—the runway would be empty of everything except wind and an occasional tumbleweed, and the dozen or so small planes tied down on the apron near a quiet maintenance hangar.

"Officer Wager"? A heavyset man whose bowed, thick legs made him even shorter than Wager aimed his reflecting sunglasses Gabe's way. The man wore sharply pressed khaki trousers and a forest green Ike jacket with leather trim at the pockets and leather patches on the elbows. He had a bolo tie with a turquoise slide that contrasted with the tan of his shirt, and although he was hatless, the span of white flesh at the top of his forehead said he usually wore one. He didn't wear a badge that Wager could see, but everything else about him said "Law Officer." "I'm Don Henderson." A thick-fingered hand tested the strength of Wager's grip. "Glad to meet you. Got any other bags?"

When Wager said no, Henderson offered to carry the clothes bag and led him around the sand-colored building to the airport's parking lot and an unmarked sedan whose very plainness said it was government issue. Then they were in the vehicle and pulling north onto a vacant highway. It pointed like an arrow towards a horizon that stretched, unbroken, between the distant glimmering peaks of two mountain ranges. The man finally cleared his throat before asking, "Your people over in Denver tell you what it's all about?" Henderson's voice had a nasal twang that Wager guessed was Oklahoma or maybe east Texas.

"Just that you wanted somebody new to the area. I was told I'd find out the rest from you. What agency are you with?"

"Bureau of Land Management."

That surprised Wager. "I thought you'd be FBI."

"You'll meet him, too. That's where I'm taking you to. But

I'm BLM—I'm their enforcement officer for this sector, and I'll be honest with you, Officer Wager. I haven't had experience with homicides before—the FBI handles those, regularly." The muscles in the heavy jaw tightened. "But that's what we're talking about here, outright murder. Sons of bitches have killed two good men—both of them real decent$human beings."

"Is this about narcotics? People growing pot on Forest Service land?"

The large head wagged. "Wish it was that simple. Tell you true, I ain't sure what all it's about. I ain't sure Special Agent Douglas D. Durkin knows what it's about, either." As if the mention of the FBI agent's name reminded him of something, Henderson steered with one hand while he fished in his breast pocket for his badge and pinned it on his shirt. "That there's my disguise: take my badge off," he said and laughed. "Hell, nobody in Montezuma County knows me, anyway, but Chief Leicht told me this here's real secret-agent stuff."

"Sure fooled me," said Wager. He leaned to glance in the paddle mirror on the rider's side of the car. The road behind was an empty notch of dwindling asphalt. "Anything at all you can tell me?"

"I can tell you it don't seem to be dope growers. Nor it don't seem to be the dog food people rounding up wild burros and horses—there's no sign of that kind of activity anywheres. And it ain't oil or gas theft—there's no wells up there. What it is, is murders. One of our USGS contract geologists, Buck Holtzer, was bushwhacked near the end of January, for no reason on earth that we been able to find out. Somebody just shot him, maybe because he was driving a government car. And the latest murder, just last week, was one of our agents, Larry Kershaw. Shot in the back—a damn good man. Family man, and I tell you I'm still tore up over it. I figure we just flat-out got some crazies that's got it in for any and all federal agencies. That's my opinion, anyway. Neither me nor Durkin's had a damn bit of luck trying to find out who, but by God we got our suspicions. You got reciprocal jurisdiction in La Sal County, right?"

"Yes. But I've been told the sheriff hasn't been too cooperative."

"You been told right. Was I you, I wouldn't even let the son of a bitch know I was working out here. Especially you don't want to do it if he thinks you're working with me. Not unless you like being treated worse than a skunk with rabies."

Wager didn't have much choice about that. "What about his deputies? Any help there?"

"He owns his deputies; there's not many ways to get a paycheck in La Sal County, and they know it. We tried—God knows we done our best to work with the man. But we don't bring in any votes for Sheriff Spurlock."

"He knows who killed your people?"

Another wag of the head. "I don't know about that. He might. Main thing is, he hasn't been too eager about helping us, and even now with this latest killing, he's dragging his goddamn feet. He doesn't want his constituents to think he likes working with the FBI or BLM, and he owes his job to them, not to us." The highway made a rare swerve, dipping to a worn and age-yellowed concrete bridge that spanned a sharp gash in the earth. Only a trickle of water darkened the sandy bed down among the tamarisk and willow branches. In a few weeks, when the distant snows began melting and thunderstorms pelted the surrounding red clay, the gully would fill with churning orange floods of mud-thick water. Then, after a couple of hours, the water would be gone and the fragile, bright flowers of the high desert would fade back into dead-looking weeds. Henderson guided the car up a low ridge and into the converging lines of the highway beyond. "Lots of the ranchers around here hate our guts. Say we're taking their grazing land away from them."

"It's not theirs."

"True. But they been using it for a long time. And now that

the government's trying to increase the grazing fees and regulate use . . . Well, they say we're putting them out of business and out of their homes."

Wager remembered what Chief Menzor had said. But he didn't have an answer. The land belonged to the government, not to the ranchers; but most of it was too poor and dry for anything except raising cows. Without the use of a lot more land than they could afford to buy, the ranchers couldn't make a living from their cattle; and without the cattle-grazing fees, the land wouldn't make any money for the government. "What about the reservation? I was told there was a murder there recently, too."

"Yeah, that was early February. An Indian. That's Special Agent D. D. Durkin's problem, though, and he'll likely tell you about that." The man shook his head. "But Durkin don't seem too excited about that one. It looks like a routine drunk fight and it don't fit his theory."

"What's his theory?"

"I better let him explain all that. He's kind of touchy, and he'll get worse if he thinks I been putting words in his mouth."

After another half hour, Henderson slowed to turn off the pavement onto a dirt road. Equally straight, it rose and fell across the rippled earth toward the glimmer of a single snowy peak that seemed to be fifty miles distant. Wager, listening to the occasional rock thrown up to thump against the car's undercarriage, studied the spread of flat earth tufted with knee-high sagebrush, smaller tufts of wiry grass, an occasional big-eared cactus or narrow-leaved yucca plant. Between weedy clumps, the red-brown dirt looked like the cracking bed of a dry lake; contorted fissures opening blackly in the clay, slabs of earth curled up at the edges in waterless agony. Narrow, windblown tongues of sand formed rippled streaks here and there, and worn shoulders of rock rose up where the sand had blown away. Except for the occasional flicker of a startled bird, there appeared to be no life at all on the heat-shimmered flats. But of course there was. It was just the kind of life that relied on sharp eyesight and camouflage for protection, on speed for the hunt—and on greater speed for the escape. It was a manner of survival, Wager thought, that anybody out here might be wise to adopt.

"There he is." Henderson nodded toward the quivering glint of afternoon sunlight on a distant windshield. It turned out to be a pickup truck painted in the pale green shade of government issue and pulled to the side of a wider stretch of road. "Douglas D. Durkin, special agent. And he's a pistol." The deputy's heavy jaw wagged. "Yessir, he is a pistol."

The pistol was a silhouette in the truck's cab until Henderson's vehicle pulled to a halt in a wind-tossed swirl of dust. Then the agent stepped out to nod at Henderson and to study Wager flatly for a long moment before he made up his mind about whatever he was wondering. Taller than Wager and Henderson, Durkin looked half as heavy and half as old, though he tried to give more weight to his boyish face with a thick brown mustache that curved around the corners of his mouth. He did not smile, but he did hold out a hand. "Detective Wager? Agent Durkin." There was no warmth in the businesslike handshake. "I appreciate your taking the time to work with us."

"A pleasure," said Wager just as insincerely. He had an image of two strange cats studying each other over a safe distance, tails twitching with tension and suspicion.

"I understand that officially you're supposed to be working on this by yourself, Detective Wager. Through the—what do you call it, the Colorado Bureau of Investigation?"

Wager nodded. "CBI, that's right."

"CBI. Right." A wag of his head said what he thought of amateurs who relied on important-sounding initials to substitute for the extensive training that real professionals received. "Well, I also understand that your independent status is supposed to make you more palatable to the local yokels. That it's supposed to make them open up to you. Frankly, I think you're going to be wasting your time, but this little plan wasn't my idea and nobody asked me." Another wag of his head for the inexplicable stupidity of superiors. "From this point in time, we'll use the telephone to exchange information. Any other personal meetings you and I have will be damn rare and clandestine. So don't be afraid to ask your questions at this briefing, because you'll be pretty much on your own after this."

"If I decide to take the job."

The man's eyes widened briefly. "If you decide to take it?"

"It's my decision, Special Agent Durkin. That's what I was told: Come out here, get a read on the assignment, and make up my mind about it."

The man's lips puffed out with a long exhale. He scuffed an expensive Gore-Tex hiking boot in the soil and glanced at the Forest Service man. "Christ, Henderson—a prima donna. I guess that's what we get when we work with local agencies: prima donnas. All right," he leaned forward as if to challenge Wager, "you can decide whether or not to take it. No skin off my nose either way. See if this makes up your mind for you: We've lost two BLM employees so far. One an agent, the other a civilian with Interior—a contract scientist doing some work for the Geological Survey. The civilian didn't have a damn thing to do with investigation or enforcement or anything remotely threatening to anyone—he just happened to be out by himself on BLM land over near the north side of the reservation. Bastards gut-shot him and crippled his vehicle and left him to die. The medical examiner said that chore probably took about fifteen hours." He added, "Toward the end, it must have hurt like hell because the man finally used a pocketknife to cut his own wrists and hurry things along."

Henderson said, "That was Buck Holtzer. Real nice young man. Lived up near Grand Junction."

"The BLM agent was murdered last week," said Durkin. "He was out on BLM land near Many Goats Canyon and somebody shot him in the back."

"That's the other one I was telling you about," said Henderson. "Larry Kershaw. I met his wife and two kids at the funeral down in Cortez three days ago, and I ain't got over feeling sick about it yet. Real nice folks. There was no reason at all for anybody to do something like that to him or to them. Two little boys, one eight, the other six."

"Same weapon?"

Durkin had the answer to that. "No. Both thirty-thirties, but different barrels."

"Do you know what either of them was looking for?"

The FBI agent eyed Wager with something like real interest. "Good question. What did you find out about Holtzer, Henderson?"

"Not much. Holtzer was probably out there on government business; he was driving a USGS four-by." The man nodded toward Durkin's government issue four-wheel-drive pickup. "But it's hard to say because the kind of project he was working on was a part-time contract: collecting long-term erosion data. Every now and then he'd drive all over BLM properties and measure erosion, which is why he was assigned a government truck. Anyway, he was found way over near Narraguinnep Wash. Some of it's BLM land, some of it's private, and most of it's reservation. Just a bunch of broken country and not much ranching—and he didn't leave any notes, so we don't know for sure if it was his own business or government business he was on. Larry Kershaw was just on routine patrol, as far as we know—keeping an eye on things, you know." He explained to Wager, "We since tightened up on patrol procedures for our personnel: Travel in pairs when possible—which ain't often, given we only got two hundred and fifty field officers to cover two hundred and seventy million acres spread across every state in the union. And always leave information about where you're going and why you're going there. The regular BLM personnel in this region's been issued radios, too, but you get down in some of these canyons and they're about as useful as a flashlight to a blind man."

"We also had another death close to three weeks ago," said Durkin. "We lost an informant. I don't know if it was a screwup on his part or the result of a leak in the local sheriff's office. I wouldn't put it past Spurlock, that asshole."

"Spurlock's the sheriff?"

"He's the one. We found the informant's body near the east side of the reservation in Squaw Canyon—but the animals hadn't left enough of it for us to determine the manner of death. No bullet holes in what parts of him we could find, and the local coroner hasn't been able to determine cause, so it's just listed as suspicious. By God, I'm suspicious, all right."

"The coroner? So the death didn't take place on federal land?"

"The body wasn't found on federal land. It was found beside a state highway, so that one belongs to the sheriff. And one of Spurlock's men was his contact, too: Deputy Howard Morris. At that time, I was instructed to go by the book—I was to advise the local authorities that I was working in the area, and get their involvement in the case in a manner that would not—ah—inhibit my own activities. Using one of the sheriff's men for contact with the confidential informant seemed the most efficacious way." Durkin's gray eyes shifted to Henderson. "You told Wager he can't rely on the local sheriff's office, right?"

"I told him."

"What was your CI looking for?"

Durkin started to speak but thought better of it, a tight little smile on his lips. "You know as much as you need to know if you pull out of this assignment. What's it going to be? And, Wager, it really makes no difference to me either way."

The two men who had interviewed Wager said only that three men had died in the last three months. They had said nothing about one of them being an informant. That was a lot more serious for what it implied about the killers' motives and the degree of threat for law enforcement officers. Captain Melrose hadn't said anything, either. Maybe she hadn't known. Then again, maybe she had, and that was why her final words to Wager had emphasized that it would be up to him to decide if he wanted to go through with it after he talked with the case agent. If so, she also probably figured he wouldn't be likely to make the long trip out to the western slope for nothing. "I'm in."

Durkin shrugged. "OK. His name was Rubin Del Ponte—half-breed, quarter-breed, something like that. Enough to have a lot of contacts among the Indians on the Squaw Point Reservation, anyway. What he was looking for was some kind of linkup between a survivalist group called the Constitutional Posse, and somebody on the reservation.

"If he found out anything, he didn't have a chance to report to me. And if he said anything to his contact in the sheriff's office, that bastard hasn't passed it on."

Henderson snorted. "Whoever it was has made it pretty damn clear they're after government personnel. They not only killed Holtzer and Kershaw and probably Del Ponte, but they've bombed a couple of BLM vehicles, too. Three in the last month."

"Same day of the week?"

"No—as far as we know, it's not some kind of anniversary thing. And I got to tell you, our people are nervous as all hell."

Wager asked Durkin, "Why do you suspect a link between this survivalist group and the reservation?"

"Something I've been following ever since Holtzer's death—rumors of some kind of deal developing between people on and off the reservation." Durkin wagged his head once. "I haven't found out anything definite yet, but that's when the bombings started. And then Kershaw was killed. And then Del Ponte himself."

"No clues at all? Nobody talking?"

"Not to me." Durkin glared at Wager as if to say nobody would talk to him, either.

"I was told there were three confirmed murders. That does not include Del Ponte's death?"

"Not confirmed, no. Whoever told you that was probably thinking of Lawrence, Walter Lawrence. An Indian killed a month ago on the reservation. That's the case I'm primarily assigned to, and to direct and provide technical assistance in the investigations of the Holtzer and Kershaw deaths. That's Henderson, here. But I don't have any evidence that Walter Lawrence's death is in any way related to these other two." Another shrug. "In fact, Del Ponte told me that he heard it was just another Saturday night stabbing over some long-standing quarrel. And I haven't found any reason to think otherwise. And no link with Del Ponte's death. Neither we nor the tribal police have found out anything more about it . . . not that the tribal police are much help"

"They don't like you, either?"

"It's not that—and believe it or not, we haven't made enemies out of everybody around here, Detective Wager. But the tribal police just aren't trained for criminal investigation—they handle parking and traffic offenses, a little security and crowd control, but nothing in the felony line. I use them for eyes and ears on the reservation, and that's about it."

"You're the only FBI man working these cases?"

"Yes. The bureau—ah—has been instructed to keep a very low profile on this. Keep your distance, so to speak, until we have enough definitive information for a four-square case. That's your job, Wager: to get me some goddamn information."

Wager studied the faint wink of the snowy peak on the horizon. Despite the half-hour drive down the dirt road, the mountain had moved no closer. Maybe it was a hundred miles away—a hundred and fifty, perhaps.

What Durkin was talking about was the muzzle that had

been slapped on the FBI since the so-called siege at Ruby Ridge up in Idaho and the Branch Davidian slaughter in Waco, Texas—two bloody eruptions of mismanagement and death that had cost a lot of civilians their lives and, more important, government agents their careers. Wager guessed that the FBI's directorate had decided to move very cautiously in any future operations that might lead to another shoot-out, especially if there was any suspicion of the involvement of local survivalist groups. So the tactic now was to place a buffer between the FBI agents and any activity having the possibility of a lethal confrontation—someone to take the blame or deflect criticism if things got out of hand. And since Durkin's first buffer, the sheriff, was not too cooperative, and his second, a civilian informant working through the sheriff's office, had not worked out too well, someone behind a desk somewhere had come up with the idea of recruiting a regional law enforcement officer to be the new buffer. Hello, Wager.

"What about the Drug Enforcement Agency or the Bureau of Alcohol, Tobacco and Firearms? They have any people assigned to this?"

"No." At the sound of those agencies' names, Durkin tried to look as if he hadn't bitten into something sour. "As far as we know, there are no drug-related offenses. And despite the bombings, BATF hasn't expressed an official interest yet."

These two other federal agencies had operatives who had been involved in various incidents, up to and including no-knock raids that tore up the wrong addresses, and agents getting into drunken brawls in rural taverns. It was a careless and ill-disciplined use of force that Wager, an ex-Marine, especially despised because it reflected badly on all competent lawmen. At its worst, the lack of discipline resulted in such corruptions as the poorly officered Ohio National Guard shooting students at Kent State; at its least dangerous, it meant that evidence was obtained illegally and thrown out of court during trial. Equally bad was the credence it gave so-called militias and survivalists who saw the federal government and—by extension—all law officers as agents of the New Evil Empire out to destroy American Freedoms.

"I'm in, Durkin. I said I would be, and I am. But I was told to make it clear that I'm neutral. I am not Officer Henderson's man. Or Sheriff Spurlock's. Or yours. Like you said, I'll be working on my own and I will be supervising coordination between your agencies."

Durkin scratched at one wing of his curving mustache as he studied Wager. "You think you're going to clean this up all by yourself, that it?"

"No. I think I'm going to try and help you people work together whether you want to or not. And we'll start off this way: From now on, I am the liaison between federal and state enforcement, including the sheriff's office. If you have information, you feed it to me; if I develop information myself or through the sheriff's office, I give it to you. It'll be a two-way trade."

"A trade."

Wager nodded. "If you have trouble with that, say so now."

"Any and every federal agency has seniority over local law enforcement, Wager."

"Not over me, they don't. My chain of command's to the state of Colorado."

"I can pull your chain as well as your goddamn federal authorization."

"You can if you have cause. And you can try it if you don't have cause. But if that's what you do, you'll want to give your chief in the Denver office a damn good explanation for your failure to work with me. Because I won't have any hesitation about filing official complaints—local and national—that describe you as being uncooperative with state enforcement personnel. And they will be filed through the state of Colorado's congressional representatives who, I have been informed by

Captain Melrose, are personally interested in the outcome of this investigation."

In the silence, Henderson, too, stared at Wager. The silvered lenses of his sunglasses hid his eyes, but his open lips signaled his surprise.

Durkin drew a long, slow breath and shifted his angry gaze to the heat-paled sky, to some distant spot on the unbroken horizon. It was finally that spot he spoke to. "I'll work with you, Wager. I've been ordered—as you obviously know—to work with you, so I'll by God do what I'm ordered. But I don't think you are going to be worth a shit around here. I don't think you're going to do a damn thing except screw up my investigation. But you go ahead and do your thing. And be sure to remember what I said: You are on your own. You can work on your own, and by God, you can die on your own."

3

HENDERSON DIDN'T SAY much until he had pulled his vehicle back onto the paved highway and the rumble and thud of the rough dirt road had changed to the high whine of tires. "Agent Douglas D. Durkin figures anybody's not with him has got to be against him."

"He ought to figure we're all on the same side."

The man's big head nodded once and he kept his eyes on the road. "Be nice if you can make Sheriff Spurlock see it that way."

"Yeah, that's true." A quarter mile away through shoulder-high brush, a flash of bobbing white indicated the backside of a startled pronghorn antelope. Wager made out, running with it, two or three other bounding, earth-colored shapes that quickly disappeared. "I take it you're working with Durkin?"

A grunt of some kind. "You got a little more independence than I do. Durkin tells me to jump, I got to ask, 'How high?' " He glanced at Wager. "FBI's got general authorization from Congress to direct operations in any joint enforcement undertakings involving BLM. That was the payoff to the FBI for letting Interior organize its own enforcement branch a few years back, and like I told you, I got no experience working a homicide. Plus, the FBI's also got control of the technical side of things. What that means is all fingerprint ID, forensic science requests, and everything else the FBI labs at Quantico can do for us have to be sent through a regional FBI liaison if we want priority service.

"Usually, it's pretty routine: We fill out a request and an agent rubber-stamps it and sends it on to be handled like a bureau item. But it doesn't have to work that smooth, and if we get into a pissing contest, it's not going to." He fell silent while the car's wheels danced across a stretch of frost-broken pavement and deep potholes caused by late winter runoff. "I forgot to tell you, even some of the routine stuff—fingerprint traces, blood and tissue samples—can take six months or more if they aren't given priority. And anything special, like chemical traces or fabric samples, can take up to a year or more."

He didn't have to tell Wager. It was why the Denver Police Department and a lot of other police departments used the FBI labs as seldom as possible.

"And there's one more thing: Federal judges tend to pay more attention to us if the FBI joins our requests for legal action. That means a lot quicker issue of warrants, subpoenas, that kind of crap."

"So what are you left to do on your own?"

"General security for BLM properties. Look for people stealing gas or oil from any wellheads on BLM land. Count cow populations for overgrazing and keep an eye out for rustlers working BLM land. Search for marijuana patches and meth labs. We do manage to find things to keep busy with, Wager."

"Poachers?"

"Not directly. The law enforcement section of Fish and Wildlife has that job—they're Department of Interior people, too, but they're independent of BLM. But there's only twenty-four of those agents to cover the north-central region—eight Rocky Mountain and prairie states, so we do keep our eyes open and call them if we see something."

"And you haven't investigated homicides?"

Henderson shook his head. "Nope. Not until now. That's one of the areas the FBI kept to itself, which has always been fine with me. But you heard what Durkin said—he's directing and advising, now, and I'm the one's supposed to do the investigating. Plus, one victim was working for the USGS and the other was a BLM agent, so we got a sort of vested interest in both cases. Which Durkin don't like particularly, but Chief Leicht said it's good for BLM morale to show we're part of the hunt for the bastards, and somehow he got the FBI regional director to go along with it. So now me and Durkin got us an officially sanctioned cooperative effort."

"It's good for morale?"

"Not as good as not getting shot, I grant you. But Kershaw was one of our people, Wager. You don't just hand something like that over to somebody else."

He could understand Henderson's point. More than once, when a metro police unit in the Denver area closed in on a cop killer, they had turned the actual arrest over to officers from the dead man's district. It wasn't just courtesy—it was a way of bringing some kind of balance to the injured department, an evening up of the score.

Henderson cleared his throat. "Tell you true, I'd just as soon leave the whole thing to you because I know damn well you know more about homicide investigations than I do. So you sort of run your own investigation, OK? I'll sort of poke around where I know I won't screw anything up, and help out when you need me, but as far as I'm concerned, you get a free field."

Wager nodded. It was what he intended anyway. "Do you think the militia group's involved, too?"

Henderson considered before answering. "Well, they have made a lot of noise about defending their rights against the federal government. And where there's smoke, there's fire, you know? But Durkin hasn't told me he's got any concrete evidence—that's one of the things Del Ponte was supposed to find out: if anybody in the group said anything about the killings. That, and if the Constitutional Posse really was trying to branch out onto the reservation."

"Why would they do that?"

"Don't know if or why. Just that the killings and one of the bombings took place on or near the reservation. No killings up in the mountains in the eastern part of the county or on the Uncompahgre Plateau up north, not yet, anyway. But we did have two vehicle bombings in the national forest land east of La Sal township."

"How much has Sheriff Spurlock been dragging his feet on this?"

"Well, since Kershaw and Holtzer were killed on federal land, and that's not Spurlock's jurisdiction, he hasn't been all that involved in those investigations. But Durkin did ask him for any information he might come up with on them, and Spurlock says he don't have none. My guess is, even if he did know something, he wouldn't be likely to give it to us if it might cause any trouble for somebody he knows. The Del Ponte death is the one Spurlock's really dragging his feet on."

"Where was he killed?"

"Alongside State Road 181, down in Squaw Canyon. That's where he was found, anyway. About a mile and a half before you reach the reservation."

"He might have been killed somewhere else and dumped there?"

"Couldn't tell. He's the one the animals got to before we did."

Wager remembered. "So it could have been natural causes?"

"Could. Or couldn't. Ruled a suspicious death."

Which was the normal label for a death that had not been sworn to by a doctor or coroner as natural. The location of the corpse made Spurlock the primary investigator on that one—his jurisdiction, his case—despite Del Ponte being an informant for the FBI. It also sounded like the case that could provide Wager with the clearest legal basis for his own involvement. "He's not copying you on his reports?"

"Hasn't yet. Far as I know, he's not doing enough work to

generate any reports. Moreover, the state district attorney just shrugs and says it's the sheriff's job and there's no evidence it was a homicide, and even if it is, there's no statute of limitations in Colorado for filing charges on a homicide, so there's no rush either way."

"Are you saying 'cover up'?"

"No. No, I'm not accusing anybody of that, so don't go saying I am. All I am saying is that Sheriff Spurlock is taking his own sweet time about doing anything, and what little he has done, he's not telling us about. Just why he's moving so slow is something else, and I don't make any guesses as to that."

"What's his name? The DA?"

"Medina. Betty Medina. She's down in Montezuma County but acts for La Sal county, too. There's not enough people in La Sal County to support a DA's office. Hardly enough to pay for their own sheriff's office, and was I Spurlock I'd worry about any one of my taxpayers getting killed off."

Talking to the DA would mean going back to Cortez, the Montezuma County seat. Wager might get by with a phone call and save that long trip—depending on what he would have to ask District Attorney Medina. And how he might have to ask it. Some things, like a person's eyes, you just couldn't read over a telephone. "There's a Colorado Highway Patrol office in Dry Creek, isn't there?"

"I think so, yeah. But they're not involved in any of this. Thank God. All we need's another agency to cooperate with."

"Just drop me off there; they're supposed to have a vehicle for me," Wager said.

A COURIER HAD driven it down from the state motor pool branch in Grand Junction. As plain as Henderson's federal vehicle, the state vehicle was a dull-white Plymouth Caravelle with official Colorado license plates and antennae mounted on the roof and on the slope of the rear deck. The boxy sedan's engine was still making little noises as it cooled from the long run along State 141.

"You want to sign this, Officer Wager?" Trooper Shonsey held out a Bic pen. Its point hovered over the line for "Receipt of Vehicle." He was lean and tall and his uniform had been tailored to fit snugly and without wrinkling. It reminded Wager of the skintight khaki uniform shirts he'd invested in when he'd finished boot camp. The Marine Corps' regulation issue, given his wide shoulders and short legs, looked baggy on him, so he'd had his shirts tailored. Along with the modifications to his dress blues, it had cost him almost a month's pay, and he'd only had a chance to wear the dress uniform for two weeks on leave before being sent to the Pacific. But he could remember the special feel of that stiff blue cloth with its scarlet-and-gold PFC stripe on the sleeve, and the sliver glitter of the expert marksmanship badges on his chest. He would, though he didn't know it then, soon rate cheery little campaign ribbons to place above those badges. That spasm of vanity had cost a lot, but it had been worth it.

"I got the keys right here, soon as you sign."

Wager traded his name for the keys strung together with a paper identification tag and asked the trooper for the local radio channels used by police and emergency units. "Do you work closely with Sheriff Spurlock?"

"Close? No—not unless it's a pursuit or a road block. Sometimes a medical call. My job's the state and federal highways, he covers the county roads."

"How about Deputy Morris? Do you know him?"

"Howie? Sure. Lives over near Egnarville. That's in his sector: southwest corner of the county. Sector four."

Wager placed the town on the Colorado highway map he held in his memory. It wasn't difficult because in this part of the state there weren't many dots with names to them. "It's near the reservation?"

"Squaw Point Reservation, yeah. About eight miles."

"Did you work on that body they found out there?"

"Del Ponte? I answered the call along with the sheriff's office—it was a state highway they found him on. But Howie and the SO cleared the scene. The death didn't involve a vehicle, so the only part I had was traffic control: a pick-up truck and two stray cows. Couple of nosy rabbits."

Wager wasn't certain if the man was joking, but he didn't see anything funny in it. "Have you worked closely with any of the FBI or BLM agents?"

"Not closely or otherwise." Shonsey carefully filed the vehicle release form in a manila folder and slid a metal drawer closed. "But you ought to know, Officer Wager, there's some hard feelings around here toward federal agents. That was Henderson who dropped you off, wasn't it? The BLM man?"

Wager nodded.

"Well, it doesn't matter to me either way. But like I say, people here don't put any trust in anything to do with the federal government."

"That includes Sheriff Spurlock?"

"Matter of fact, it does. He and that FBI agent—Durbin? Durman?—traded some hard words. The way Spurlock tells it, he and Henderson came in here from Denver or Washington, D.C., or somewhere and begun to tell Spurlock how to run his county and what he should do on the Del Ponte case and I don't know what all. The upshot was one hell of an argument, I understand, and Spurlock told both of them he didn't want to see either of their ugly faces in his office again. Ever. So if you're thinking of getting some help from the SO, you might want to think twice about palling around with Henderson anymore."

"I'll remember that."

A shrug. "Like I say, it doesn't make any difference to me—as long as it doesn't have anything to do with the state highways."

4

THE SO DISPATCHER told Wager that Deputy Sheriff
Howie Morris was on patrol somewhere, out of reach of their
radio equipment. She would have to relay his request to meet
the next time Deputy Morris made his hourly check-in. In theory, "on patrol" could mean anywhere in the approximately 350
square miles that made up the southwest quadrant of La Sal
County and which was Morris's sole responsibility seven days
a week, twenty-four hours a day. Studying his topo map, Wager
saw that most of the local vehicle lanes in the flat, western edge
of the county were made up of section roads. On the map they
made a dozen or so clusters of short, straight lines and right
angles that tended to end in the dark tan of tightly bunched
contour lines, indicating steep canyon walls and washes impass-
able for vehicles. Three or four of those county roads turned into
stray squiggles that managed to link various clusters together
before they disappeared across the state line into Utah, and a
couple more angled into remoter corners of the Squaw Point
Reservation before stopping. The mountainous, eastern portion
of Morris's quadrant was colored green for national forest land
and was just about empty of any roads at all. Only two paved
highways crossed the western side of the entire county. One was
U.S. 666, which Wager and Henderson had driven up from
Cortez; it angled northwest toward Monticello, Utah. The other

was State Highway 181, which was the main road west from the
county seat of La Sal township, down Squaw Canyon and into
the reservation. Its pavement ended at Dark Mesa Village,
which is where the government offices and the tribal council
center were located. All the other roads on the reservation were
the parallel dashes that indicated unimproved dirt. Along those
two paved highways were three settlements big enough to have
names and to be shown as clusters of tiny black squares marking
the towns' buildings. Two of the towns were in Morris's quadrant, and Wager figured that if he drove slowly along State 181
toward one of the clusters—Egnarville—he would be reasonably close when the man made his hourly contact with the dispatcher.

It was the right idea but the wrong direction. The woman's
voice finally came up on Wager's radio with the message that
Deputy Morris would be waiting for him at the cafe in Gypsum.
Wager acknowledged and turned his vehicle around, heading
back toward U.S. 666 and the second cluster of half a dozen tiny
black squares.

Like the other municipalities of Colorado, this town's name
signs—here mounted back to back on one post—gave Gypsum's elevation rather than its population: 6,843 feet. Wager
guessed the number of people above ground was quite a bit less
than the number of feet above sea level—around 6,800 less. But
even with a population of at most a hundred or so, they didn't
like living too close to each other. Two dirt section roads met
the pavement to form the center of town. On one corner was the
Gypsum Motel and Restaurant, a long two-story rectangle of
pink stucco with a pink neon sign glowing VACANCY. Another
sign said TELEPHONE AND FREE TELEVISION IN EVERY ROOM. A
large receiving dish, angled to the sky and resting in a corner
of the almost vacant gravel parking area beside an empty horse
trailer, said the sign told the truth. Facing the motel from across
the highway was a combination service station and grocery store

whose dusty and sun-bleached false front said MCPHEE'S MAR-
KET. Behind that was a small frame house that must have belonged to McPhee. A two-story redbrick building sat a few yards
down the highway beyond the store. Its lower windows were
covered with irregular sheets of weathered plywood, the upper
windows glassless and black. The only other construction was
a large metal Butler building surrounded by rusting farm ma-
chinery. Someone had printed in black paint the large word
"Welding" halfway across its side. A quarter mile away, tucked
under a fringe of leafless cottonwoods that wandered along a
streambed, were scattered a handful of mobile homes, and beyond them a two-story sandstone ranch house with a stubby silo
and a barn. The rest was flat emptiness dotted with gray-blue
sagebrush and broken by a swell or two of land and the occasional dark blob of a lonely cedar tree. In fact, if he'd wanted to
spend half an hour, Wager could probably have counted each
tree. Over it all was a vast overcast grayness streaked with wind-
sculpted, low-lying clouds that leached color from the afternoon
sun and turned it into a pale white disk that—to Wager, who
was used to the mountains being on Denver's western horizon—
seemed strangely low in the sky.

He stood for a moment beside his car and listened to the
wind. Far off a dog barked. Each yap was separated from the
next by a long pause that accentuated the silence. The loose
collection of weathered buildings, the line of crooked, skinny
telephone poles—black against the gray sky—that paced down
the vacant highway to sag wires to the few roofs, the sandy
footpaths straggling on each side of the highway's frayed asphalt, all spoke of transiency and isolation—as if the wind had
blown these buildings and their people into a loose collection
like trash in a corner, and would, everyone knew, one of these
days blow them all away to leave the high desert empty once
more.

It was an atmosphere of rootlessness, of suspicion toward

community that was far different from that seen in the Anasazi ruins found in the canyons and cliffs of the surrounding deserts. There, the ancient ones had gathered together to share the stone walls and stick-and-clay ceilings that formed their honey-combed villages. They must have been happy to have their fellows busy in the fields around them during the days and gathered close beside the cooking fires in the nights, pleased to share each other's nearness in the small rooms of the pueblos and in the secret wombs of the men's kivas and the ceremonial buildings of the women. It was as if their sense of community—heightened by the boundlessness of canyon and plateau and mesa, where a hunting son or father could vanish into emptiness—had found focus and harmony in building, out of the very earth that supported them, the physical representation of their life together. As if, being so rooted, they might last forever. But of course they hadn't. The wind now blew through the cold and empty fragments of their stone walls just as it swirled around this collection of flimsy and decaying buildings. And that thought made Wager wonder if the Anasazi, too, had had their murderers and thieves, their selfish violators of community. Probably—ancient ones or no, they were human, too. But perhaps, because they valued the community that was so much a part of their collective and individual sense of self, they had fewer violators. Perhaps, because they understood so deeply the threat of the waiting emptiness surrounding them, and the importance of those who joined in creating a place against all that emptiness, they were more civilized.

He sighed and pushed away from the chill metal of the car's fender and through the sticking glass door that opened to the motel's unstaffed reception desk. Filling an alcove between the desk and an open double door leading to the restaurant was a small lounge area with a dimly lit three-stool bar fronted by four or five small tables. It reminded Wager of some of those tiny bars in the Far East, the closet-sized kind that popped up in villages just outside a base's main gate: so cramped that if more than three or four Marines entered, they had to take turns breathing. This one was empty now and had the feeling of usually being that way. The restaurant's blank sterility echoed the surrounding sweep of empty land. A dozen tables were dressed up in red-and-white checkered cloths that tried to bring some warmth; the only other attempt at decoration was a cluster of potted plants in a far corner—the kind with long skinny leaves sprouting at the top of a crooked trunk, and which Wager associated with a dentist's office.

Only one table, set beside the plate-glass windows, was occupied. A thin-shouldered, potbellied man in a western shirt and Levi's stood to shake hands. The chrome badge on his vest pocket said Deputy Sheriff, La Sal County, and the man said "Officer Wager? I'm Howie Morris. Want some coffee?"

Wager nodded yes to the coffee.

"I was about to come out and see if you froze to that car out there."

"Just admiring the scenery."

"Well, we got a lot of that," said Morris. He wagged two fingers toward the open kitchen door. A few seconds later a tall young woman, attractive in a worn but carefully ironed tan waitress uniform that had been tucked and pleated to fit her slim figure, brought out a cup for Wager and a glass pot of steaming black liquid.

"Would you like a refill, Officer Morris?" Her voice was soft, almost shy.

"Sure, honey—just top it off."

She filled Wager's cup, refilled Morris's, and asked, "Anything to eat?"

"Not just now," said Wager. "I'll be needing a room, though."

She looked slightly surprised but nodded her head, the light-brown ponytail bobbing. "Yessir, I'll tell Verdie."

"Verdie's the owner." Morris admired the girl's slender legs as she went back to the kitchen.

"And that's Verdie's daughter?"

"Naw. I don't know that Verdie ever had any kids. Or ever wanted any. Only things Verdie's interested in is this motel and her horses. That's Paula Ree. Her grandpa runs the welding shop, but I think she makes more from Verdie than he does in his business." He winked at Wager. "Verdie pays her pretty good because there's not a cowboy or rancher in the county doesn't come by a couple of times a week for a cup of coffee and to look her over."

"She's very pretty."

"She is that. Plus, there's damn little competition around. A few squaws, if you like 'em darker than Mexicans." He glanced at Wager's face with a twitch of guilt and, after an awkward silence, offered a kind of apology made up of free information. "You wouldn't guess it from her light hair, but Paula's one quarter Indian. Her grandpa on her daddy's side, he was a full-blooded Squaw Point Ute. Came back from serving in Korea and didn't want to live on the reservation anymore. He sold off his share of reservation land or something and used his G.I. Bill to start that garage and welding shop over there back in the mid-fifties. Married a white girl from up around Grand Junction. She died a few years back. They had Paula's pa, George Ree. He hooked up with an eastern girl going to college down in Durango, Shelly something—strawberry blond, which is where Paula gets hers, that and her grandma. She lasted here about five years, then run off somewhere and left George with Paula. Then he run off, too, and left her with the grandpa. But the grandpa's done a pretty good job of raising her when he's not too liquored up; Paula's turned out real good. She's real bright—knows all the regulars by name. Hears a name once, and she knows it. Me, I got to write a name down before I can remember it, and even then I likely forget if I don't use it a lot. What'd you say your name was?" He smiled. "Smith?"

Wager's lips rose and fell in return. With less than five

hundred people scattered over his quadrant, Morris probably used the names enough to remember them. And probably knew the life story of each family for three or four generations back. But Wager's interest was focused on the ones that were more pertinent. "What can you tell me about Del Ponte?"

"Poor old Rubin." He shook his head. "He was a quarter-breed, too. Used to be a member of the reservation tribe but since he was more Mexican than anything else, the government wouldn't recognize him as an Indian anymore. His family buried him over near Manassa where his pa's folks mostly live, Conejos County."

"Do you think he was murdered?"

"No way to tell." He asked a question of his own. "The CBI interested in him? That why they sent you out here?"

"That and to work with the federal agents on their homicides," Wager said.

"You gentlemen need a refill?" The girl, silent in her soft-soled shoes, held the globe of hot coffee over their cups. Wager nudged his toward her. As she poured, Paula told him, "Verdie says to ring the bell when you're ready to register and she'll take care of you. She's in the back."

"OK."

Morris waited until the girl had refilled his cup. "Why'd they send you to work with the feds?"

"Mostly on the chance the Del Ponte case is tied in with the killings they're working on. And because your boss and the federal agencies don't get along."

The deputy's eyes once again followed Paula's legs as she headed back to the kitchen. But his mind was on what Wager had said. "You talked to Sheriff Spurlock yet?"

Wager shook his head. "I plan to tomorrow."

"That FBI man, Durkin, thinks he's pretty hot shit. Henderson might be all right by himself, but he won't wipe his own nose without Durkin lets him." Morris pushed his cup in a tiny circle, sending its muddy coffee swirling almost to the rim.

A gust of wind made the large window quiver and hum, and from its surface—darker, now, and reflecting the restaurant's lights and tables—Wager felt cold air slide down the glass to pool around his ankles. "Was Del Ponte's death tied in any way to the BLM agent's death?"

"Not that I ever heard of."

"You were his contact, weren't you?"

The deputy's eyes, a shade between blue and green, studied Wager. "You already talked to Durkin? That son of a bitch as much as accused me of getting Rubin killed. That what he told you?"

"I'd like to hear what you have to say."

"I say he's full of shit's what I say!"

"What do you think happened to Del Ponte?"

"Could have been anything. Rubin could've asked too many questions or talked to the wrong people about what he was doing. God knows he couldn't keep his mouth shut more'n five minutes—I warned him about that. I think he dropped hints to every son of a bitch and his son-in-law that he was working for the FBI. Made him feel like hot shit, but he wasn't worth a damn as an informant. I told Durkin that." The deputy gulped at his coffee and winced at its heat. "Could've been killed by accident, too—drunk and sleeping on the pavement to keep warm, most likely. Happens all the time with Indians. Or died some other way. Wasn't any evidence of murder."

"He was on foot, alone, a long way from anywhere. No car. Did you find any trace of tire tracks at the scene?"

"No. He'd been there maybe a week or more: rain, wind, animals. Wasn't much left of him, let alone the site. We did pick up a couple of cigarette butts—filter tip. Rubin didn't smoke, but God only knows how long they'd been there. They could as easy been thrown from passing cars. There was nothing more to show anybody else had been around the body."

"What had he been working on?"

"Durkin had him looking into something."

"What?"

Morris leaned back in his chair, its joints making tiny crackling noises that sounded loud in the quiet room. Wager heard a drawer slide shut in the kitchen and the brief hiss of a faucet splash water into a sink. "He probably already told you—his version of it, anyway. I'll tell you mine: Durkin's got a hard-on for this civilian militia a lot of the ranchers belong to. Call themselves the Constitutional Posse. He wanted Rubin to find out if they were meeting with anybody on the reservation."

"Why would they do that?"

"Ask Durkin. It was his idea."

"Did Del Ponte find out anything?"

"Hell, no. Was a damn-fool idea to start with. The ranchers and the Indians mostly don't get along, unless a rancher happens to be a Mormon out to save their souls. Ranchers say the government uses their tax money to give the Indians everything they ask for, and the Indians say the ranchers run their cows on reservation land and take reservation water with their wells."

"Del Ponte told you nothing?"

"Far as I can figure, there's nothing he could've told me that I didn't already know, so I don't think he was killed—if he was killed—for knowing anything dangerous." A snort of disgust. "And like I say, everybody knew he was working for Durkin; a worse goddamn secret informant I couldn't think of!"

"Is this Constitutional Posse a serious threat?"

"Who to? They don't go running around shooting and bombing."

"Somebody is."

Morris considered that. "Well, I don't think it's them doing it, Officer Wager. I know a lot of them—good family men. Hard, by God, working, pay their bills, do the best they can in a hard country that's having hard times. And generally stay out of trouble."

"Can you give me some of their names?"

"It's no secret. Brad Nichols is sort of the organizer—they mostly meet out at his ranch, anyway. And Stan Litvak generally runs the training sessions."

"Who else?"

"Just drive around the county and read the goddamn mailboxes."

"All the ranchers belong?"

"I don't know about all. A hell of a lot of them do."

And probably all voted alike, which would carry a lot of weight with any publicly elected official such as a sheriff. "Did Del Ponte infiltrate them?"

"You sound just like Durkin—infiltrate! He was maybe invited to join them, I don't know. Maybe he even went to a couple of meetings. Hell, everybody over twelve years old they ask to join them. They don't make any secret who they are. Be pretty hard to do around here, anyway. They have monthly training sessions when the weather allows—third weekend of every month, if you're interested in going: weapons familiarization, target practice, survival techniques. And no, Rubin didn't tell me this—he didn't have to. I was told when they invited me to join!"

Wager looked at the narrow-shouldered man. "Are you a member?"

"No. Didn't feel right about joining since I get my money from the government—it's county, but it's government just the same. And, anyway, Sheriff Spurlock said he'd fire me if I did join. Said the deputy's oath doesn't allow membership in any outfits that challenge government, local or federal." He shook his head, voice dropping as the surge of anger passed—or was stifled. "Rubin didn't tell me anything I didn't already know, Officer Wager. That's what I said to Durkin. Told him just what I'm telling you, but the son of a bitch didn't believe me. As much as accused me of getting Rubin killed because I was the contact for that sorry son of a bitch and must have shot my mouth off to somebody about him."

"Who do you think is killing federal agents?"

Morris shook his head. "It might be somebody from around here. Nobody has any cause to love the bastards. But I don't have any suspects, and I don't know anybody crazy enough to shoot them."

"Not even some of the Constitutional Posse?"

The man's jaw worked a time or two before he answered, his words growing heated again. "Whoever it is is working on his own. And that's not saying it's somebody from around here, even. It could be somebody on the reservation, it could be somebody coming in from another county. If it was somebody doing it for the Posse, Wager, I'd've heard about it, because there's not that many people in the county. Tell me, just how close are you working with the FBI and BLM? You taking your orders from Durkin?"

"I'm an officer of the state of Colorado and that's who I work for—just like you. But somebody killed two men who happen to be federal employees, Deputy Morris. And a law officer, any law officer, wants to see murderers caught."

"Didn't happen in my jurisdiction, Wager. And don't you tell me how I ought to feel about doing my job. I do my job. I take the county's money and I do my job. You want to listen to what them goddamn federal people tell you, you go ahead. But don't you or anybody else tell me what my job is." He squared his hat on his head, its wide brim shading his flushed face from the now-bright fluorescent lights overhead. "Been nice talking to you."

Through the glass, Wager watched Morris's dim shadow rapidly cross the pale gravel, saw the lights of the deputy's car flick on, and watched the red taillights pull hotly onto the highway and turn right toward Egnarville.

"More coffee, sir?" Paula, silent on her crepe-soled waitress shoes, stood at his elbow with her glass bowl of coffee. As Wager held up his cup, her soft voice asked, "You're from Denver, ain't you?"

"Yeah." Wager, still thinking of Morris and his defensive anger, cleared his throat and tried to make his voice into something polite. "You been there?"

"No, not yet. I'd like to, though." A quick frown pulled her eyebrows together. "It's not as big as Los Angeles, is it?"

"No. You like Los Angeles?"

"Never been there, either. I just seen pictures of it. And on TV." She added shyly, "I've never been much of anyplace except here."

"It's nice here," said Wager. "Nice scenery, relaxing."

"Yessir. But I been here all my life." There was another question she apparently had planned to ask, "Can you get work there? You know, like a waitress?"

"Sure." He paid closer attention to her, now. "But you won't earn much. And it's still a big place. It could be pretty scary without any family or friends around."

She considered that while she wiped the lip of the coffeepot with a cloth. Then she glanced toward the cashier's stand. "If you want to register, Verdie's there now."

"OK. How late is your kitchen open?"

"Nine."

"I'll be back before then."

5

THE BRIGHT SUN, a hard yellow against his room's drawn roller shade, woke him, and he lay a few moments in the strange bed. The still air brought the stale smell of old cigarette smoke from the worn carpet and faded drapes, the raucous squawk of a magpie somewhere outside, the murmur of a single car passing slowly on the highway.

Liz had been glad to hear his voice last night, and he was just as glad he had remembered to call her and let her know he'd arrived all right and where he was staying. They really hadn't had much to say to each other that was important—Wager told her he was meeting with local law officers and she told him about Committee Chairman McGraw's latest ploy, sponsoring a bill that would exempt United Airlines and the Broncos, Nuggets, and Rockies from paying city property taxes. "He claims they earn enough for the city in sales, seat, and occupation taxes, as well as bringing in out-of-town customers. He said it's unfair to expect them to pay property taxes, too."

"Everyone else pays their share, including stores and movies that collect sales and seat taxes and bring in visitors."

"You know it and I know it. But McGraw wants to give his rich friends a little more. He says if they make more, they'll invest more in Denver—the old trickle-down theory."

That had been the kind of things they'd talked about, but it wasn't exactly all that their words told each other. He could hear it in her voice as they spoke: the shift from an early brisk tension to a lower, more relaxed, and intimate tone, so that when they finally said good-bye, it was as if they had really been saying how glad they were to listen to each other regardless of the topic. And when she told Wager that she missed him, his answer was just as simple, and as sincere—"I miss you, too." Neither used the word "love," but he guessed that was what they'd meant.

Propped against the hard pillows, he let out a long, slow breath. Liz and his mother had become friends—possibly because they didn't see too much of each other, or, more likely, because they both suffered him. And there was really no reason why he and Liz shouldn't marry. Except that she didn't seem to want to and he didn't think it was necessary. Even, it suddenly struck him, his mother hadn't asked whether or not he planned to marry her. It seemed like a paradox, as if the legal distance between them gave more weight to their emotional ties. Occasionally in Denver the issue had crossed his mind; but here, in silence and loneliness and three hundred miles from the varied and constant demands of daily life in the Homicide division, he had the stillness and solitude to reflect on how much Liz meant to him. And how deep a sense of loss he would suffer if she were to go.

It was something he would feel good telling her right now, and he glanced at his watch to see if it was too early to call. But he was surprised to find it was too late—almost eight—and she would be in whatever morning meeting filled today's seven-thirty slot in her own varied and demanding schedule.

He had slept far later than he usually did. The altitude, maybe—fifteen hundred feet higher than Denver—or the almost total silence broken only by the faint tink of radiator pipes and, just then, by the thud of a door closing three or four rooms away. Or maybe he had been a lot more tired than he had thought. But it was late now, and time to move—things to see and people to do.

Heaving from under the blankets and thick comforter, he showered and shaved and had breakfast in the restaurant, the house specialty: huevos rancheros with your choice of green or red chili sauce. The morning sun made the faceless box of a dining room a little less blank, though not much. Paula worked this meal, too, moving so quickly and quietly that she was almost invisible, bearing plates and coffeepot between Wager and the three or four other tables occupied by tourists and salesmen. They ate quickly, filling up before heading for their cars and the long roads ahead. The only table where people lounged on their elbows and smoked over cups of coffee was at the far end. Three ranchers, faces chapped and red with wind and sun, and thick fingers dwarfing the mugs they gripped, had fallen silent when Wager came in. Occasionally, as he ate, they glanced his way, voices a low rumble. One of them asked Paula something and she, too, glanced at Wager, then shook her head as if to say she didn't know.

Wager, finishing, wiped his mouth and went out past the tiny bar with its OPEN 11 A.M. TO 11 P.M. sign to the cash register. He could feel their eyes follow him across the room.

Verdie, the thin woman with curly hair dyed flat black who had signed Wager in the night before, smiled and asked how he'd liked his breakfast. Then she paid no attention to his answer as her sharp eye checked the addition. She quickly made change, which was fine with Wager, because his answer had been as formulaic and pointless as the question. Intent and as quick as a sparrow, she handed Wager his money; Wager pushed a couple of ones across the glass-topped counter as a tip. "Those three men over there, they have ranches around here?"

The woman craned her head around the doorway, showing Wager the back of it, with its hair colored evenly down to its gray roots. "Two of them do. One's a foreman."

"Know their names?"

"Bradley Nichols—he owns the B Lazy N over on Cross Creek. Louis Gregory, he's the foreman on the Rocking K. And Stan Litvak. He owns the Bar L Bar."

Wager studied the three men. "Which one's Nichols?"

She looked again, jerking back as one of the faces seemed to feel Wager's interest and turned their way. "The dark-haired one. Sitting with his back to the window."

Wager studied the man. He was lean, dark complexioned; somewhere in his late thirties or early forties. His hair, cropped close on the sides, rose to a tall pompadour that was combed back from his forehead. "Litvak?"

"Sitting next to Nichols. Crew cut, blond hair."

Wager caught that man's eyes, too: chips that stared back across the room with a glint of pale blue light, and the thought crossed Wager's mind that Deputy Morris probably made a phone call or two last night. "Come here a lot, do they?"

"About everybody in this part of the county comes by one time or another." Her eyes were black dots in the leathery, wrinkled face of a longtime smoker. She wore no makeup, but her fingernails had been painted a dark red and looked so perfect that Wager wondered if they were false. "There's not that many other places to go without driving a lot of miles." A muffled bell dinged from the serving window and a couple of seconds later Paula crossed the dining room with another tray of breakfast plates.

"Does Paula have a boyfriend?"

Verdie's eyebrows, narrow lines that had more ink than hair in them, lifted. "Nobody special I know of. A lot would like to be, and she seems to like a couple of them, but nothing special. Why?"

Wager shrugged. "She's a pretty girl. Seems someone would have claimed her by now."

"Maybe, maybe not." The woman's voice closed the subject. "She's a real smart girl—too damned bright for the men around here. And a good worker." Her dark eyes glanced at Wager and sharpened. "And a good girl, too!"

"That seems to go together." Wager looked again at the three men who had turned back to their own business, then went to his room to brush his teeth. The sky had cleared overnight and the sunlight held a hint of summer's coming heat as he locked his room door and headed out to his car. Even the wind had quieted and, from the high grass of a roadside ditch, the sharp whistle of a meadowlark gave its seven or eight rising and falling notes. A dusty pickup truck pulled onto the highway from one of the county roads; the rattle of its worn shock absorbers faded as it slowly picked up speed, heading toward the northwest and the Utah line. Even the still air smelled of peace. As Wager started to unlock his car, his reaching hand told him that something wasn't quite right. But his eyes hadn't noticed anything yet. Then he paused and looked at the vehicle—something about its height—and stepped back to gaze at his tires. Both on the driver's side were flat. Gaping lips of sliced rubber scarred their pinched black walls. He walked around to the other side, and they, too, pressed, airless, against the dusty gravel. Glancing in the restaurant windows, Wager caught the three men staring at him. Their eyes were eager but their faces showed nothing before they turned back to huddle with each other. He could almost hear their laughter through the glass.

IT WAS ALMOST ten before he pulled onto the highway and headed toward the county seat of La Sal. The AAA service truck had taken a good hour and a half to show up, then another half hour to replace the tires. The mechanic, in his twenties with his straight hair pulled back into a ponytail, looked out of his truck window at the cut tires and asked if someone was trying to give Wager a message. Wager nodded. "I guess whoever it was didn't know how to write."

The young man glanced at the antennae and then the state license plates. "You a cop?" That had been his last comment until he'd finished the fourth tire. Then, as he made out a receipt for parts and service, "Hope the rest of your visit's better than this."

"I plan on that," said Wager.

"But if it ain't," he handed an oil-smeared business card to Wager, "just give us a call. Twenty-four-hour service." The card repeated the sign on the truck's door: "La Sal Conoco Service." Then he tossed his jack and tools into the truck's sponson, wiping grease-smeared hands first on a stained rag and then across his long hair to smooth it down. "Think I'll have a cup of coffee and say hi to Paula before I go."

The three ranchers had long ago strolled to their pickup trucks, ignoring Wager and his car, and had disappeared down the highway; Wager, finally mobile, pressed hard on the gas pedal as he steered east on State 181 for the county seat.

AFTER GYPSUM, LA SAL seemed like a large town with its tavern and hardware store, restaurant and clothing emporium. It even had a traffic light at the main intersection, and Wager guessed at a population of around seven or eight hundred. The county metropolis that boasted a car dealer and a small supermarket also advertised the league championship of the La Sal Eagles high school six-man football team; he passed the Conoco station with its stenciled notice, TOE-TRUCK SERVICE, 24 HRS, and saw the blue state-supplied sign SHERIFF with an arrow pointing down a side street. It was one of the half dozen paved lanes that led out the block or two into the quiet residential area around the shopping district. The sheriff's office was in the county courthouse, a narrow brick building set back behind a mowed lawn with a flagpole and a World War I monument. The ground floor was half basement, and white stone stairs led from the walk up to the second level, whose arched entry said it was the main floor. A central pointed tower formed a narrow third story. The building looked as if it had been put up in the late nineteenth century. Across the street, behind its own patch of lawn, stood a redbrick school dating from about the same period and designed by the same architect. There must have been a lot of tax money in the county at that time. Mining, probably, though long played out by now.

Wager pulled into one of the angled parking places and spotted a second blue-and-white metal sign for the sheriff's office; it pointed to a small door tucked beneath the worn white stone stairs.

The whitewashed door opened to a tiny cubicle and three steps down to a second door. Wager pushed through that and found himself facing the barrier of a cramped, chest-high service counter. A sign pointing off to a reinforced door on his left said HOLDING CELLS. A smaller one said PLEASE RING FOR SERVICE and had a wired button at its foot. Wager pressed.

"Yes, sir. Can I help you?" A woman came from behind a bookshelf filled with loose-leaf binders, manuals, papers, and row after row of manila folders of varying thicknesses. She wore a blue work shirt bearing a name tag—D. LAMMERS—and black slacks that made her lower torso look like a large ball supported by two thin sticks of short legs.

"I'm Detective Sergeant Wager, Denver police. I missed my earlier appointment with Sheriff Spurlock—car trouble. Is he still around?"

"We wondered what happened to you, Officer Wager. Let me see where the sheriff's at." She disappeared into the crowded office space behind the bookshelf and Wager heard her talking into an intercom or a radio. Then she came back. "He's back in the jail. He'll be out in a few minutes. You want a cup of coffee?"

Wager's Styrofoam cup was half empty when the locks on the reinforced security door rattled and the man stepped out.

Spurlock was big. Probably in his mid-fifties, though it was hard to tell because of the combination of wrinkles and the tanned, healthy-looking flesh of his full cheeks. He ducked under the door frame, wide of shoulder, his waist even wider, with a swelling stomach bound by a cartridge belt of glossy, tooled leather; heavy thighs stretched flat the remnants of creases in his khaki trousers. He was clean-shaven, but Wager thought a mustache might have reduced the size of the fleshy, almost purple nose that had been broken at one time and spread like a fist in the middle of the man's face. If his office clerk looked like a golf ball on a tee, Spurlock looked like the tree she could get lost behind, and like a tree he seemed to sway from the roots of his large cowboy boots to swallow Wager's hand in his own.

"Heard about you, Officer Wager. Good to meet you." His voice rumbled with half-swallowed phlegm.

"Sorry I'm late—car trouble."

"Those things happen. Dorothy's fixed you up with coffee? Good—come on back. Tell me what all you're doing out here."

The man's office, made even smaller by his bulk, had a tiny window protected by a mesh of heavy metal. It looked out into a corrugated steel well on the other side of the basement wall. The top of the well had a barred grate over it. While Wager told the sheriff what he thought Spurlock had a right to know, the large man stared up at strips of blue sky.

"Howie Morris called me last night. Told me you two'd talked some."

The deputy's telephone had been pretty busy. "He thinks I'm working for the FBI or BLM. I'm not. I was asked to come out here and see if I could help coordinate between your office and the feds, and that's what I'd like to do."

"You were asked to come out here? By who?"

"The FBI, through Captain Melrose, Denver Police Department. The initial request came to the CBI from the state attorney general's office." Then he played the big card. "The governor signed off on the request, too."

As chief executive of the state, the governor had the power to name replacements for elected officials who, for one reason or another, failed to serve out their terms; the state attorney general had direct supervision of all district attorneys as well as the state court system in Colorado. That office's power over sheriffs was in the hazy area that called sheriffs and their deputies "officers of the court." Under law, the court system was one structure leading all the way from local small-claims courts up to the state supreme court. However, like judges, sheriffs were elected by district and had wide latitude in performing their duties. Reported irregularities in that performance were assessed by the state attorney general's office, which had the power to empanel grand juries to investigate complaints. But the distinction between local and state powers was a flexible and sometimes competitive line. While no one at either state or local level was ever eager to investigate charges of malfeasance, it had happened occasionally. And no sheriff enjoyed the idea of explaining to the voters at the next election why he had been investigated by the SAG or why the governor had threatened to appoint someone else to the job.

The heavy flesh of Spurlock's face hid any emotion, as did his baggy eyes, which rested, unblinking, on Wager. "The governor did, huh? So just what kind of 'coordination' you have in mind, Officer Wager?"

"Whatever it takes to solve four homicides."

"Three, none of which was in my jurisdiction. We're not sure the fourth's a homicide."

"It's listed as a suspicious death. I'd like to clear it up one way or the other."

"You'd like to do that, would you?" He folded large-knuckled hands comfortably across his stomach. "Well, just what makes you think I won't be able to do that without your help?"

"I don't doubt that you can. And I know for sure I couldn't do it without your help. But my job—what the governor and the attorney general sent me out to do—is to help you and the federal people work together to determine if any of the deaths are related." He added, "If they are, then maybe working on one will lead to a break on the others."

"And just why does the state attorney general's office think they're related?"

"Four homicides—possible homicides, I know—in a three-month period and in a population this small is suspicious in itself. Then you add the facts that two were federal employees killed by snipers, and the third was an informant for the feds. It becomes a possibility too strong to ignore."

"That's the way the people in Denver see it?"

"If it happened in another county, wouldn't you wonder?"

The sheriff didn't answer, but only hissed a long breath through his nose. "La Sal County has 1,658 people in it, Officer Wager, and 1,280 square miles. I got four patrol deputies and myself to look after that many square miles and the people therein, twenty-four hours a day, three hundred sixty-five days a year. Don't get me wrong—I'm not complaining. I ran for this office, and I'll keep running for it as long as me and the people think I can do the job. What I'm telling you is me and my deputies get called to everything from hippies camping out on somebody's range land to robberies and killings, plus the court's business in this county, as well as running my four-room, free-rent hotel, which tends to get pretty full on payday weekends. To do all that with what little support the county commissioners let me have, Wager, means I got to have a system—I have to do things my way if they're going to get done at all. Now," another long breath, "I'm happy to work with those people any time they want to work with me. But I'll be damned if I have the time or the resources to turn me and my people over to Special Agent Durkin so things can be done the way him and Washington,

D.C., think they should be done. To the people that put me in office, Wager, moving them hippies off the land they squatted on is a hell of a lot more important that whether or not Special Agent Durkin's confidential informant was a homicide. And that, Wager, is the way it is and the way it is going to be."

And that gave Wager his angle. "Which is the other reason I was sent out: I'm a homicide detective—been one for almost ten years. I might be able to help you out if you want me to, and you can still run your county your way."

"I didn't ask for no help, damn it!"

"No, you didn't. Neither did Durkin. He thinks he can do it all by himself. Henderson's the one who had the sense to make the phone call, Sheriff. He's the one who doesn't give a damn who gets the credit as long as he can find a way to solve the murders. And personally, I think he's got the right attitude: Forget the politics and get the job done. And do it before another man is killed and somebody else's wife and kids have to stand around staring at a fresh grave."

The strips of sky above the window well must have been interesting because the sheriff took his time studying them. When he began speaking again, it seemed off the subject. But Wager knew the man well enough by now to understand that that was the way the sheriff worked toward something he was angry at or wasn't really comfortable with. "We have a real population boom in La Sal County. Have had for the past few years—four or five new people move in each year, most of them from California. Looking for God knows what. Some of them don't find it and leave pretty quick, and some hang around and try to change things so they have whatever it is they're missing. Whatever will make La Sal County into what they ran way from: Orange County, or whatever. Can't just let things be."

Wager waited through the long pause. He had expected the sheriff to be a redneck who shared his constituents' suspicion of federal officers and outsiders in general, and maybe the man did, down deep. But so far, all Wager had seen was a sheriff who figured he knew how to run his county, and damn well knew how the law defined his authority. And he didn't intend to let Durkin or Henderson or Wager poke their noses into the way he ran his office. It was a territorial attitude Wager had seen before and one he could understand.

"More than half my county belongs to the federal government, Wager, and it don't pay any local taxes—national parks, national forest land. And we got some bits and pieces of the Indian reservation, but they're not my worry, thank God. And now we got people want to build great big retirement communities on the edge of the forest land—say that's where money's going to come from: aging baby boomers who want to retire in the mountains. Of course, it's not really the mountains they have in mind. It's golf courses, it's better highways so the retirees can get in and out with their Winnebagos. It's better medical facilities—hell, we don't even have a county hospital! But now there's talk we should legalize gambling and build up the tax base so we can afford all these things, and to do it by making the place more attractive to high rollers. Set up big hotels, whatnot, because high rollers have to have some place nice to roll in. Open up the forestland to more than just fishing and hunting: winter sports like skiing and snowmobiling. Start subdividing the ranch land and put in roads and put up schools for more people who want to bring California with them. Damn it, the land can't take that kind of use, Wager—we live in a desert!"

"Is that what has the ranchers worried?"

"Yeah, that's the big part of it. Change never does come easy when people are happy with their lives, and now there's a lot of that kind of pressure. That and the federal government's policies on grazing and land use that's squeezing the small outfits till they can't make a dime, year in and year out. Most of the land around here's just plain scrub—you need five hundred, a thousand acres for each cow, and it's not good for anything else anyway." He finally stopped staring up at the window. "I reckon I can use some help at that, Officer Wager. But only if you take care of that damned Durkin—you keep him away from me—you do that and I'll turn this Del Ponte thing over to you. That what you want?"

Wager nodded. "That'll do."

6

THE DEL PONTE file was one of the thinner manila folders
propped up in the bookcase behind the reception counter.
Dorothy, the sheriff's clerk, didn't have a check-out form—"I'll
remember who's got it, Officer Wager"—and Wager, given a
closet-sized corner of the copy room and a folding table and
chair—"Sorry, it's all we got"—settled down to scan the papers.

He had asked Sheriff Spurlock who might have slashed his
tires; the answer didn't rule out the three ranchers or calm any
fears Wager might have had: "Anybody who thinks you might
be a fed." And he'd asked Spurlock how that somebody would
have known Wager was a cop. "You got a state car? State license
plate and radio antenna on the back? Don't take a genius to
figure that out, Wager. That, and being a new face at the only
motel in that part of the county." He added, "I'll tell everybody
you're working with me. Maybe that'll keep your wheels safe.
As well as your scalp."

And maybe it wouldn't, but that was something Wager didn't
want to waste time worrying about now. Instead, he put the
incident into that corner of his memory labeled "Don't get mad,
just get even" and focused all his attention on the Del Ponte file.

The body had been reported at 11:14 A.M. on 24 March by
one Gordon Hunter, State Highway Maintenance, who had been
doing a routine survey of the road's condition and had noticed

a shoe lying at the shoulder. He'd also noticed that it wasn't your everyday empty shoe, curled and split by weather and perhaps flattened by a passing tire. In fact, there seemed to be a ragged knob of something poking out of the shoe, which looked suspiciously like a chewed-on ankle. Hunter stopped the maintenance truck for a better look and his belief that the shoe was no ordinary discard was reinforced by a thick column of busy ants. That, and, carried by a gentle breeze, the smell that came from somewhere over in the high grass filling the berm. Following his nose, Hunter discovered what was making the smell, and a small stack of glossy black-and-white Polaroid photographs showed what Hunter had seen: a swatch of mashed grass and the scattered and partially eaten bits of the body strewn across the broken weeds. The last photograph was of Del Ponte's torso with its head—the distance marked by a ruler to give dimension to the photo—tumbled into a depression between two rocks. To judge from the black, desiccated flesh running from left eye to right jaw and covering half the face, he had lain partially facedown in the hot sun for at least a couple of days before animals began their playful feast.

Identification had been by the man's wife, one Sharon Del Ponte of RR1, Egnarville. She stated that her husband had left home on 17 March and that she hadn't seen him since. No missing person report had been filed—Del Ponte had been self-employed as a small-time trucker and had had his own tractor-trailer for transporting livestock and other cargo. March was a busy time for him ordinarily, bringing cows from lower winter pastures in the canyons to the better grass of the highlands at the east end of the county. It wasn't unusual for him to go off to a job that lasted several days and which she would not be told about. She knew of no one who wanted to kill her husband.

His last haul, at least that Sheriff Spurlock could determine, was March 15 for the Butte Springs Ranch, moving cattle to their summer range in BLM land east of La Sal.

The analysis of the remains—conducted by the coroner down in Montezuma County—showed no causative wounds located in the bones of the victim; too much damage had been done by animals to determine if death was the result of trauma in the soft tissue. In short, the coroner's report was inconclusive on everything except the fact that nobody would be in that condition who wasn't dead.

Neighbors or known associates of the deceased who had been interviewed were listed: B. J. Haydn, Egnarville; Pete Stine, Egnarville; Joseph Dorfin, RR 2, Egnarville. None offered any information about possible assailants.

Del Ponte's car and his diesel tractor were found parked and locked behind Mallard's Garage at Lewis Corners, where he usually stored his truck and trailers.

What wasn't in the file were the steps of investigation that a larger department would do routinely: lab analyses of body fluids and tissue samples; fingerprint search of the victim's vehicles; canvass of all local residents who used that stretch of highway daily; forensic medical specialists to examine the victim's clothes, intestines, fingernails, hair, teeth for any indication of where he'd spent his last hours. It was too late for any of that now, and the only thing left for Wager was legwork.

Or car work. He couldn't help a glance at his tires as he unlocked the Plymouth and headed back west toward Egnarville. Twenty-five minutes later, he passed the Gypsum Motel. In the parking lot outside the restaurant, he noted two dusty pickup trucks bearing La Sal County plates and a dark Lexus sedan with Denver's code: it was the car a salesman was likely to drive in this country—speedy but easy to handle and soft to ride in. Another twenty minutes of fast driving brought Wager to Egnarville.

This town didn't have a crossroads. Its center was a wider shoulder on the north side of the highway where a combination gas station and grocery store sat. It held the single public telephone as well as the contract post office. The scattered mobile homes and small frame houses were all on the same side of the highway. The south side was fenced rangeland, and Wager guessed that the houses were located where they were because that was where a spring had been found and where water wells could be sunk without much drilling.

The name of the Egnarville store was Store, and the name of the man who worked the cash register as well as the post office counter was Jesse.

"Jesse Herrera." He looked at Wager's ID and then at Wager. "What can I help you with, Officer?"

"Rubin Del Ponte. He lived around here, didn't he?"

"Sure did." A tilt of his head indicated somewhere behind the crammed shelving that formed the wall behind him. "Just over there. Terrible thing, him dying like that."

"Did you know him very well?"

"Not as well as I know some of the other folks around here. He wasn't around home that much. I know his wife, Sharon, a lot better." His cheeks suddenly darkened with a blush. "I mean, she comes in the store to do shopping and mail letters, you know. So we have a chance to talk some. Rubin was always off somewhere with his trucking business, so I didn't know him so well." He added, "Seemed like a nice fella, though. Always friendly."

"You've lived here long?" Wager glanced across the dimly lit store. The aisles were narrow and flanked by a little of everything, ranging from canned and dried foodstuffs to hardware and beauty items. A chiller near the entry held soda pop and beer, another just beyond the cash register and fronted with sliding glass doors showed dairy goods, ice cream, popsicles, a small variety of frozen dinners, bags of frozen vegetables, wrapped packages of meat and fish and poultry. There were no shopping carts—they wouldn't fit through the cramped aisles—but a short stack of plastic tote baskets sat beside the check-out counter. That was a small space cleared between displays of candy and tobacco, most of which was the chewing kind.

"Afout three years now. Came from California about three years ago when I bought the store. Love it here—it's peaceful, you know?"

"Ever hear of anyone who might want Del Ponte dead?"

"Oh, no. Maybe some of his relatives over on the reservation could tell you something." A tilt of his head in another direction. "But I never heard anything like that."

"Have you ever heard of the Constitutional Posse?"

Herrera's eyes widened momentarily and he blinked. "Just that some folks belong. I don't. I don't really know much about it. I can't tell you much about it."

"Is Mrs. Del Ponte home now?"

"Sure—she's . . . I mean, she's usually home. . . . Got her two kids and only one's in school, you know, and so she has to stay home."

Wager asked a few more questions about local people Del Ponte might know and where they lived. Egnarville was different from Denver and far more spread out. But the network of a victim's friends and acquaintances, relatives and enemies, was familiar; and despite the empty sky, the distant glimmer of snowy peaks, the wind that made the only sound, Wager was beginning to feel at home.

Sharon Del Ponte had one of those faces that seemed to be dried down to basics: small, triangular eyes, thin nose, full lips. She wasn't what Wager would call pretty, but she wasn't exactly plain or ugly, either. She might have been better-looking when she was in her teens—probably when she married Del Ponte— but there was enough left which, with the bushy red hair that made her face seem even more doll-like, could cause some men to look twice.

"I heard he was telling people he worked as an informer. We didn't talk about it, though." Her full lips pressed together a bit. "Somebody told the newspaper he was. It was in the newspaper with the story about him being found." She sat in a turned-wood rocking chair placed to look through the picture window at the swing set in the sandy front yard. There, a child climbed alone up the small slide, carefully slid down, and then turned to climb again: he or she did it over and over, deliberately, learning early what life was all about. "I don't think they should've put that in there."

The house was a prefab, the "wide load" kind you saw being trucked in halves down the highway on flatbed trailers, to be set up on a cinder-block foundation somewhere. Early American. That was what the wooden chairs and table, the red-and-white checkered curtains and wall paneling were called, Wager remembered. Early American, maple stain. Framed pictures of mountains and lakes hung here and there on the dark walls, and children's toys had been dropped and not yet picked up. The urgent knock of a dog scratching a flea bite bumped against the closed front door.

"He never spoke to you about anything he might have found out? About anyone who might have been interested in or afraid of what he was doing?"

"No. If he knew something like that, he never told me."

"Did he ever mention the Constitutional Posse?"

"No!"

"Do you know anybody who belongs to it?"

She chewed at her lip. "Some around here probably do—it's mostly the big ranch owners and the ones who go along with them. Not Rubin—he didn't have any reason to join up with them."

Wager nodded. "Any idea what he was doing over in Squaw Canyon without his truck?"

A frown pulled her pale red eyebrows together. "I don't know. I have wondered some about that. But you ought to talk to his brother over on the reservation—Luther. Rubin was always going over there to see him."

Wager asked a dozen or so other questions, but they were the same thing in different words and received similar responses. When you didn't know exactly what you wanted, when you were going by hunch and guesswork, you tried repeating the same thing in two or three different ways. It was one of the basic techniques of interviewing witnesses that Wager had learned over the years. More than once, early in his career, he had found himself unnecessarily delayed until a witness—on a third or fourth interview—brought out something vital that hadn't been mentioned earlier because, "You didn't ask me about it that way!" The worst kind were those witnesses who, being helpful, limited their answers strictly to what the detective asked. But Mrs. Del Ponte didn't seem helpful as much as reluctant—her answers were terse and they all came back to the same point: She knew very little about her husband's job or even about his life away from Egnarville.

"Did you or your husband know Larry Kershaw, Buck Holtzer, or Walter Lawrence?"

"No . . . Walter Lawrence, maybe. Ain't he the Indian they found dead on the reservation a while ago?"

"Yes, ma'am. The other two are the slain federal employees. Your husband would have been asking about them."

"Oh." Then, "No. I didn't know them. Rubin probably knew Walter Lawrence—everybody on the reservation knows each other. They're all some kind of kin, mostly." She shook her head again. "I didn't know him."

"Do you like living here, Mrs. Del Ponte?"

That question surprised her and drew her eyes from the cheery yellow-and-red plastic swing set dwarfed by the expanse of sagebrush and horizon. "Like it? Well, I reckon. It's where I've lived all my life."

"You have family nearby?"

"My uncle and his wife, but I don't see much of them. Most of my family's up near Fruita—in Mesa County. It used to be like this: real pretty and nobody around. It's grown a lot up there, though." She added, looking at a future Wager couldn't see, "Jesse says it's going to grow like that around here, too. I don't think I'll like that."

"Who says?"

"Jesse. Herrera. Owns the store."

"You talk to him a lot?"

She shrugged. "When I go over to the store. The post office is there, too." She added, and her tone of voice told Wager to make of it what he would, that she didn't have anything to hide. "Around here, anybody you see you talk to. It's not like some places."

"Do you intend to stay here now?"

"Well, it's paid for . . ." Which was either as far down the road as she had thought or as far as she was willing to let Wager see. He wasn't sure which.

"Does Jesse Herrera live around here, too?"

"Yes." She wagged a hand over her shoulder. "Over there near the store. Why?"

"Is he married?"

"What's that mean?"

"Just trying to understand your husband's life, Mrs. Del Ponte. Maybe something will help explain his death."

"Well, you understand this, Detective Whatever Your Name Is: There ain't nothing between me and Jesse Herrera—nothing at all! We're friends and that's it!"

B. J. Haydn told another story. His house was about a mile down a dirt section road on a quarter acre of lushly irrigated greenness. It was fenced off from the expanse of open range with its greasewood and sagebrush by an electrified wire.

"Hell, a man runs around and leaves his woman alone all the time, he's got to expect somebody'll sniff around when he ain't there."

The unshaven, wiry man in dark blue overalls grunted as he

wrenched tight a hose connection on the pneumatic line of his drilling rig. Wager stood in the shade of the metal Butler building and pushed the wet, insistent nose of Haydn's dog away from his crotch. The dual-axle pickup truck parked between the weathered frame house and the tin building had HAYDN DRILLING SERVICE on the door in sun-worn letters.

"Is Herrera married?"

"Sure. What difference's that make? So's she. Or was."

"Did Del Ponte think there was anything between his wife and Herrera?"

"Hell, I don't know. If he didn't, he didn't say anything to me. And I wasn't about to tell him. Little place like this, you mind your own business, know what I mean?"

"You were his friend, I understand."

"Well, yeah, I suppose. I hired him and his truck sometimes when I needed extra wheels on a job. And we're neighbors. Hell, around here, it's hard not to be a neighbor."

"Did you know he was working for the FBI as an informant?"

Haydn grinned and scratched an oil-grimed knuckle at his earlobe. "Yeah, I read something about that. They even had something in the newspaper about it. Damn waste of the taxpayers' money, but that's nothing new."

"Did he ever say anything to you about what he was looking for or if he might have discovered something about the deaths of two federal agents?"

"No. Nothing like that. No reason to."

"Have you heard of the Constitutional Posse?"

"Sure. Everybody around here has. Half the ranchers in the county belong or have relatives in it. Why? You think they had something to do with Rubin's death?"

"I don't know. Did he ever mention them to you?"

"Naw. What for? They're not like the goddamn KKK—they don't go around burning crosses and lynching people. That what you think?"

"I don't know anything about them," said Wager. "What kind of work did Rubin do for you?"

"Transport—drove his truck or mine to the site, depending."

"You do a lot of well drilling around here?"

"Here, Montezuma County, Montrose County. The reservation. Sometimes over in Utah, depending. Business's been good. Promises to get better—more people coming in all the time. How long the water'll last is another question—that and the water rights on the subterranean flow. That's what'll make or break the future of La Sal and every other county around here: how much water and who owns it."

"Can you think of any reason at all why someone might want Del Ponte dead?"

"No."

Neither could Pete Stein, who Wager found under the shaft of an irrigation rig and wearing rubber boots coated up to their shins with gluey mud. The long aluminum tube ran like an axle through the centers of a dozen spoked wheels spaced fifty feet apart and which stood about twice as tall as Stein. The farthest wheel, tiny and fragile-looking across the wind-rippled grass whose green was so dark it almost hurt the eyes, was anchored near a well pump or a hose connection. The water from that source built up pressure in the long shaft, its jets pulsating feathers of water from rotating sprinkler heads, and the turning sprinkler heads levered the wheels in wide circles around the pivot. It was the same principle as a crawling lawn sprinkler, and like that device, occasionally broke down.

"No reason at all why anybody might kill him that I know of." Stein had a big chin made bigger by a wad of tobacco in his cheek and by the strain he put on a nut that held against the torque of his wrench. "Som'bitch set here half a day running water before I saw it." He pointed to a six-inch-wide track of dredged mud where the frozen walker wheel had been dragged across the soaked earth by the effort of the other wheels.

"This your hay crop?"

The brown-haired man glanced at Wager and nodded. "Get it grown, get it baled, get it stacked, get through the winter." He spat a long brown stream. "And then get started again." He grunted with satisfaction as the nut finally yielded a fraction. "There—you som'bitch!"

"How well did you know Rubin Del Ponte?"

"Well enough, I reckon. Hired him off and on—he was a pretty good worker, if he did talk your ears off."

"What did he do for you?"

"Field work—moving irrigation pipe—general farmwork when he wasn't trucking. Anything he could to scrape in a few dollars cash."

"Would that include being an informer for the feds?"

Another long squirt of brown spit. "What I hear, yeah, I guess it did." Stein glanced at Wager again. "Was it you he was working for?"

"I'm not federal. I'm state."

A wordless nod.

"Did he seem worried or afraid of anything before he was killed?"

"He definitely was killed? That what they saying now?"

Wager corrected himself. "Maybe killed. We don't know for sure."

"Then maybe you don't want to go around saying he was."

"Why?"

The man rattled in his large toolbox for a tube of something and squeezed a blob into the opened axle plate. "If it ain't true, you don't want to say it. That's all."

"Did he seem afraid or worried before he died?"

"Quiet. He was quiet. Like he was thinking something over real good."

"Any idea what that was?"

"No. I didn't ask and he didn't say. At least he wasn't talking a hundred words to the minute."

"How long before his death was this?"

"Week, maybe. I hired him to move some steers for me, and we worked almost a full day loading and trucking." He added, "I gave him a full day's pay for his time, anyway."

"Did he say anything at all unusual? Anything that at the time struck you as odd?"

"Didn't say much. That's what was odd. Usually he had all sorts of crap to talk about—who he was working for next, what job he'd just finished, who he'd run across over in the canyons. I didn't much care, but he liked to talk about it."

"Did he say anything about his wife?"

Stein paused in his work to swing his arm and loosen a stiff shoulder. The flannel of his shirt was dark with water dripping from the pipe. "What's that mean?"

"I heard Mrs. Del Ponte might have played around."

"Sharon? Who with? Who said that?"

"Did you ever hear of anything between her and Jesse Herrera?"

"Herrera? Hell, no. I don't know him that good—he's new around here. But Sharon wouldn't do anything like that. I don't think, anyway." He frowned at something on the horizon. "Who told you that?"

"Mr. Haydn."

"Aw, hell—that sawed-off little turd. You don't want to listen to anything B.J. says about women or much else. He's been trying to get in Sharon's pants since Rubin brung her out here. And his chances won't be much better now Rubin's dead."

"How about Herrera's chances?"

The full jaw swayed slowly as the man chewed. It reminded Wager of a cow. "She's a widow now. Got to find some way to support herself and them two kids, because the county's not going to give her much help. But Herrera's wife might have something to say about it. If there's anything to it, which—seeing's who told you about it—I doubt."

"What about the other two killings—the government men? Any idea who might do something like that?"

The jaw stopped for a long moment and the man's pale gray eyes, still studying something on the horizon, blinked. "No."

"What about somebody in the Constitutional Posse?"

The eyes turned to Wager and the jaw moved faster, now, before Stein finally spoke. "I'm a member of that Posse, Mister. And damned proud to be. There's not a man among them who won't fight back at anybody who attacks them first." He spit and rubbed the corner of his mouth with his thumb. "And not one who'd shoot somebody who didn't. They sure as hell would not shoot somebody in the back, and they would not kill an unarmed man. So if you're thinking of blaming the Posse for those killings, you're barking up the wrong tree. And you sure as hell ain't welcome on my property any more."

Wager felt the glare of the man's eyes follow him back to the car.

7

WAGER REMINDED HIMSELF that often the result of being a professional snoop was to cause discombobulation among the local citizenry, and even occasional mild hatred toward the snooper. In itself, that didn't bother him—Wager could not think of more than one or two people whose attitude toward him he cared much about. The problem was purely tactics: Most people—especially tight-mouthed cowboys—didn't tend to give as much information when they felt they were being pushed. They got hard-jawed and stubborn, like some of the horses they rode, and an interview could turn into a mental or even physical wrestling match where the only thing that counted was to show Wager—the outsider—that being a cop didn't carry much weight out here. And so far, even though he might be influencing people, Wager certainly wasn't winning many friends.

He eased the Plymouth through a stretch of rough pavement and accelerated again. The AM radio could pick up only two stations, one that sounded like an old man speaking a language with a lot of "ah" and "sh" sounds and soft grunts. Navajo, Wager guessed, because it was sort of like the World War II code-talkers he had seen in one of the Marine Corps' training films. The other was a nasal voice that sang, "While we were waltzing, the heel of your heart stomped on the toe of mine." It was hard to tell if the singer was happy or sad about that, but it didn't make much difference; the wailing guitar and voice were only fillers between long advertisements for feed prices, farm and ranch supplies, wedding and birthday catering, used cars and trucks, well drilling and maintenance, auctions, appliance repair services, hunting and fishing centers, dressmaking, large and small animal veterinarians, heavy equipment rental and maintenance, grocery specials, LP gas deliveries to home and shop, automobile and truck repairs, local farm-fresh produce and all the other ways the population scattered thinly across these empty miles scrabbled for a living. Wager finally shut off the radio and listened to the hum of the motor and tires. If you could get some money out of it, do it; if it took money from you, fight it. But money did not seem to be behind the deaths; in fact, aside from the connection with the federal government, there was little to indicate any pattern in the killings: a USGS geologist, an informer, a BLM agent. And then there was an Indian whose murder seemed even less connected to the other three.

The reasons for killing someone, the reasons Wager had usually run across, were several: hatred, greed, mindless terror, a twisted sense of justice, and, most popular and to Wager the most damning, just plain carelessness. Carelessness about the results of one's acts, carelessness about the worth of another human being. Those usually ranged from drive-by shootings to murder in the course of a robbery. But it wasn't clear yet which, if any of these, was behind the deaths of Del Ponte or the others. Nor, Wager cautioned himself, should he start getting impatient yet; out here he was a stray dog in a strange neighborhood, and getting things done would take more time than in Denver—to understand, he would have to see wider and read more deeply than he did on his familiar turf. Which, he reminded himself, was why he had volunteered for temporary additional duty in the first place: because he was tired of the routine his work had fallen into. It was only yesterday at this time that his airplane had been circling for a landing, and he'd even taken eight hours out for sleep since then. Besides, there were a lot of people he hadn't yet talked to, and a lot of facts he had to learn before he could start making things happen.

He passed a wooden sign whose carved, blue-painted letters said "Squaw Point Reservation. Home of the Blue Sky People. Welcome to the Ute Nation. Please Observe Our Laws." On the map lying open beside him, Wager noted sixteen miles from the boundary line to Dark Mesa Village; he also noted that the quality of the pavement had improved—wider lanes and shoulders, newer road surface, no potholes. And an expensive stock fence now lined both sides of the highway with taut wire and metal posts painted a fresh, bright blue.

Occasional breaks in the fence, protected by cattle guards, opened to dirt roads that wound away into the sagebrush and grass clumps. There were no names tacked up or mailboxes on posts, but he could glimpse houses tucked into draws or against the shelter of low hills and buttes. Some were a single story and boxy, almost square. They looked a lot like the prefab homes found off the reservation. Others were the kind of split level with attached garage that you could see in any subdivision anywhere else. There seemed to be no people around them, but most had a corral of some sort and a few of those held horses that stared off at nothing. Now and then he saw a house with an outbuilding that looked like a low, clay-covered haystack with a stovepipe poking out of the top of its dome and a low door in the round wall. It wasn't a hogan—Wager knew what the Navajo hogans looked like with their eight straight sides made nine logs high and domed with a clay roof over the octagonal. These looked more like frozen bubbles of clay that had erupted from the red dirt around them, and he guessed they were sweat lodges. Trucks, some shiny and new, many broken in one way or another and sitting forever in the sun. An occasional cottonwood tree, where there was enough underground water to feed one; usually a large, dully white fiberglass tub lifted on a frame beside the house to be filled once every month or so with drinking water from a tank truck. Even now and then a teepee, the kind Wager associated with the Plains Indians who used to wander around the eastern face of the Rocky Mountains—Arapaho, Kiowa, Pawnee. The steeply pointed tent with its inverted cone of poles sprouting out of the top looked somehow alien in this land of no grass and abrupt walls of red rock.

In about ten minutes, he saw the village, three or four miles ahead, a scatter of tiny, low buildings half hidden along a tree-marked watercourse and spreading a little way up the side of the stone face of a mesa. Other mesas—some big enough on top to graze cattle, others standing like broken smokestacks—dotted the heat-wavered glare of the treeless desert. Unlike many of the surrounding ones, this wide mesa was capped with a band of black rock—lava, maybe—that spilled in tongues from its irregular lip down a face of red, yellow, and white striations. Along its rim and against a hard, blue sky, a dark green fringe of cedar and Douglas fir made the stripe of black rock look wider and thus, Wager patted himself on the back, the name: Dark Mesa.

Here and there, in the draws and beside washes that had begun to cut the dry plain into rough, cedar-dotted desert were more of the boxy houses. Government issue and made on a standard plan, some were nestled among outbuildings while others stood stark and isolated, bleak and fragile, unprotected from the sun or the wind. As the highway widened into the main street of the village, he passed a platted subdivision of the houses, uniform in color and design and with a regularity that reminded Wager of the quarters on a military base. But unlike a military base, their upkeep varied; some of the quarters were neat and even had a few struggling flowers planted in the shade near their foundations; others, despite looking new, were already sagging and chipped and unkempt. A few were boarded up and empty.

Along the highway, which now formed the village street, each building wanted to be by itself. Widely spaced, they were separated by weedy stretches of earth or by broad sandy parking areas. The most modern buildings were a gas station with its convenience store and a sprawling cast-concrete box with a flat roof and a sign naming it TRIBAL HEADQUARTERS. Half a dozen pickup trucks were parked in front of that, many with slatted wooden sides framing the truck bed as a pen for carrying livestock.

He slowly drove past an old-style adobe building, flat with roof poles sticking out like fingers just below its rim. It was fronted by an American flag and a cast-concrete sign saying BUREAU OF INDIAN AFFAIRS, DEPARTMENT OF INTERIOR. Then a large prefab building with a wide and sun-scorched gravel parking lot and its sign: DARK MESA CLINIC. A smaller building off to the side was labeled ALCOHOL ABUSE CENTER. A few hundred yards down from that, a similar prefab building, which had a taller flagpole with a bigger American flag, was what Wager looked for: DARK MESA JUSTICE CENTER. Across the street, sitting by itself on half a block of weedy sand, was a small brick post office, brand new, with a wide, glaringly white concrete walk leading from the road's unpaved shoulder to its shiny aluminum-frame door.

Wager pulled his car into the justice center's parking lot and plodded through the baking heat to mount the four concrete steps toward the double doors of glass. A painted directory listed the offices inside: TRIBAL COURT, LEGAL RECORDS AND PERMITS, TRIBAL POLICE HEADQUARTERS. The last was left, down a corridor leading off from the cool and shadowy lobby.

"Yessir? Help you?" A young woman—black hair, black eyes, smooth round face—looked up from the computer screen on her desk behind the service counter. The rest of the small office held a table and transmitter, three tall metal filing cabinets, and the inevitable bulletin board cluttered with notices and messages. The clerk wore a dark denim vest over what to Wager looked like a white, short-sleeved muscle shirt. It didn't show any muscles, but what it did show caught his eye and said "fashion magazine" more than "Indian reservation" or even "police headquarters."

Wager leaned on the counter and dangled his ID over his forefinger. "I'm investigating the death of Rubin Del Ponte. I'd like to talk with any of your officers who could give me information about him or his family."

She glanced at Wager's photograph and pushed her chair back on its squealing rollers. The heels of her cowboy boots, peeking from under the narrow legs of her nicely rounded Levi's, thumped hollowly across the floor as she went to a partition and leaned around it. Wager couldn't hear what she said, but a moment later she looked his way and nodded. "Ray says he might be able to help you."

Ray was about Wager's height and build but at least ten years younger. He had a last name, but Wager hadn't caught it clearly—something like "cantaloupe," but there was no nameplate on his desk that spelled it.

"Rubin Del Ponte? Sheriff Spurlock finally find out something about his death?" On one light brown wall hung a collection of diplomas and certificates bearing the policeman's name: Ray Qwana'tua. One certified in ornate script that he had completed the requirements for a bachelor of science degree in criminal justice from Ft. Lewis State College. Another not quite so fancy told the world that he had "Achieved a Certificate in Managerial Sciences." A smaller one simply stated that he had completed the course of study for the crime scene search and physical evidence program at the FBI Academy, Quantico, Virginia. Above them and head high was a rack of deer horns with a canteen dangling by its strap from one point. The other wall held large displays; two were a pair of scheduling charts covered with acetate and marked with grease pencil. A stained wipe rag hung on a string between them. Another large sheet was a detailed topographical map of the reservation and surrounding land. It, too, was covered with acetate and ready for the grease pencil.

"No. He turned it over to me. I'm from Denver Homicide. CBI sent me out to work with the sheriff." Wager accepted the single straight-backed chair the Indian officer gestured toward. Through the open window over the man's shoulder, Wager could look across the fenced police parking lots into a backyard of one of the military-style houses. Like Sharon Del Ponte's yard, it held a brightly colored kiddie gym, but no child clambered up its sun-heated steel bars. "I'd like to interview members of his family—see if they might be able to tell me anything about him."

Ray's black eyes watched Wager's face. Some bad acne had pitted his brown cheeks. He had straight black hair trimmed close at the sides and neck but long on top. Like the office secretary, he wore mostly ranch clothing: Levi's, probably cowboy boots—though Wager couldn't see them when the man had stood for a brief and light handshake—olive-colored uniform shirt with a black-and-yellow shoulder patch that said Squaw Point Reservation Tribal Police. He waited until he was certain Wager had finished speaking. "Luther Del Ponte, Rubin's half brother. They were closest, anyway, more than with his half sisters or stepmother. Luther lives over in Narraguinnep Wash. You want to talk to him?"

"If you'll tell me how to get there, yes."

Again there was a pause, giving Wager as much time as he needed to add anything. "Be better if I show you." He tilted his head toward the desert on the other side of the office wall. "It's a long way out there, easy to get lost if you don't know the country. Be better if we take my truck, too."

After the first mile or two, after the road had changed from gravel to graded dirt to just a two-rut track through the sagebrush and wind-worn rock, Wager was glad they had the stiff but high-sprung pickup truck instead of his spongy and low sedan. Ray seemed to drive too fast for the road, but he managed somehow to miss the biggest holes and stones and to talk to Wager at the same time. At first he wanted to know about Wager: what kind of assignments he'd had, what the job in Denver was like, what the pay and benefits were, information about the politics and administration of the DPD. It was the kind of stuff cops asked each other when they were trying to make up their minds as to how helpful to be. Wager told as much as the man wanted to know. Finally Ray moved closer to what Wager was interested in.

"Have you touched bases yet with the FBI? Agent Durkin?"

"I met him yesterday."

"What's he say about you coming on the reservation?"

"He doesn't have any trouble with it. In fact, he arranged jurisdiction for me."

A grunt that didn't decipher well.

"How does your office get along with his?" Wager asked.

"We get along." He glanced at Wager. "Most of what the tribal police handle is misdemeanor stuff. A little theft, family violence, search and rescue, rounding up drunks. By charter we don't handle much in the way of felonies, and never homicides." If there was any resentment about that, it didn't show in his voice.

"How do you think Rubin Del Ponte died?"

A snort that was half laugh, half scorn. "You know you're the first one to ask me that? Sheriff Spurlock does things his way, Agent Durkin's not too interested in Rubin, and neither one of them thinks the tribal police would be much help anyway." He braked as the road fell suddenly into a gully whose vertical walls, carved into fluted columns of dark red sand, twisted away, higher than the vehicle. "Some truth to that, I guess. A lot of Indians don't talk to each other about dead people—bad manners because it brings bad luck." Shifting into first, he eased the truck up the other side, going slowly so the rear wheels would not kick loose on the stony road. "Tabeguache Wash—leads off into Tabeguache Canyon maybe ten miles that way." He wagged a hand toward the lowering sun. "All the land around here runs off west that way—'The Leaning Land,' my people call it. Another hundred and fifty miles, it all drains into the Grand Canyon." He shifted through the gears as they picked up speed and the bumps came more rapidly again. "That's air miles. You follow one of the canyons, it could be two, maybe three hundred miles, it winds around so much." Then, "I think he was maybe killed by somebody."

"What makes you think that?"

"He was on foot."

Wager waited for more explanation, but none came. "What about an accident? Hitchhiking and hit by a car, or drunk and passed out?"

"Didn't drink—hated the stuff, his stepmother says. And no Ute with a car's going to walk or hitchhike unless it's broke down. His wasn't broke down, what I heard."

Gabe considered that. "Any idea who might want to kill him?"

A flash of white teeth. "Somebody who didn't like him, I guess."

Wager didn't laugh; it was true, not funny. "Why didn't he live on the reservation with the rest of his family?"

Ray glanced at Wager. "How much do you know about the Utes?"

"Used to haul in my share of drunk Native Americans when I patrolled Larimer Street. Some of them were Utes, I guess."

Another quick grin, this one with a slightly bitter twist. "I can't tell a German from a Frenchman, either, and you Native Hispanics all look alike, too." The truck tilted heavily to Wager's side as the two-rut track swung across a wide shoulder of slickrock webbed with cracks that held sprouts of tough grass and stunted sagebrush. "Rubin didn't want to live here. And under the new tribal rules that came in three years ago, he was no longer eligible to even if he'd wanted to; only half-bloods can live on the reservation, now. That was so the government doesn't have to give money to so may people. Rubin's dad, Marshall, his father was Mexican and his mother a Squaw Point Ute from here. Mildred Bow. That made Marshall Del Ponte half Ute. The grandfather took Marshall's mother over to the San Luis Valley, raised cattle on a ranch owned by the Del Ponte side of the family. That's where Marshall was born. He married a white woman over there and had Rubin—quarter Ute—then he divorced her and left San Luis and moved back here to Squaw Point Reservation, married a Squaw Point girl, Isabel Sena. Marshall died maybe five years ago. Drank himself to death, of course. So Rubin's brother and sisters are three-quarters Squaw Pointe Ute and they can live here. That's generally the tribe on this reservation, Squaw Point Utes. Them and a few from the White River and Uncompaghre tribes." He explained, "Most of the Ute Mountain Utes are down on the Ute Mountain Reservation—down in Four Corners near Cortez and Towaoc. Most of the Uncompaghre and White River tribes are up in Utah—Uintah and Duray reservations. The Southern Utes—my tribe—are on the Southern Ute reservation over by Ignacio: the Kapu'ute band and my band, the Mowhache. We're all Utes, but we come from different tribes and different bands. So even if we all look alike, we're not all like, see what I mean?"

Wager nodded. "I see." Some of it, anyway. The general picture, which was all he wanted to have to know right now. The complexity of Rubin's family ties and the tangle of his cousins sounded even worse than Wager's own, and if it wasn't going to bear on the case, Wager wasn't interested.

"What we got on this reservation is a mixture, people who didn't want to go to those other reservations for one reason or another: some Paiutes and even a few Apaches. Even a couple

Navajo families who bought out some of the Utes and moved in.
A real American melting pot, you know?"

"How did you get here?"

"I was hired to come: no tribal ties, no family bias." A slight
hesitation before he added, "They've had a lot of trouble here
for a long time with a couple of families running the tribal council, stealing the tribal money, taking over the common land,
hiring their own relatives, that kind of thing. So after the last
election, which was mostly honest, the new tribal council went
to BIA and asked to hire an outsider to run the police. So I got
the job. It's better this way, but sometimes it makes things hard."
A mild shrug that dismissed a lot of personal loss. "There's weird
stuff goes on around here sometimes and it's better I'm not part
of it. This way I'm everybody's enemy."

Wager could understand the man's feelings: a lot of cops
were outside the communities they were hired to protect and
serve. "What kind of weird stuff?"

"Family feuds, one group jealous of another. They're always
maneuvering, you know? Always think some other family's getting more than they are."

"Why did Rubin's father come here?"

"So he could register into the tribe and get his share of the
tribal royalties money." He moved his hand, palm down, over
the dash. "Looks like shit out there, don't it? Sand, rock, sky.
Nothing. Except for the oil, gas, coal. Uranium, too, but the market
for that's gone bad. And we finally won some court cases; started
getting property settlements for the stolen lands and broken treaties.
But only registered tribal members can share it."

"That means full-bloods, right?"

"Half-bloods." Another shrug. "Too many people had already married outside their tribes to limit it to full-bloods. Some
of the bands didn't even exist anymore, if you only counted
full-bloods. Anyway, after the property settlement of 1952, a lot
of people came back to the reservations. Got a house, some

money, food stamps and medical care, land for horses. Damn near doubled our populations in a couple of years.

"The Utes were the last Native Americans to be put on reservations—1880—and we filed court claims in 1932 for compensation for lands taken in violation of the treaties. It was finally settled in 1952 and the indemnity distributed in 1961. Hell," he smiled again, "we only signed a peace treaty with the Comanches in 1977. We're still pretty much savages, you see."

"Rubin's father came here in 1961?" The file Wager had read said Rubin had been born in 1965.

"No. Later, maybe seventy-two or seventy-three. That was when the tribe started getting royalties from gas and oil companies. He missed out on the first disbursal, so he didn't want to miss the oil money."

"And he could just move in and get a share?"

"He was half Squaw Point Ute and had his mother's relations living here—the Box family. And at the time, the tribe was trying to build up its numbers, too; so the council let in about anybody who could come up with any kind of blood claim." He tugged at a corner of the brim of his baseball cap. "You see, the way it was for a long time, the tribes got welfare per capita—the more people, the more money came into the tribe's collective account. That's starting to change, now—Washington found out it's too expensive. People started having too many babies, some of the tribal councils opened membership to quarter-bloods and even one-eighths. Like on this reservation, where all the I am money still goes into the central account and then gets used for tribal expenses, management costs, disbursal, eighteen money, twenty-one money, so on." A shrug. "But the government said 'Enough already.' Now the government's got a new idea, the sovereignty policy, they call it. Now only half-bloods and full-bloods are supposed to live on this reservation and collect benefits. But legally, it's all screwed up—quarter-bloods can't live here or claim benefits anymore, but they can inherit land allotments if they're legitimate heirs. That means they can own and even sell reservation land, but they can't live on it. It's really screwed up."

Wager shook his head. "You lost me somewhere in there. What's I am money and eighteen money?"

" 'I am,' that's what the government pays you when you say 'I am a Squaw Point Ute' or 'I am a Southern Ute.' Those payments start when you're born. When a child turns eighteen, they get a lump sum from their trust fund of I am money, which the tribal council manages. Eight, ten thousand dollars. Then more when they turn twenty-one: eighteen and twenty-one money. Unless some of the council members steal it. That's what happened here, a while back. It's supposed to give kids a stake to get started with. Buy a house, get married, start a business, go to college, whatever." He shook his head. "Most of the kids here, if they have any eighteen money, they go down to Cortez, buy a new car, party it up, and end up back on the reservation with nothing." Another shake of the head. "We do better: my tribe, the Southern Utes. A lot of these Squaw Point people, they just don't care."

"Why not?"

Ray took a while to answer, the silver of his mirrored sunglasses staring somewhere down the twisting ruts ahead. When he spoke again, the brittle irony of his voice had been replaced by a kind of weariness. "They've been broken, I guess. Their great-grandparents were broken when they were pushed out of the mountains and over into the desert. That was when almost all of the tribal leaders—adults and old folks—died: TB, whiskey, suicide. For thirty years, just about no death on this reservation was from natural causes; they were all caused by whiskey. Suicide accident, overdose, homicide. All caused by whiskey. And nothing had been written down, none of the stories, none of the chants and songs—it was all oral. So when the old ones died off, most of that went with them. There's not even any more Ute medicine men on this reservation—somebody wants a traditional cure, they have to hire a Navajo medicine man. A Navajo! They charge, too; a thousand, two thousand dollars—more than they charge their own people. So what happened, those first kids, the first ones born on the reservation had to just about raise themselves. Then they had their own kids and grandkids who did the same. And," his voice grew ironic again, "the only people to teach them were the white men and the BIA; so they learned what a dollar was worth and how to steal from people who trusted them and that Jesus loved them. It broke their spirit."

Wager said nothing. He had nothing to say.

"But it happened a long time ago. Now it's time they changed. It's goddamn hard, but other tribes have done it." His hand slapped the steering wheel for emphasis. "It's time, man!"

They rode in silence for a long while. Wager felt as if he ought to have a hard time imagining the fragmented and bewildered lives of those reservation kids, but he didn't; it sounded depressingly similar to life in the Denver projects, like the things he saw as a cop in the inner city, like the throwaway kids who drifted through the alleys and dimly lit parks of nighttime Denver. It sounded depressingly like the forgotten corners of the rest of America, like the lost lives that the nation's business and government leaders said were worth nothing and deserved the punishment they got because to do something might cut their own profits or reduce their own tax breaks.

"Did you help Durkin investigate Walter Lawrence's death?"

Ray nodded. "A little bit—rounded up some witnesses so Durkin could question them. That's all I was asked to do."

"How'd he die?"

"Knife in the back. Blood test showed plenty of alcohol, so Durkin decided it was a fight between a couple of drunks."

"Do you agree?"

"I'm not as sure as Durkin is."

"Why?"

"No other signs of a fight. And Lawrence mostly stayed by himself: no kids, no close relatives living on the rez, his wife died a long time ago, and he never visited his wife's relatives. A real loner—just him and his sheep. Who would he fight with?"

Wager didn't have an answer to that. "Any ties to the deaths of the federal agents? Holtzer and Kershaw?"

"Doesn't look that way. Far as I know, Lawrence had as little to do with them as he did with anybody else. Maybe less, since he made no secret about not trusting any white men. He ran a few sheep on some land on Narraguinnep Wash, a couple of miles above Luther Del Ponte's place. Came into Dark Mesa maybe once a month or so for salt and tobacco." Ray shifted into a higher gear as the track pulled out of a rock-choked valley and onto a sandy flat covered thinly by sagebrush and yucca spikes. "If he hadn't been stabbed in the back, there wouldn't be any reason to think anybody killed him; he hardly ever saw anybody, didn't have anything anybody would want. And nobody's talking about it that I've heard of. But like I said, they think it's real bad luck to talk about the dead."

"Where'd he get killed?"

"Found him about a mile and a half east of Dark Mesa Village. Looked like he was drunk and trying to walk home, maybe, when somebody knifed him."

"Where'd he get the whiskey?" Wager remembered passing a sign at the entrance to the reservation warning that no alcoholic beverages were allowed in the Ute Nation.

"It's easy enough to bring it on the reservation." Ray nodded as much to himself as to Wager. "A lot of people do. And Lawrence's section's right on the reservation boundary; when he wanted whiskey badly enough, all he had to do was get on his horse and ride across Narraguinnep Wash. Might take him half a day to ride to a liquor store and back, but he could have gone cross-country to Egnarville or Dry Creek, if he wanted.

That still doesn't tell me he was drinking with someone in the village the night he was killed; in fact, I never found a horse he could've ridden to town. And nobody I've talked to gave him a ride to town or saw him in the village or knew who he had a feud with."

They rode in silence again, Wager half listening to the rocks being kicked up that struck the truck's frame and fenders.

"There's Luther Del Ponte's place." Ray wagged a single finger toward the horizon.

Wager noted the odometer and the miles they had covered since leaving Dark Mesa: twenty-three.

8

IT WAS ANOTHER of the split-level, suburban tract homes whose isolation on a tilted plain between two widely separated mesas looked both lonely and incongruous. Dark-colored, it stood near a spur of red sandstone that rose like a rooster comb. Beyond the house, glimpsed here and there as a deep fissure writhing through the rise of sage and cedars, was Narraguinnep Wash. A corral, made of old rubber tires hung in a line between horizontal poles, penned a pair of horses whose heads were up and turned in the direction of the approaching truck. One of those mud-covered domes could be seen, half hidden behind a screen of shoulder-high sagebrush in back of the house, and on the sand in front of it a television dish was tilted to the sky. A line of anemic, twisted telephone poles brought electricity and telephone wires from somewhere over a rise of brush-dotted land.

"Is that a sweat lodge? That mud hut?"

"A wickiup. Sometimes they're used for sweat lodges. Other times like a Navajo hogan. They're made of sticks and limbs and covered with mud. Some of the old people like living in them better than in a white man's house—cooler, and they have their own space. Kind of an Indian mother-in-law's apartment, you know?"

Wager nodded and looked over the half-dozen vehicles that

sat around in the house's clearing. Most were trucks that had been more or less stripped for parts; a motorcycle frame lay on its side beside a rusting cab and flatbed that lacked glass and wheels. In front of the house, angled in different directions, were parked two vehicles that apparently still ran: a newer minivan and a pickup truck that didn't look too much better than the derelicts. From the doorless shade of one of the abandoned vehicles, a lean dog came out and stared at their approaching truck, ears raised intently, tail half lifted between alarm and wag.

Ray slowed to a gently lurching pace and approached to within a hundred yards or so of the house and then shut off his motor.

"We'll wait a couple of minutes," he told Wager. "Give them a chance to know we're here."

Wager listened to the silence and the faint stir of the wind in the stiff branches of sagebrush and across the sand and shoulders of pale, bare rock. "Thay didn't hear us come up?"

"Probably. But it's their house and they didn't know we were coming. Pretty soon somebody'll be out. Won't be long."

That's what happened. After maybe five minutes of listening to their truck's hot engine tick as it cooled, the front door opened and a bow-legged man wearing a black cowboy hat and denims slowly came down the steps to the grassless dirt of the cluttered yard. The dog started to approach him but the man gestured it away and it turned, tail down, back to its rusting truck. In no hurry, the man strolled toward them. He said something to Ray that Wager didn't understand, and Ray answered. Then to Wager, "He says he's glad to see us. Asks us to visit with him."

"He speak English?"

"When he wants to, sure. Speaks some Ute and some Navajo, too, don't you, Luther?" Through the cab window he introduced Wager in English as a policeman working for the state of Colorado. "He's not with the federal government."

Luther, black eyes magnified by the thick lenses of his teardrop glasses, studied Wager.

"He's come here to find out about somebody," said Ray. "Might be this somebody is related to you—a half brother, maybe. Might be this half brother had some bad trouble not too long ago. Might be this half brother's wife said he came out to visit you three or four weeks ago, not too long before he had his trouble. This man," he nodded to Wager, "wants to know what this half brother maybe said to you."

Ray had explained that the bad luck, which came from talking about the dead, arose from using their names and thereby calling their spirits back to cause mischief for the living. A lot of Utes believed that what was good about a dead person went on to a good place; what was bad stayed here as an evil spirit, and that explained why there was so much trouble and pain and suffering in this life. Even most nontraditional Utes felt uneasy talking about the dead; many of them still believed in bad spirits that had a lot of power. So what you did was talk around the dead—avoid direct mention of their names, speak conditionally so the listening ghosts couldn't be certain you meant them.

When someone died they were still buried as quickly as possible. A long time ago, they had been placed in an out-of-the-way crack in the rocks and covered with stones to keep animals from disturbing the corpse and its spirit. Now the BIA made them bury them in a cemetery whether or not they were Christian. It was said that some of the Uinta Utes used to build a platform to lift the corpse closer to heaven, but that information came from white men. What the other tribes did in their traditional burials was something a Ute just didn't talk about if he had manners.

The place where a person had died was avoided; most Squaw Point Utes didn't use the community swimming pool at Dark Mesa Village anymore because a boy had drowned there a few years ago, so it must have had evil spirits. They called it *ihupi'arat tubuts*—a place where ghosts waited. If someone died in a house, it was abandoned. That was why some of the bungalows in the Dark Mesa compound were boarded up. Like many Southern Utes, Ray's parents were Christian and did not fully believe in the traditional ways of the dead. Ray, himself neither Christian nor traditional, had as hard a time believing in all the ghosts and bad spirits that haunted many of the Squaw Point Utes as he did believing that a man from the Jewish tribe rose from the grave, walked around awhile, and then flew up to heaven. "I'm sort of typical of my generation, I guess. Not much faith in any kind of spirits; everything depends on what we do ourselves—no god or ghost is going to help or hurt us. We got to do it ourselves." He snorted. "If anything, whatever god there is needs our help, not the other way around." But many of the Squaw Point Utes did believe in spirits and hexes because that was about the only cultural past that had been handed down to them—"It's the stories their mothers and grandmothers learned from their grandparents and told the kids at bedtimes. And I guess it does support their belief in what happens to the dead: As a culture, the Squaw Point Utes are just about dead, and only the stories of bad ghosts and goblins are left; the good of their spirit world is gone away with their *po'rats*—their medicine men."

Luther Del Ponte looked to be in his thirties. He had a short nose and a wide upper lip that rose out over his lower one. His jaw tapered to a fragile point. If it had not been for the two thick braids of black hair that hung in front of his shoulders, Wager thought he would look more like a Japanese scholar than an Indian.

"Why do you want to know this?" The man spoke to Ray but the question was to Wager.

"In case it wasn't an accident," he answered.

Luther used a scarred thumb to push his glasses up his nose while he thought over what Wager had said. "OK. Let's go to the shade house."

He turned and led the way, the heels of his cowboy boots leaving dents in the dry earth. Wager and Ray followed around behind the split-level house with its big fiberglass water tank. A patch of churned sand made the backyard distinct from the unfenced brush and weeds that surrounded it. Well-used toys littered the sand and a few half-buried tires made kid-sized seats. At the vague outer edge of the yard, a path wound between clumps of sage and leafless scrub oak for about fifty yards, to what looked like a six-foot-high table whose four legs were made of heavy sticks and whose top was a roughly woven mat of cottonwood branches with the dead leaves still on. In the shade beneath it, two children played in the sand, a boy around seven and a girl a year or two younger. When they noticed Wager, they froze like rabbits and stared at him with wide, black eyes.

"I would thank you if you kids went to play somewhere else so we could use the shade house now. These men have come a long way to talk to me."

Wordless, they grabbed their toy trucks and plastic dinosaurs and ran off through the brush.

Luther led them under the low roof and then settled himself in the shade. Ray and Wager followed.

"Cooler here. Quieter than the house, too." He tugged a blue stegosaurus from under his leg and set it near one of the roof's uprights, out of the way. "No damn television here."

Somewhere behind him, hidden by the gnarled, flaking trunks of the scrub oak, Wager heard the scuffle of small feet.

Ray settled into his cross-legged position. "This is nice. You sleep out here?"

"Sometimes—when the house is too hot. Good place to come when we got family visiting, too. Nice and quiet so a man can think."

There was a silence and Wager, feeling his knees begin to twinge from the unaccustomed stretch, hoped they weren't going to sit like this for too long. Luther fished in his shirt pocket for a package of cigarettes and offered them. "Smoke?"

Wager shook his head. "No thanks. I don't' smoke."

Ray took one but just held it in his hand, not lighting up.

Luther lit his with a paper match and bobbed his head back to pull the smoke into his lungs.

Ray waited until Luther had set the cigarette package and matches on the sand beside him. "How's the horses this spring?"

"Pretty good. Got two mares coming into foal. Stud by Three-hands. Maybe one of them will be pretty good."

Ray explained to Wager. "Three-hands is one of the fastest quarter horses on the reservation. Damn good horse."

"Better be good. Stud fees cost me enough."

"What about the stock? Get through the winter OK?"

"Real good, a mild winter this time. Grass could be better but there's lots of spring lambs—enough to make a Navajo jealous."

Ray laughed. "How's your mother doing?"

"OK, I guess. She moved to the village to live with Cynthia. She can visit her friends more there. She's closer to the clinic, too."

Cynthia, Ray told Wager, was one of Luther's three sisters. She had a job with the food-stamp agency. "How's the family? Wife? Kids?"

"They're OK."

And apparently less important, if Wager judged by the dismissal in Luther's voice.

But not without problems: "My daughter Janie wants to get married now. I told her fifteen's too young."

Ray nodded and ran some sand between his fingers. It made a small sound like the bottom of an hourglass. "Who's she want to marry?"

"Parley Red Bird. He just turned eighteen."

"Well, they'll have his eighteen money."

"Yeah, I hope so. Then Janie's eighteen money, then his twenty-one money, then hers. That's what they think, anyway.

Just like me and Cerise had, they think." He shook his head.
"But I don't know how much money that's going to be anymore.
Nobody knows, now. Be what the Many Coats don't take, I guess,
and that won't be much." Another shake of his head. "Besides,
it's still too young. She'll drop out of school, have kids, pretty
soon even if they get some eighteen and twenty-one money, there
won't be nothing else."

The two men fell silent. Apparently, it was a familiar story
and one they had no answer to.

"Kids do what they want to," Ray said at last.

Luther nodded. "It's still too young. Her mother thinks it's
too young, too." There was another silence, and something inside one of Wager's knees started to twitch.

Luther offered more cigarettes. Wager shook his head; Ray
held up the one he still held. When Luther had taken a few puffs,
Ray said, "Maybe you can tell us something about this person.
Anything he told you about what he was doing. Why he was
where he was."

A long, meditative draw on the cigarette. "This person was
not Squaw Point Ute, only a little. Maybe this person will not
get mad if I tell you. But," and there was a long silence while
Luther thought and smoked his cigarette down to a tiny stub
before carefully rubbing it out on the arch of his boot, "maybe
he would."

That was the way it went, and Wager lost count of the times
he shifted his weight to relieve the numbness in his butt or the
stiffening ache in his knees. And when Luther finally started
telling his story, it was oblique, removed as far as possible from
his half brother, and it teased and irritated Wager with missing
facts.

"You know who runs our tribal council."

"The Many Coats."

Luther nodded. "Mostly the Many Coats family. They have
for a long time. They look out for themselves first. They take the

trust money, they pay themselves a big salary and expenses, and if anybody complains they tell the BIA that that person is no good. That person should get his payments cut or he shouldn't get any more tribal work or he shouldn't be given a house." He added in a lower voice, "And they use hexes. I know you don't believe in these things, Ray, but people who argue with the Many Coats family get sick and die. They commit suicide, they have accidents, they go off by themselves into the canyons and live with their sheep all alone. I know these things."

It was Ray's turn to nod but he waited until he was sure Luther was finished. "Whether I believe or not is unimportant. What's important is that the Squaw Point Utes believe in the Many Coats's magic."

Wager said, "That's federal money those people are misusing, isn't it? Hasn't the FBI been called in to investigate?"

Luther stared at the sand, and finally Ray answered for him. "Sure. FBI agent came in six or seven years ago, went through all the receipts. Found a lot of things wrong. Found Douglas Many Coats had charged the tribal account for three hundred ninety days' per diem for one year."

"For one year?"

Luther snorted. "And a year only has three hundred sixty-five days. You know it and I know it. But Douglas Many Coats forgot about that—he was so greedy he forgot how many days in a year."

Ray laughed. "Douglas gave greed a bad name with that one."

"So what'd the FBI do?"

"Nothing," said Ray. "Submitted the report to the BIA. The Many Coats family has the BIA in its many pockets, so BIA turned it over to the tribal council to handle. Which, of course, is run by the Many Coats family. So the FBI went away and things stayed the same."

Luther lit another cigarette, this time not going through the ritual of offering. "Around here, if you kiss the asses of the Many Coats, you can get things: extra money, credit at the trading post, interest-free loans from the banks down in Cortez and up in Grand Junction. If you don't, you got to wade through shit just to get your annuity. About ten years ago the tribe even went broke for a while—the Many Coats family had spent the tribe's whole annuity money and eighteen money. I heard Ramey Many Coats bought six cars that year."

"That was the worst time," Ray said. "I wasn't here then, but we heard about it over on the Southern Ute reservation. Sounded like there was going to be shooting, people were so mad."

"Would have been, except Douglas Many Coats can put a hex on anybody he doesn't like. He's done it—made one of Charley Buck's sons shoot himself in the head." He pinched some of the fine sand and tossed it away from him as if to cleanse the air of the dead man's name. "They're like that: They figure you might give them some trouble, they hex you and your family, and you don't even know it until something bad comes along." His voice dropped into gloom. "And now they're talking 'tribal sovereignty'—just another way to take away what little we got left."

Wager wanted to ask if Rubin had troubles with the Many Coats, but this time he held his tongue; the question had to be in Ray's mind, too, and he would know the best way to get around to it.

"The tribal council's elected," Ray told Wager. "But there's no voter registry so it's easy to stuff the ballot box. The Many Coats family have at least four of the seven members elected to the council every year. Have for as long as I can remember."

"Me, too. First the older ones, then their sons. Now Douglas's son Ramey and his brothers and cousins." Luther shrugged. "It's the way things are. The way they always will be unless things get worse."

Ray didn't like to hear resignation like that, Wager saw, but the younger man didn't say anything. They sat in silence for a while. Finally Luther started speaking again. "Anyway, since all the trouble a few years back when the tribe went broke, the Many Coats family hasn't been stealing as much from the tribe, so people got enough to get by on for now. But now maybe something else is going on."

After a polite wait, Ray asked, "You mean the sovereignty policy?"

Luther shook his head. "No. Something else, maybe. I'm not sure. This person told everybody that something was going on—some big deal, maybe."

Wager forgot about his aching knees.

And Ray, though he still sat, dragging his fingertips through the sand, seemed more alert. "Something that Ramey Many Coats was mixed up in?"

Luther grunted. "I don't know for sure, but I think so. This person talked about some deal. I guess he talked about it to everybody; I got asked about it from some other people who'd heard about it, anyway. He always did talk a lot." He fell silent and Wager wondered if Luther expected them to agree.

Ray finally asked, "Have you talked to Ramey?"

"I don't talk to no Many Coats. Got nothing to say to them." Luther's silence turned sullen. "That's just what this person said. Said there were some white men in on it talking to Ramey about it, too. Told me and a lot of other Indians that there would be big news in a while."

"How did this person find out?"

A shrug. "This person went to a lot of places in his work. He heard a lot of things—he talked to people and they talked to him. Maybe this person was getting paid to find out things, too." Another shrug. "Ask whoever else he told this to. He liked to talk, so ask them."

Again Wager made himself keep quiet; Ray finally got

around to what Wager wanted to ask: "Maybe this big news had to do with some white men getting shot? Some federal government men?"

Luther thought that over and then shrugged. "I don't know. Maybe that was it. This person, he was always asking around about things like that for the FBI. Maybe that was it. You ask Ramey."

Wager could keep quiet no longer. "Did this person belong to the Constitutional Posse?"

The man's silence apologized for Wager's rudeness. After a while he wagged his head. "I don't think so. I don't know, but this person didn't go to no meetings—didn't have time."

"When was this? When did he tell you about this deal?"

Luther mumbled. "The last time I saw him. Maybe a week before he met the sheriff."

"Met the sheriff?"

"Before the sheriff found him," say Ray.

"This person," Luther studied the sand in front of his folded legs, "you think somebody maybe killed him? Is that why you're asking these questions?"

Wager answered, "It's what I'm trying to find out. There's not enough evidence to say for sure, only suspicion."

"Any idea who?"

"He was an informant for the FBI. He was told to ask about the Constitutional Posse. And about who had shot those government people."

Luther sat still, eyes half closed, as if forcing himself not to hear Wager's voice.

"Did this person ever talk to you about his wife? Say they were having troubles?" Wager asked

"No."

Ray said, "That's something only women talk to each other about. And white men. If he did talk about his marriage, it wasn't to an Indian."

Wager persisted. "Did you know his wife?"

"Met her."

"Do you think she could have killed him?"

Luther absently fingered one of the leather thongs wrapped around the end of a braid. "Maybe it's better to stop asking things about this person. Better to leave this person in peace."

"The law says I can't do that. It's a suspicious death and it has to be investigated." Wager added, "Did Ru—did this person know either of the white men who were shot?"

Luther stared at the sand. "I don't know. I don't know any more."

Apparently that was all Luther was going to say about that. Even a question about Walter Lawrence—called "your old neighbor who maybe lived up the wash" by Ray—was answered with only a puff of cigarette smoke. Ray finally turned the talk back to quarter-horse racing and who had won what where. After another half hour of that, he handed back the unsmoked cigarette he had held. "Thanks for your help, Luther. We better get going now."

The man tapped the cigarette into the box. "You didn't hear anything from me."

"No. We talked about horses."

"That's right."

Wager asked the man to call him through Ray or Sheriff Spurlock or at the Gypsum Motel if he remembered anything else that might be helpful. Then he limped back to Ray's truck, his legs stiff and awkward. "What do you think?"

"I'm not sure. But if Rubin did find out something about the Posse that he wasn't supposed to know, I don't think it involved anybody on the reservation."

"Why not?"

"Because they knew he was working for the FBI."

"Everybody on the reservation knew that?"

"Aw, sure! Durkin asked maybe half a dozen people to work

for him before he got around to asking Rubin. And Rubin told Luther what he was doing—he wasn't the kind who could keep his mouth shut, from what I hear about him. If he told Luther, he probably told somebody else as well. Hell, Rubin was a magpie, always squawking. Everybody on the reservation knew better than to tell that man anything they wanted kept secret."

9

DESPITE THE ROUGH road, Wager's knees thought the trip back was bliss. He kneaded the flesh of his legs and stretched and bent the tenderness out of his joints. For a while, neither man talked much; Ray kept his mirrored glasses facing the dirt track ahead, and Wager was trying to build a system for determining Rubin's last few days.

"I figure Rubin came out to visit Luther a day or two before he died," Wager finally said.

"Yeah. Maybe even the same day. He was dead, what, a week before he was found?"

"That's the coroner's estimate." For what that was worth. The coroner for La Sal and Montezuma counties was an undertaker down in Cortez. As was true in most rural counties of Colorado, he lacked both a medical degree and any forensics training. Which the coroner's report clearly showed. That county office was just a way to earn extra cash from the taxpayers. But, in fairness, it would have been a tough case even for an MD. "From what little he had to work with."

Ray grunted. He might not have been as superstitious as the Squaw Point Utes, but the details of an ugly death scene still seemed to verge on the obscene for him. "Looks like the people are getting some rain over there." He nodded toward a billowing pile of mounting clouds that reached high enough to brush the jet stream and form an anvil head. Icy blue lightning flickered behind different spurs and boils of cloud, and from its flat, dark bottom, a gray beard of rain slanted toward the earth. "Hope it's a two-inch rain and not a six-inch rain."

"Flash-flood danger?"

"Too early in the year for that. Naw, out here, a two-inch rain means the drops land closer together than in a six-inch rain. By four inches."

"Oh." Maybe that was supposed to be a joke—the young Indian seemed to be smiling to himself. "Could Luther belong to the Constitutional Posse?"

"No. Nobody on the reservation does—that's a white man's organization and they don't want Indians near it."

"But he knew about it."

"Sure. Everybody does." Then, "Oh, you mean he might have known about the Posse because of Rubin? You still think Rubin might have been trying to infiltrate the Posse and they're the ones who killed him?" When Wager nodded, Ray said, "Well, Luther said Rubin didn't belong, and I believe him. You have to understand: The Posse's as much social as it is political, and those ranchers wouldn't mix socially with many Indians."

"Even a quarter-blood?"

"Even one drop of blood. Some of those ranchers call us 'red niggers.' And some of us Southern Utes do have some Negro blood—from buffalo soldiers who married into the tribe, and I'm damn proud of it. No, I can't see Rubin or any other Indian being even a fringe member of that bunch. And, by God, I wouldn't want any of them in my tribe, either." He shifted down to cross a gulch, working the gears with a bit more force than necessary. "But you better ask Spurlock about the Posse—he gets their vote every election! Rubin might have sympathized with them— or said he did. He'd have to, I reckon, since a lot of his customers are members. But they'd never invite him to join—hell, they might have to drink out of the same bottle."

"He was an FBI informant. He was told to look into the deaths of those men, and Durkin believes that the Constitutional Posse might be involved in the shootings."

Ray considered that. "I suppose that's possible. And maybe Rubin did find out something that could incriminate somebody, and that's why he was killed. Killing an Indian wouldn't mean much to some of the ranchers around here. If so," Ray's mirrored sunglasses swung Wager's way for a long moment, "you might not want to ask Spurlock about the Posse. He does owe his job to those people. And then there's Rubin's wife."

"What's that mean? Rubin's wife?"

"She's Spurlock's niece. And from what I hear, he wasn't very happy when she married an Indian."

"That's her uncle? The sheriff?"

Ray nodded. After a while, he added, "Maybe even Luther thinks the Posse killed Rubin—God knows he clammed up fast enough when you started asking questions about them."

"Do you know the Posse leaders?"

He shook his head. "I don't know too much about the Posse at all, just that they're around. I don't know if they have elected officers and such. Like I said, it's more a social group than a military one; my guess is that they get together and talk out a consensus—maybe if somebody comes up with some kind of plan, he's the leader for that, and whoever wants to, joins him." Another of those wry grins. "Sort of the way the Indians used to do it."

The vehicle lurched across a spine of rock and then its tires churned through a wind drift of fine, pink sand.

"Have you heard of Bradley Nichols or Stan Litvak?"

Ray frowned slightly. "Nichols has a place up Narraguinnep Wash, I believe. I'm not sure where Litvak's spread is."

"Nichols is supposed to be the Posse's organizer. Litvak takes care of the training, I hear."

"You hear more than me, man—blows hell out of my theory of consensus, doesn't it?"

It did. Wager watched a startled rabbit scurry into a thicket, its tail a bouncing white dot. "You think Luther is a pretty reliable witness?"

"Good question. He wants to get the Many Coats into trouble. Most of the people would be happy to see trouble come to that family. But I don't think Luther would lie. He might forget to tell everything or not tell exactly the truth, but I doubt he'd outright lie like a white man. Even the Squaw Point Utes have a little pride left."

Wager wondered if he was considered white or brown. Probably just blue—a cop, which was all right with him. "I'd like to talk to Ramey Many Coats."

Ray nodded. "Figured you would. But Ramey might not want to talk with you."

"Why not?"

"Because you're a cop and he's up to something. That whole family's always up to something—they always got a guilty conscience, and with good reason. Indian Snopses, that's what they are."

Wager didn't know what an Indian Snopses was, but he let it go. "Even if all I want is information about Rubin?"

"Anything you want, he won't want to talk about it. He's that suspicious of the law—especially a white lawman. Better let me see what I can find out."

Wager nodded. "As soon as you can?"

"Do my best," Ray said. "Old Luther was worried about you, too, at first."

"Why's that?"

"Probably his kids. He's claimed that his three youngest kids are retarded. He gets some extra government money for them that way. Special education allowance." He laughed. "That's why I made sure he knew you were a state policeman, not a federal—he thinks you've got no jurisdiction on the reservation."

"And they're not retarded?"

Ray shook his head.

"Won't that cause problems when they have to go to school?"

"Probably. But what the hell, the BIA teachers will treat them like they're retarded anyway."

"Does he need money that badly?"

"The tribe's finances are pretty insecure now. What with the Many Coats running thing their way, and the government talking about doing away with allotments and even selling off parts of the reservation, nobody knows what's going to happen. It's all part of the new sovereignty policy: Get rid of the reservation, give everything to the people who live there and let them make their way without any more government support. Here, it means turn everything over to the Many Coats family. And besides, Luther's just a crazy Indian: He wants the money now, and tomorrow will take care of itself."

Wager weighed the bitterness in the young man's voice. "You use your Indian name, don't you? Your last name?"

"Yeah. My name translates into 'Eagle Son' and that's what my folks are still called: Joseph and LaDonna Eagle Son. I changed it back into Ute. I figured Carl Yastrzemski didn't have to change his name, and there's Kareem Abdul-Jabbar and Kristie Yamaguchi. Even Cecil Traumerhauser."

"Traumerhauser?"

"Kid I roomed with in college: Cecil Traumerhauser. His ancestors came over from Germany about the time mine were first meeting white men. Means 'Dream House,' but he didn't change it into English. So I changed mine back to Qwana'tua. I figured if I'm Indian, I might as well be Indian." He laughed again. "I guess I'm just as crazy as the rest of them."

10

WAGER FIGURED ON two stops after he left Dark Mesa
Village on his way to the Gypsum Motel and something to eat.
One was directly on his route back—Egnarville and the small
house of the widow Del Ponte. The other was south on Highway
666, a somewhat longer drive and a much longer shot. But it
had to be done. Why? Well, given how little he'd found out so
far, there wasn't much else to do.

By the time he pulled into the unpaved driveway that looped
in and out of the Del Ponte yard, the shadows of the cottonwood
trees had begun to lengthen and point east toward the rampart
of high, pine-covered plateau and the distant, snowy peaks behind
it. Sharon Del Ponte heard the sound of Wager's vehicle and came
to the screen door. He climbed the two concrete-block steps to the
wooden platform that served as an unroofed front porch.

"Sorry to bother you again, Mrs. Del Ponte."

She didn't seem disturbed to see him. "That's all right. You
like a cup of coffee?"

"No thanks. I won't take much of your time. Do you happen
to know where your husband kept his business records? Jobs
bid, expenses, income, the kind of things he'd need to fill out
on his tax forms each year?"

"His tax records? Well, yeah, I do remember him fussing
over that last year. This year, I don't know. He . . . he died before

taxes were due. He always waited until the last minute." She added, "But he didn't fill out his own tax forms. He used the H & R Block people over in La Sal."

"Did he have a log book or a driving record for daily entries? Something he could use for a running account?"

She frowned and absently stroked the small head that had appeared at her leg to stare from behind it at Wager. The child's large and solemn eyes were almost green. "I haven't seen it around here. He has a drawer where he keeps his business stuff, though. Let me go look."

The small face stayed, hanging mostly out of sight to peek around the door frame. Wager smiled at it, but it only stared back in silence. He'd never had much of a way with babies and little kids; came from having none of his own, he supposed.

"Here's all I could find. Will this help?" She handed him a wrinkled manila envelope that contained a clutch of loose receipts; most were monthly statements from Conoco; Mallard's Garage in Lewis Corners had several: lube and maintenance receipts, brake repair for $473.62; vehicle insurance premiums, State Farm. Apparently it was the cache of bills that were routinely mailed to his home address or were one-time business expenses. "Did he keep any daily record of miles traveled? Or income?"

"He had a business account at La Sal bank." Her eyes blinked as if masking something. "I had to close it out to pay the funeral bills. There wasn't more than a couple thousand in it."

"Any record of people paying into the account?"

"I don't know. The bank statement doesn't say who, just how much."

"How about a mileage book or calendar with his appointments?"

She shrugged. "In the truck, maybe. It's over at Lewis Corners, still. Harvey Mallard said he'd try to sell it for me."

Wager nodded. Lewis Corners was the second place he had planned to stop.

"Do you know of any appointments your husband had just before he died? Anybody he planned to meet?"

"No. Like I told you this morning, we didn't talk much about the business. That was all his."

"Did your husband drink, Mrs. Del Ponte?"

"Drink? Whiskey? No—he was afraid of it. His daddy was a drinker. Said he had too much Indian in him to drink. He wouldn't even drink beer, much."

At the edge of hearing, a car sped down a dirt road. Wager couldn't see it—it was maybe half a mile away—but he heard the rise and fall of its clattering tires over bumps and through gravel. "Did he ever say anything—anything at all—about some kind of big opportunity coming up soon?"

"Opportunity? What kind of opportunity?"

"I'm not sure. His brother, Luther, mentioned that he was excited about some deal that was supposed to happen soon."

She stared at him, mouth sucked in so her lips made a tight line. "No. He didn't tell me anything like that. He might have had something on his mind, but he wasn't worried about anything. Just thinking." She half apologized. "I didn't remember that when you were here earlier. But now you mention it, I recall I wondered a little at the time."

"Anything at all that he said?"

"Not to me. To Luther maybe, but not to me." There was the faint aroma of bitterness in the words. "When we first got married, I used to tease him about not telling me anything about his business. He said that was the Indian in him—men's business was men's, and squaws didn't need to know about it, so after a while I stopped asking." A deep breath. "What kind of deal did Luther say it was?"

"He didn't know. Just that your husband mentioned it to him and some other people." Wager waited, but she didn't say anything more.

"I understand your uncle's the sheriff."

She nodded.

"How did he feel about you and Rubin getting married?

"Feel? I don't know. OK, I guess. He came to the wedding—gave us a nice wedding present. What do you mean, feel?"

"Did he object because Rubin was an Indian?"

"No! Where'd you get that idea? I never see much of him, but that's because he's so busy. But he never said anything against Rubin or did anything, either! Who gave you that idea?"

"I heard that he and the Constitutional Posse dislike Indians."

"Well, I don't know about the Posse—maybe so, maybe not. But not Uncle Malcolm. We have dinner—had dinner—together from time to time and he always got along well with Rubin, so I don't know why anybody should tell you he didn't."

Wager studied the woman's angry eyes. "Do you know Mr. Haydn well?"

"B.J.? I know him. Why? Is he the one told you Uncle Malcolm didn't like Rubin?"

"I heard he made a pass at you."

"I hope you also heard it didn't get him anywhere!"

Wager nodded. "Did your husband know about it?"

"I didn't tell him. It made me feel too . . . dirty." Her head lifted. "Who told you?"

"One of the people I talked to. All he said was that Haydn made passes at every woman, you among them."

"B. J. Haydn is a shit. When you talk to him next time, you tell him I said so."

"If I do." He told her that she could leave messages for him through Sheriff Spurlock's office or at the Gypsum Motel if she remembered anything more. She nodded and stood watching through the screen door as Wager swung out of the driveway. The green-eyed child was back, clutching her leg.

LEWIS CORNERS WAS just that: four corners formed where a graveled county road crossed the pavement of U.S. 666.

Wager must have passed it coming up from Cortez, but he didn't remember it—that's the kind of place it was. The only sign bearing a name was at the front of a rambling building and said MALLARD'S GARAGE. The building had grown this way and that over time. Apparently it had started out as a two-story log house, probably a ranch house, and then had a covered boardwalk added to its front when it became a store. Then, on one side, the store had been enlarged by a frame addition whose flat roof slanted from head high up to the eave of the old house. Behind the addition, an almost square column like the block house of a fort rose a couple of stories and bore a television antenna, and off that, in another direction, lay a large tin shed. An island of 1950s gas pumps sat out in front with sun-faded advertisements for Conoco's hot brand, and—near the tin shed—stood one of those ancient gas pumps, empty now, the kind with the graduated glass cylinder at the top that let you see how many gallons drained into your tank. A dozen or so cargo trailers, some listing with age and inaction, and a few trucks were pulled into an irregular line in the stunted brush and weeds behind the tin building. Wager figured that the one with the fresh FOR SALE sign propped behind the windshield was Rubin's.

"Yep. This is his." Harvey Mallard, a man who looked like a bent straw, slapped a bony hand on the thick fender of a gray-and-white Kenmore tractor. Scrolled letters on the door spelled "Del Ponte Trucking Company. Egnarville, Colo." and listed Rubin's home telephone number. "Told Sharon I'd try and sell it for her. Told her I wouldn't charge no commission—just advertising costs. She's got a hard row, a widow with two little kids."

Wager agreed. "Rubin didn't leave any insurance?"

"Don't know. But even if he did, Sharon'll need all the money she can get. Hell of a thing, him dying like that."

Wager watched the man climb up to unlock the driver's door and search for the vehicle's log book. "Why didn't Rubin park his equipment at home? He had plenty of land for it."

"This way saved time and fuel. It's easier to park his rig here, just off the highway. One-eighty-one's just a long, dead-end road—don't go anywhere but the reservation. I told him he could leave his rig here, seeing's he was getting his fuel and repairs done here anyway." He wagged a narrow, long-fingered hand at the other vehicles. "Couple of truckers around here do that. Some park the tractor and trailer, some just the trailer and drive the tractor home bobtail. Saved Rubin almost sixty miles round trip every day he drove his truck. Three, four, five times a week, that adds up. And it's free parking—a service for my regular customers."

"I understand he left his car here before he died."

Mallard stopped rummaging around in the truck long enough to look over a narrow, curving shoulder and down at Wager. "You're right, Officer. He sure did. After they found him, Sharon had to get that Herrera fella to give her a ride up here so she could drive it home."

"Did you see him leave with anyone?"

"Can't remember that I did." The man, hand full of a thick booklet and some loose papers, relocked the door and swung down the mounting rungs to the ground. "Important, is it?"

"It is if someone killed him."

He scratched at the white bristles of his chin with oil-grimed fingernails. "I hadn't heard that's what happened. Just that he died. Nobody said what of."

"He might or might not have been killed. That's what I'm trying to find out." Wager was getting a little tired of saying that, but repetition went with the territory when you were investigating things.

"Well, now . . . well. That puts a somewhat different light on things, don't it?"

"Why's that?"

"Makes it a lot more important who he left here with, for one thing. I ain't paid much attention, you know, to trying to remember all that kind of thing. Sheriff Spurlock just wanted to know if Rubin's car or truck was here, which they both was, and that's about all he asked me." Absently, he held out the bundle to Wager. "I just can't remember him leaving with nobody. Drove up and parked next to his tractor, messed around there a while, and when I noticed again, he was gone." He explained, "I get busy in the garage, I can't see much back here. I just don't know."

Wager nodded, his attention on the booklet and papers.

"That's the vehicle maintenance log. I got to have that back, Officer. Somebody buys the tractor, they want to know how it's been maintained, what parts been replaced, that kind of thing."

"OK." A narrow book with "1997" inked on the cover in ballpoint pen looked promising; it held standard forms for receipt of payment and a worn piece of carbon paper. A smaller spiral notebook, bound at the top, also had "1997" on the cover, and it looked like the daily log of jobs undertaken. "All right if I sit in my car and look through these?"

"Use my office if you want."

"Thanks, the car'll do."

The maintenance log was just that, a listing of mileages and dates and services performed. The loose papers were a variety of certifications and inspections that operators might have to produce: proof of insurance, safety and pollution inspections, a couple of weight verifications. He leafed through them quickly and then turned to the notebook, starting with the last entry, "Rocking W: twelve head, 29 March." That date was after the date of his disappearance, the seventeenth; obviously, he wasn't planning on dying before then, so that made suicide doubtful. The next two scheduled jobs were similar, the twenty-seventh and the twenty-sixth, also for moving cattle. Wager slid his finger up the sheet of lined paper. There was a note for "Haydn, 23-24," and another for "Bar L Bar" on 22 March. On the seventeenth through the nineteenth of March, he was apparently scheduled for a run to Phoenix for the Lastwell Furniture Store in Grand Junction. That would be the job he was headed for when his wife waved good-bye for the last time. The next entry was 15 March: the Butte Springs Ranch. This entry was followed by three numbers—158—and, looking ahead, Wager noted that the rest of the earlier entries also had numbers behind them: mileages, he finally figured out. Which meant that those later jobs without mileage numbers behind them had not been completed. The run to Phoenix for the furniture store either had not been made or, for some reason, Rubin had not entered the miles traveled.

Wager cross-checked his suppositions against the carbon entries in the receipt booklet. Many but not all of the dates of payment received matched dates of the jobs listed in the log book. It looked as if some of the employers paid in cash or by check at the completion of a job, while others were billed and would pay at the end of the month. Sure enough, Rubin had not recorded any payments received after 16 March.

Thumbing through the spiral notebook back to January, Wager noted one other point: Occasionally, an awkwardly penned five-pointed star followed a mileage entry. There was no obvious reason for the marks; they came at irregular intervals, though most were applied to short hauls, the mileage said, which took a day at most. Two or three followed ranch names, the rest came behind a last name: Turney, Hegendorf, Briscoe, Archibeque. Wager looked back through the daily log again; in all there were six entries that had the little star. He looked at the list of starred names he had jotted down and a thought struck him; paging through the receipt book, he verified what he thought he remembered: There were no carbon sheets bearing those six names. The star seemed to mean that those people had not paid. Credit? But there was no notation of what was owed, and Wager doubted that Rubin would be able to carry so much delayed income. Cash? Barter? Maybe that was it—whatever he was paid for those six jobs, Rubin had not listed it as income. Shaving a little off the reported income for tax purposes; possibly gave a cut rate for cash, possibly jobs for members of the Constitutional Posse who hated supporting the federal government with taxes. Yet Rubin had kept a record of the mileage so he could maintain an accurate service schedule on his vehicle. And that hinted to Wager that he tended to be careful about his business, even if putting some things in writing wasn't the smartest thing to do.

He found Mallard in the tin building, working on the axle end of a jacked-up truck. "I'd like to keep these job and payment books, if I can."

"Sure thing—maintenance log's all I need."

Wager set that on the oil-stained and cluttered planks of the long workbench. "I'll leave it right here. Do you remember what time it was Del Ponte came in that last day?"

Mallard, squatting on a low stool beside the dismantled hub, tilted his head back to stare in thought at the fluorescent ceiling light. The movement made his large Adam's apple protrude even further. "Late morning, I think—maybe ten or eleven. Wasn't early. Most of the time he got here early when he had a run." He explained, "I open at seven. Some of the truckers like to top off before they go. Unless they're heading into Utah. Diesel's a lot cheaper across the line—less state tax."

"Did he speak with you? Say anything at all?"

Another stare upward while his fingers felt their way around a part half submerged in a bucket of muddy-looking solvent. "Didn't come in the shop to talk like he usually did—I wouldn't't've known he was here if I hadn't had to go out back." More thought. "Just said good morning. He did seem kind of excited about something, but he didn't say what. Now, when I saw him before, by a day or two, he said he might be in the market for a new truck soon. He talked like he was expecting to get some money soon, but a lot of times he talked like that. Always had a big new job promised or was going to make a killing. But he never did—just talk."

"Can you remember exactly what he said that last time?"

"Let's see . . . " Even his fingers stopped moving as he thought. "He was kind of fidgeting around; kept looking toward the highway for whoever. Said something about he had a lot to do . . . Wait—he did say something. Said, 'Harvey, my allotment's finally worth something.' " The bony head bobbed with satisfaction. "That's just what he said."

"His allotment?"

"Yep. I don't know what he meant, but that's what he said, all right."

"Anything else? Anything about why it was worth something?"

Mallard shook his head. "Nope. That was all he said. I didn't pay much attention to it at the time. Like I told you, he always had some kind of big business deal going, or said he did."

"Mention the name of whoever he was waiting for?"

"Nope. He was just excited, that's all. Then I came back in here to work, and next time I went out, he was gone."

11

THE DISPATCHER REACHED Wager before he reached
the Gypsum Motel. "Sheriff Spurlock wants you to phone him when
you get a chance."

"Does he need to see me?"

"No, he just said to give him a call when you can."

"Will do." And no, the dispatcher said to Gabe's question,
there were no messages for him.

Wager parked his car outside his room's window so he could
glance through the curtains if he heard anyone near it. It wasn't
much in the way of security, but it was all the motel had to offer.
Spurlock was still at the office when Wager called.

"Just want to know what you've been up to, Officer Wager.
You work for me, I expect daily reports."

Wager managed to stifle the comment that came to his
tongue; it had to do with who was and who wasn't paying his
salary. "I just got back from the reservation, Sheriff. Talking to
Del Ponte's brother."

"Find out anything?"

"Nothing that definitely says Rubin was murdered. He was
excited about some kind of deal about to happen. Did you run
across anything on that?"

"Some kind of deal? What kind of deal?"

"His brother didn't know."

"I never heard anything about it. Does that make it look like a homicide?"

"Not yet. I understand Del Ponte's widow's your niece."

"Yep. My youngest sister's daughter. I sure hate to see something like this happen to anybody, but it's especially hard when it happens to kin."

"Did you and Del Ponte get along?"

"Get along? Mostly. Some things about him I didn't care for much—talk the ears off a mule if the mule stood there long enough. But he took care of Sharon and the kids, and I didn't see that much of him anyway. Couple times a year, when me and Gracie had them over for dinner or went over there."

"Do you know if Del Ponte and his wife were having troubles?"

A silence. "You mean like marriage troubles?"

"Yes."

"No. But I never asked about that. Never had call to. You find something there?"

"His wife seems to be friendly with Jesse Herrera—runs the Egnarville store. But I don't know how friendly."

Another silence. "Sharon was fool enough to run away and marry too young, but I don't think she's fool enough to do something like that. I sure don't. I don't know Herrera—he's new to the county. One of those refugees from California." He added, "But he's married, I do know that. If it was something like that, his wife would learn about it damn fast, and as far as I know, she's still around."

"I'm just looking for possibilities, Sheriff."

"You mean the possibility that Sharon and this Herrera might have killed Rubin?" Wager let his silence be agreement. "Well, it sounds like you're scratching goddamn hard to find your possibilities. Like I say, Herrera's got a wife. And I can't see Sharon killing anybody." But they both knew stories of husbands killing wives and wives killing husbands. "You got anything you can take into court, Wager?"

"No," Wager admitted. "Do you know what kind of allotment Del Ponte might have had?"

"Allotment . . . ? He was quarter-breed. Might've had something that way."

"I thought the quarter-bloods were bought out. Couldn't live on the reservation anymore."

"That's the way it is now. Wasn't that way before. But those damn Indians have things so screwed up out there, God only knows who's getting what anymore."

Wager turned over that possibility in his mind. "One thing I haven't found yet is any connection with the other killings."

"If you think Sharon did it, I'm not a bit surprised to hear that. You tell your theory to Durkin?"

"Not yet."

"Well, unless you got some evidence, Wager, I'd just as soon you keep your suspicions to yourself. I understand you got to have those suspicions—it's . . . well, it's the way an officer has to think. But unless you got some damn good evidence, I'd just as soon you didn't start mouthing Sharon's name around. I'd just as soon you didn't cause that girl any more hurt."

"No need to say anything to Durkin."

"Fine."

Durkin answered on the second ring and, from the broken sound of his transmission, Wager figured the man was using a mobile telephone. He let Wager make his report without interruption, then asked his first question, "Did you find out if Del Ponte joined the Constitutional Posse?"

"Both his wife and his brother say he didn't. She did know about his work as an informant. In fact, everybody seems to have known he was an informant."

"Well, that's what they say now. It got in the paper when the story on his death came out."

"How? Who told the reporter?"

"I did. Figured I'd pressure the sons a bitches a little—make them worry about how much Del Ponte might have told me and who else might be an informant."

It wasn't the way Wager would have done it, but Durkin was getting paid more than he was. And every man had a right to make his own mistakes. "I haven't found anything to rule out the Constitutional Posse, but nobody I talked to seems to think they'd kill anyone."

"Sure. That's why they practice weaponry and military maneuvers—because they don't want to shoot anybody. All right," Durkin's voice said he was through, "continue working on the Constitutional Posse angle and keep me closely informed, Wager. Daily reports."

"Wait a minute—I have a couple of questions for you. Did you ever run across anything about a deal coming down that Rubin was involved in?"

"No. The only thing we talked about was the Posse."

"You didn't hear that he was excited about something just before he died?"

"I haven't been investigating him, Wager. Not my case. That's why you're here, remember?"

"Was there any deal the federal men might have been involved in?"

"Deal?"

"Either one of the victims. Were they doing business with somebody?"

"Not that I know of . . . Kershaw worked full time for the government. Holtzer probably had some jobs in the private sector, but I don't know what. You might ask Henderson, if you really think it's important."

"How about some kind of illegal business?"

"What the hell, Wager, are you suggesting malfeasance?"

"It's an angle. It has to be looked at."

"That angle has nothing to look at. It doesn't exist. You just keep on Del Ponte and the Posse. I'll handle the deaths on the reservation. That clear?"

AT LEAST LIZ was glad to hear his voice and to listen to what he had to say about the Del Ponte case. Possibly because she wasn't expecting a daily report, and certainly because it gave her a chance in turn to blow off steam about the latest on her fellow councilman, Weldon McGraw: "I'm not certain what he and his cronies are up to, Gabe, but I think he's getting some kind of under-the-table money for that new River Park project."

"Why's that?"

"Remember I told you he tried to pass a tax break for the Broncos and all?"

"Yeah."

"I get the feeling that was a red herring—something he knew would get shot down. Something to make the other council members feel bad so they would be more inclined to pass his next proposal." Liz had long ago told Wager that most council members kept very accurate scorecards on each other, and if they couldn't support one of a fellow member's bills, would try to make it up on something else. It was the way deals were cut in council chambers. "He and Ronald Pyne went out to lunch with some members of the state gambling commission. They're obviously trying to buy their votes for something, and my guess is it's the River Park project."

Colorado already had a state lottery and three communities in the state where casino gambling was legal: the old mining towns of Central City, Blackhawk, and Cripple Creek. Denverites who wanted to gamble were offered cheap and convenient rides courtesy of those towns' various casinos. So Wager couldn't see that legalizing gambling in Denver, provided the voters supported it, would corrupt the municipal morality. Which is what he told Liz.

"That's not the issue, Gabe! Currently, I don't have an opinion about legalized gambling in Denver because I haven't seen any studies of its impact on the city. What I do care about, however, and the point I'm trying to make, is that McGraw and Pyne are involved. And where those men go, the public trust suffers."

"Hey, Liz, get off your soapbox. The River Park's going to be in the city limits, right? Nobody can put a casino in there without a public vote. A statewide vote, at that."

"What about a gambling boat in the river? It's a navigable waterway and that makes it a federal jurisdiction that supersedes local laws. What about that possibility, Gabe?"

He hadn't thought of that. "I guess they could open a casino. But it would still be subject to state regulations. Has McGraw been having lunch with any federal officials?"

"Not that I know of."

"What about the Coast Guard?"

"Of course not!"

"Well, when he does, then you can start worrying about a gambling boat—which, we both know, would have to be a damn small one to float in the South Platte." He pictured it. "A rowboat, maybe. Could hold a four-hand poker table and an ice bucket."

"It's not funny, Gabe. He's up to something," she said stubbornly. "I know he is!"

But Wager did not intend to get into an argument, even a friendly one. For one thing, McGraw was, from Wager's point of view, a pretty silly thing to argue over; for another, when it came to the topic of city politics, Liz usually won. He changed the subject. "I ran across Evelyn Litvak's husband."

"You met him?"

"No, just saw him drinking coffee with some buddies. I didn't speak with him or anything."

"I saw Evelyn yesterday. She looked awful. Apparently he's

been making threats of some kind if she tries to fight for custody."

"Where's the case being heard?"

"I think she said Montezuma County."

That made sense; La Sal County didn't have a court. A judge came up one day a week from Cortez to try local misdemeanor cases. "Litvak has a lot of friends out here."

"That's one of the reasons she's so worried."

"You'll be talking to her again, right?"

"We're having lunch tomorrow. She needs some support."

As if Liz didn't have enough to do. But that was one of the reasons Wager liked her as a person: She thought of others and was willing to put her own interests aside to help them. "Ask her about her husband—about the Constitutional Posse, about any trouble he's ever been in, about his friends—especially a Bradley Nichols."

"Wait a minute, let me write that down." Silence. "Why?"

"Their names have come up in this case I'm on. I just want to know more about them."

"Is it anything that might help Evelyn's custody hearing?"

"It might be worth looking at, but I can't promise anything."

An extra note of excitement came into her voice. "I'll ask her!"

"Don't get her hopes up. Or yours, either."

"I won't!" Then, "I miss you, Gabe. It's only been a couple of days, but it seems like a lot longer."

He missed her, too—at least he did now that he heard her voice and had a few minutes to think about her. He told her that, too—or part of it, anyway. When they finally said good night, she warned him to be careful.

"Hey, I can name a dozen streets in Denver more dangerous than this place."

"I suppose. But you're away, and that makes it seem scarier."

"Since when are you scared of anything?"

"I'm not scared of, I'm scared for. Just take care of yourself."

"No sweat."

AFTER DINNER AND after he had turned off the television and slipped into a heavy sleep, the telephone bored into his consciousness. At first, still mostly asleep, he thought it was Liz calling back: It was a woman's voice. Then he realized that it wasn't hers—it was different—it was nervous, muffled, with an attempt at disguise—possibly a handkerchief over the mouthpiece—and spoke quickly. "You're in danger. They're going to hurt you. Leave before they hurt you."

"What? Who's this?"

"They're going to hurt you. You've got to go away!"

The line clicked into silence and Wager tapped the receiver's cradle, getting an empty hum in return. He replaced the telephone, thoroughly awake now. Funny how death threats could wake a guy up. He stared at a ceiling dim from the light leaking around the window shade and realized he was half listening for sounds of a prowler around his car on the other side of the picture window.

Knowing it was pointless, he nonetheless gave in and peeked past the heavy roller shade. The car sat, tires full, isolated in the orange glow of the walkway light. No sounds came from the black world beyond.

A real threat? Or an attempt to scare him off? He sat on the bed and, wide awake, propped the pillows behind his back. The voice had been tense and muffled, but female. And disguised—which meant she did not want him to recognize her voice. Someone he had either already talked with or who expected to talk with him soon? The only women he had spoken with were Sharon Del Ponte, the sheriff's dispatcher, and the clerk in Ray

Qwana'tua's office. The voice sounded as if it could belong to any of them. Or none. A real warning or a scare tactic? Either way, what the warning meant was that he had made someone nervous. Something he had done, someone he had talked to, one of his several aimless probes had made someone nervous. And it also meant that he was damned if he'd go.

12

HIS ALARM WOKE him, groggy from rolling and tossing
half the night. He had been unable to get back to sleep until,
feeling the chill of early morning, he had added the bedspread
to the layer of blankets. Despite its smell of chemicals and heavy
ironing, he had finally drifted into an uneasy rest.

The first thing after prying himself out of bed was to look
through the window at the wheels on his car. Then he stood for
a long time under the hot water and steamed the sleepiness from
his mind. Shaving helped, too, though in scraping the whiskers
around his mustache he nicked a corner of his nostril. That was
a bad place and it always irritated him to be careless enough to
cut himself there: The blood vessels were near the surface and
the little scraps of toilet paper kept coming off wet and red from
the nick. He didn't want to go into the restaurant with either
blood dripping down his face or a flag of paper waving from his
nose, so he ignored the angry rumble of his stomach and started
the first telephone call from the list he had formulated while
tossing back and forth during the night.

It was to the Butte Springs Ranch, Rubin's last known job.
Wager figured a ranch family would be up and working this
early, and he was right. A woman who sounded breathless from
running to the telephone answered and Wager identified himself
and asked for the ranch manager.

"He's out on the range right now. He's got a mobile phone, but I don't know if you can reach him on it. Sometimes the phone doesn't work, he gets down in those draws and canyons. Maybe I can help you."

"Maybe you can. I understand Rubin Del Ponte hauled some cattle for you on the fifteenth of March. I wonder if you had a chance to talk with him."

"Only at lunchtime. I read what happened to him. That was terrible—I feel so sorry for his family."

"Yes, ma'am. Can you remember what you talked about?"

"Oh, that was so long ago. . . . It wasn't anything important. You know, just how life was treating him, that kind of thing. He did have young children, didn't he?"

"Yes, ma'am. Did he seem in any way excited or nervous or behave differently in any way?"

"Differently? No. Not that I remember." The telephone line crackled distantly. "He was in a hurry to get loaded—helped run the cattle up the chute. But I supposed that was because he had another job to get to."

"Did the ranch manager notice anything about Del Ponte? Anything he mentioned to you?"

"He's my husband. And no, he didn't say anything to me."

He thanked her and asked her to call him through the sheriff's office if she or her husband remembered anything at all.

Most interviews went that way, Wager knew. Only on television did the detective get a clue every time he talked to a witness. But then they only had sixty minutes to solve the crime, and that included car crashes, love scenes, shoot-outs, and advertisements. Gently, Wager tugged at the shred of paper stuck to his nose and it peeled off; it was dry. That was the signal for breakfast—for which his stomach thanked him with a spasm of eagerness—and then more phone calls.

The store manager of the Lastwell Furniture Store did not have much good to say about Rubin. "He was supposed to, yessir. But he never showed up. I didn't hear a thing about it until late that afternoon—the afternoon of the seventeenth. The distributor in the Phoenix warehouse called to ask where our truck was. He had our load all ready to go but no one had come to load yet and he was getting ready to close."

"Can you remember what time that was?"

"Certainly, I can. I glanced at the clock: four-thirty. Mr. Del Ponte usually arrived there between three and four. I supposed he had a breakdown, so I told the distributor not to worry, that Mr. Del Ponte would probably be there first thing in the a.m. But he wasn't. The distributor called again the next day around ten and said he was still waiting."

"No call from Del Ponte?"

"Not one word! I phone his office, but the woman there didn't know anything. Just said he'd left the previous morning. Didn't have any idea where he was, and I haven't heard from him since. Not one single word of explanation!"

"His office?"

"Well, I think it's his home, really. I think he works out of his home. But it's the only number I have for him—the one on the side of his truck. I tell you, I'll never hire Mr. Del Ponte again—we almost had to cancel our April Fools' Day sale. Would have, if I hadn't been able to locate another trucker on short notice and pay extra for the trouble. No, sir. No more of our business for Mr. Del Ponte!"

"He's out of business."

"Good thing!"

"He's dead."

"Oh? Oh—is that why . . . ?"

"That's what I'm trying to find out. When's the last time you did see him or talk to him?"

"Oh, my . . . It must have been February something. Early February, when we finalized our plans for the April Fools' Day sale."

"You didn't talk to him after that?"

"No. I called his number and left a message for him, and he called back and we scheduled this run. That's the way we usually did it, over the telephone. I'd tell him when to pick up our load, and what he usually did was to drive straight down to the warehouse in Phoenix on one day and load up and get back to the store the following afternoon. That's when I'd see him. Supervise the unloading, check the invoice and the cargo for any shipping damage . . . Dead? Well, I didn't hear about that. I mean, I wouldn't have been so angry with him if I'd known that."

"How often did he make a run for you?"

"At least once a month. Sometimes twice, depending on how much inventory the sales staff moved." The slightly lilting voice went on, "We had an on-call arrangement rather than a contract. That way we only paid him for actual work performed, and he was usually both available and reliable. Except, of course, for this last time . . ."

"What time of the afternoon did he usually get back from Phoenix?"

"Between two and three. I wanted it no later than three, so our warehouse staff has time to unload before five. That way I don't have to pay them overtime."

"Did you pay Del Ponte in cash or by check?" The Lastwell Furniture Store was among those many names without the little star behind it.

"Check. He gave me a bill with the invoice and I paid at the end of the month. Made out to Del Ponte Trucking, through a bank in La Sal." He said again, "It never crossed my mind Mr. Del Ponte might have died."

Wager let the man make his apologies to the dead and then hung up to think over what he'd learned. According to Harvey Mallard, Rubin had arrived at the parking lot in Lewis Corners no earlier than mid-morning; according to Rubin's wife, he'd left home early. According to Rubin's routine, he should have been on the way to Phoenix in time to get there by late afternoon ... Wager unfolded his road map of the western U.S. and found the mileage chart. Eight-eighteen from Denver to Phoenix—less the three-fifty or so from Denver to La Sal County. Figure about five hundred miles, and, according to the map, a lot of it on secondary roads. Rubin probably took 666 to Cortez, then 160 through Tuba City, Arizona, and 89 down to join I-17, running from Flagstaff to Phoenix. At least eight hours, with two-lane traffic and mountain passes slowing him down, probably ten hours. Then the return drive through the night, taking out five or six hours somewhere to sleep, and make it to Grand Junction by mid-afternoon of the next day. A fixed routine and guaranteed money once a month.

Something had happened to make Rubin kiss off a steady customer. No apology, no warning so the customer could hire a replacement vehicle, nothing. And that was what Wager had to find out about somehow: the morning of the seventeenth of March. Rubin, an informant for the FBI, a man careful enough to keep records even of his tax-dodging mileage, had broken his schedule without telling anyone. Had planned to meet someone when he should have been on the road. Apparently met them and then disappeared. Why? And who had he been waiting for at Lewis Corners? And—the thought came to Wager from a different angle—why did Sharon Del Ponte say she knew nothing of his business when all of her husband's customers used her home phone to reach the man?

DEPUTY SHERIFF HOWIE Morris's small ranch was about three miles beyond Egnarville; he told Wager that he would wait until ten and, yes, his wife would be there, too. The deputy hadn't sounded too pleased to hear from Wager, but he sounded a lot calmer than the last time they had talked. And when Wager parked in the weedy gravel in front of the low frame house, Morris even met him at the door with an offer of coffee.

"Sounds fine," said Wager. He didn't really want any more—Paula had filled and refilled his cup at breakfast—but a yes was friendlier than a no, and might lead to more information than a blunt question about Morris telephoning Nichols to warn him of Wager's presence. "I appreciate you and your wife talking with me," he said and smiled.

"I don't know what good it'll do, Wager. Anything she knows she'd've told me about already. And I haven't found out anything more in the past two days."

"You're right. But other people have told me a few things that I'd like to get your opinions on."

"Like what?" He led Wager through the formal-looking living room with its furniture covered in matching black-and-white cowhide design to a comfortable area off the kitchen. It was glassed in like a greenhouse and filled with enough potted plants to give the air an earthy, leafy smell. A gaunt woman with her hair in a single large braid down her back smiled a welcome. Despite the warmth of the room, she wore a flannel shirt tucked into Levi's. The Levi's were tucked into cowboy boots. "Rosemary, this is Officer Wager. He's the one I told you about."

"I've heard a lot about you. Coffee?"

Wager could imagine what she'd heard. "Please—just black."

"Like what?" repeated Morris.

"Have either of you heard of any kind of trouble between Del Ponte and his wife?"

Morris's eyebrows lifted and he turned to his wife. "I sure haven't! Rosie?"

"No . . ." She poured a cup for herself and rejoined them at the glass-and-metal garden table. It was shaded by a large climbing bougainvillea plant whose pink leaves made a waterfall of color down what had once been the outside wall of the house. "Does this have to do with his death?"

"I'm not sure. Right now, I'm just chasing down any and every rumor. I was told Sharon Del Ponte and Jesse Herrera might be seeing each other. Have you ever heard anyone mention that?"

"I'm not around town enough to know that. Rosie? Is there anything?"

She paused to sip gingerly at her steaming coffee before she answered. She was a dry-looking woman, the flesh taut across her prominent cheekbones, and her lips were thin, like a man's. For some reason, Wager assumed the couple had no children. "Nothing definite. And I wouldn't want to say anything that would cause trouble."

"It won't cause any trouble unless it has a bearing on his death."

The woman glanced at her husband and then through one of the glass panels to the open desert and a distant ripple of snowy mountains that peeked above the curve of the earth. "I'm not sure—I saw Jesse coming back to the store from her house a couple of times. I'd be driving by, you know. He'd be walking across the field back to the store. And they seem pretty . . . friendly. At least when I've gone in the store and they're both there it's sort of like they stopped talking the minute I walked in. You know that feeling?"

Both men nodded.

"But that doesn't mean they're, you know, doing something. I can't say I've seen anything like that actually going on."

"Where there's smoke," said Morris darkly. Then, to Wager, "You talked to Sheriff Spurlock about this? You know she's his niece?"

"We've talked. He didn't think she would play around, but he didn't know for certain."

"Well," the deputy rubbed his bony hands along the thighs of his trousers, "you never know. You think she could've killed her husband?"

"Howie! That's a terrible thing to say! Even if Sharon might be having an affair, she would never do something like that!"

"Rosie, this is police work—you got to ask questions like that."

"Police work or not, Sharon would never do anything like that. She's a gentle person—she loves her children, and that says a lot about a woman!"

"It doesn't say she might not be getting it on with Herrera."

"Well, if she is, who could blame her? Being stuck out here all alone, week after week. Her husband gone all the time!"

"Did either of you ever hear of any domestic violence between the Del Pontes?"

"No. And I never saw any evidence of it, either—no black eyes, no bruises. None of that kind of thing you men are always doing to your wives."

" 'You men'! Rosie, I've never hit you! I can't even remember the last time we had an argument."

The bitterness in her voice sharpened. "That's because between your job and the National Guard, you're never home long enough to argue with!"

Morris, jaw sagging, stared at someone he suddenly did not recognize.

Wager asked, "Do you talk with Mrs. Herrera? Has she ever said she was suspicious of her husband?"

"Heidi? No." The woman's slender fingers brushed back a strand of lank, black hair as she took a deep breath. "I don't know her that well, but she doesn't seem to think anything like that. In fact, she seems quite happy. She seems to be real friendly with Sharon whenever I see them together."

"Did Rubin or his wife ever say anything about some kind of allotment he had?"

Morris, still studying his wife, let her speak first. "It wasn't an allotment—not money, not like the Indians on the reservation get. It was more a settlement. They joked about it once—he did, anyway. She wasn't too happy about it. When Rubin's father died, he left Rubin some land on the reservation. But it didn't do them any good because Rubin can't sell it and he's not allowed to live there. Not that Sharon wanted to move out there anyway—it would be worse than Egnarville. Some of those places are so lonely . . . !"

"So what did Rubin do with it?"

"Nothing. Sharon told me there was nothing they could do with it. Let his brother run sheep or cattle on it, I believe."

"Did she or Rubin say anything about some kind of deal, lately?" Wager clarified the question. "A couple of people said Rubin was excited about something big that was to happen soon. He was supposed to be working on some deal that might have involved some white men and Indians."

"Deal?" Rosemary shook her head. "Nothing I was told about. Sharon's certainly said nothing like that." She looked at her husband. "You hear anything about it?"

"No." His sarcastic tone said he was thinking more of his wife than of Rubin. "I'm not around enough to hear things like that. I'm too damn busy trying to make a living."

Wager asked quickly, "Did Sharon help her husband with his business? Take care of the billing? That kind of thing?"

"Sure. He ran the trucking company out of his home. Or she did, anyway, when he was on the road. Which—" she glanced at Morris "—was most of the time."

"Rosie, you know this job brings in the only cash money we can—"

Wager interrupted, "So she would know his trip schedule?"

"I'm not sure about that. I think she just took messages and let Rubin call back to arrange his schedule. In fact, I know that's how it worked because she told me once they'd lost some jobs because she couldn't tell the caller right then when Rubin would be available and the caller had to know for certain. She said she wished Rubin would let her draw up his schedule. But he wouldn't. I'm not sure why. He just wanted to do that himself."

"What about billing and tax forms? Did she handle that?"

"I don't know. She never said anything about that."

Wager sipped his coffee, now that it was cool enough not to blister his mouth. Beside him, he felt Morris radiating a different type of heat. "What kind of plant is that?" He pointed to a shrub that dangled clusters of fleshy-looking pink blossoms under its wide leaves.

Rosemary stared at the plant for a long moment before answering. "A bleeding-heart plant. They do real well here."

Morris started to make some kind of noise but Wager interrupted him to say it was a flower he remembered from his childhood—his mother had a bunch of them in a shady corner of the yard—and then he asked about a few other plants, and that's all they talked about until he quickly finished his coffee and thanked them for their time.

Morris walked him out to his car. He gazed around the horizon as if studying it for the first time. "I always thought Rosie liked it here. I thought it was what she wanted."

"Maybe she just wants to see a little more of you."

His teeth nipped at a spur of dried flesh on his lower lip. He seemed to want to talk about his personal life but Wager hoped he wouldn't; the trouble between Morris and his wife sounded painfully similar to that between Wager and his ex-wife. Lorraine had been one of those women who stifled their grievances until they finally exploded, and by then it was too late—her anger and her hatred of Wager, just and unjust, had been engraved too deeply to be overcome. There had been nothing left to reconcile in their marriage and it had ended in the failure of divorce.

Morris stood silent for a few moments. But all he finally said was, "We can't have children." Then he glanced at his watch. "Well, I better get rolling—got to serve and protect."

"Got time to look at some names from Del Ponte's appointment book?"

"Names? Sure."

Morris's firmer tone of voice told Wager that the deputy, too, found relief in getting back to the job; Wager showed him the page.

"Turney. That's probably Dave Turney. Owns a little outfit over on Disappointment Creek. Hegendorf has the QT ranch. That's a big spread near the Utah line. Archibeque manages the Flying W. It's over near the Utah line, too—down Squaw Point Canyon, alongside the reservation." He frowned, remembering something. "That place changed hands a couple of years ago—was owned by some Texans, and they sold out. Somebody in Denver, I think I heard. I'd say Rubin was moving cows for them." He handed the booklet back to Wager. "It sounds like you don't think the Constitutional Posse had anything to do with his death."

Wager wagged his head. "I still don't know about that. But I haven't found any evidence tying the deaths together."

"I doubt you will."

"Have you seen or talked to Bradley Nichols lately?"

The man's head wagged no. "I'll tell you how to get to his ranch if you want to go over and see him."

"How about Stan Litvak?"

"Nope."

There had been a third man at that table in the restaurant yesterday morning. "What about Gregory—Louis Gregory? Is he a Posse member, too?"

"Probably. I don't know for sure." Morris studied Wager. "I can't see any of those men shooting anybody. Like I told you before, Wager, I can't see any of the Posse shooting anybody. Unless somebody shot at them first."

"Or was some kind of threat to them?"

"What kind of threat was either of them federal workers? No

way, Wager. It was probably some damn drunk Indian shot those men, and I don't know what happened to Rubin. But there's no evidence even that he was murdered; and I don't care if he was an FBI informant, he didn't have anything to inform about! I mean, Rubin was no threat to nobody, let alone the goddamn Constitutional Posse! I wish to hell Durkin would get that through his goddamn skull."

Rubin could have been a threat to someone without knowing who. So could Holtzer and Kershaw. Just like, thought Wager, remembering last night's telephone call, he himself was.

"Any idea who might have wanted to slash my tires?"

"Slash your tires?"

"Night before last. Somebody cut all four."

Morris, jaw slack, stared at Wager, who went on, "Nichols and his friends happened to be at the motel restaurant the next morning. It looked like they were waiting to see what I'd do with four flat tires."

"Well, what . . . ? Why . . . ?"

"I figure it was a warning. I figure somebody thinks I'm a threat, too."

Morris, a worried frown pulling his thick eyebrows together, watched in silence as Wager backed the car around and pulled out onto the highway.

13

THE FEMALE VOICE on the other end of the line asked Wager to hold on a minute, and a second or two later Ray said, "Glad you called—I talked to Ramey Many Coats. He says he'll talk to you. Sounded like he wanted to, in fact."

"When and where?"

"His place. Come on out and I'll take you over there."

The drive to Ramey's house wasn't as far as that to Luther Del Ponte's. Ray took one of the three or four sandy village streets that crossed the highway; it passed a couple of old building made of cut sandstone and at some vague point left town and entered the desert. They followed its long, meandering curve around the base of a small butte that looked as if it were once part of the larger Dark Mesa. "I have to admit I'm kind of surprised, Gabe. Figured if he'd talk to you at all, he'd do it on Indian time. You know, 'One of these days.' But he said to bring you out. Said he'd be home all day today and I could bring you out any time."

"Any idea why he'd do that?"

Thoughtfully, the tribal policeman ran the side of his thumb along his pockmarked jaw. "There's got to be money in it for him somewhere. I mean, he's a Many Coats, and the only reason a Many Coats does anything is for money." The bill of Ray's baseball cap, with its red-and-black tribal police emblem, slowly wagged. "I don't know if one of them would even walk across the street unless it was to pick up a dime."

"Could that be the deal Rubin was excited about? Something he was doing with Ramey?"

"I hadn't thought of that. It could be, I suppose. Ramey's always working some deal or another. But Rubin didn't have any money, I don't think, and Ramey doesn't have time for anybody who's broke." He was quiet for a few seconds. "Maybe Rubin's truck—maybe Rubin was using his truck for collateral in some way."

"That still doesn't say why Ramey wants to talk with me."

The road threaded between two massive slabs of dark rock, pieces of the mesa cap that had, some time long ago, tumbled off the lip of the butte that rose above them. As the truck passed close to them, Wager saw that they were part of the old lava flow, roughly pitted, like Ray's skin.

Ray shook his head again. "Yeah. It doesn't. Maybe he just heard you were talking to people on the reservation." The tribal policeman corrected himself, "His reservation. That's the way he thinks of it, anyway."

Abruptly, they crossed into the butte's shadow and Wager felt the sun-heated skin of his arm relax in the cooler air. "Do you know if any of the victims reported threats before they were killed?"

"Threats? Not that I heard. But then, Special Agent Durkin doesn't talk to me much about his cases. You have to figure, though, if Kershaw had gotten a threat, he wouldn't have gone out by himself—not after Holtzer was shot. And I think Luther would have told us if Rubin had said anything like that to him. Why?"

Wager told him about last night's telephone call.

"A woman?"

"Yeah. Is that important?"

"I don't know how important it is. It's kind of weird, though."

Ray shifted into high gear as the road straightened out. This one was a lot smoother than the two-rut track to Luther's place. A road grader had scraped shallow ditches on each side to protect its surface from runoff, and gentled its occasional dips into the washes. "I bet it was a white woman."

"Why?"

"Women on the reservation, they wouldn't likely know if their men were threatening or planning to attack somebody. And the men wouldn't ask them to make a call like that because then they'd have to explain what they were up to. Around here, there's still a pretty deep division between what's proper for men and for women, and women are supposed to take care of the home and kids and not mess in men's business. You've seen our secretary? Patty? Everybody thinks that little girl is a real hellraiser because she's trying to organize a women's center. Even most of the older women in town think she's some kind of troublemaker, think she's poking her nose into what the men are responsible for doing. All she's trying to do is bring them into the twentieth century. Not the twenty-first, just the twentieth." His cheeks swelled with a puff of disgust. "And if somehow one of the women did find out, why would she warn you?"

"Why would a white woman warn me?"

"Good point. So maybe it was just to scare you off."

"I've thought of that, too." He told the tribal policeman about his slashed tires.

"Welcome to friendly La Sal County! You have a weapon?"

"Pistol."

"Well, better carry it. In case it's more than just a scare call." He drummed his fingers on the steering wheel. "Of course, a pistol's no match for a thirty-thirty." Which they both knew was the recent weapon of choice for killing federal workers.

The pickup truck swung around a shoulder of talus and back into the heat of the sun. Ahead, almost against the base of the mesa's cliff, a large stand of budding cottonwood trees looked pale green against the red-and-orange rock. Nestled among them was a small community made up of a sprawling ranch house surrounded by half a dozen outbuildings: barn with a stubby silo, several sheds, a large corral with its stables, three or four house trailers up on concrete blocks, two television dishes tilted to the sky, a scattering of trucks, cars, and motorcycles. This ranch had no fiberglass holding tank; a windmill near the corral told Wager it had the luxury of its own well water. A pair of dogs ran toward them, barking, and kept pace with the truck as they drove under the crossbar between the gate's tall posts. A man in a white cowboy hat stepped down from the shade of a long gallery that fronted the house and waited for them; a large eagle feather rose above the hat's deeply creased crown and stood as unmoving as the man.

Ray did the introductions. Wager thought that Ramey Many Coats looked more like an Indian should look: high and prominent cheekbones, a strong chin. Thick black eyebrows made an almost continuous line over his black eyes and straight nose, and the hairless flesh of his dark, wide face was heavy, making his head seem almost overlarge for his stocky body. Two thick braids of glossy black hair hung down behind his ears to his chest. He said, "Welcome to my lodge," and shook hands like a white man, squeezing Wager's fingers in a signal of strength.

"I hear you're investigating the death of my cousin."

Apparently, Ramey wasn't as superstitious as Luther about speaking of the dead. Wager glanced at Ray. "I didn't know you and the Del Pontes were related."

"Through his grandmother. She was the aunt of one of my wife's mother's cousins."

"Just about everybody at Squaw Point is related, more or less," said Ray. "Same thing on my reservation."

"It is our way," said Ramey. "We are all family. It's how we have survived what the white man has tried to do to us."

"It's also what happens when you have less than eight hundred people living together for four or more generations," said Ray.

"What can you tell me about Rubin?" asked Wager.

The long feather bobbed stiffly as the man's head nodded. "Let's go out of the sun." He led them up the scarred steps to the veranda, which held a miscellaneous collection of well-used lawn furniture. "Sit down—be comfortable in my lodge. You've come a long way in the heat. You want some soda pop? Ice water?"

Wager shook his head; Ray nodded.

"I'll get you something to drink." He went through the open door into the quiet dimness of the house, stepping lightly and quietly despite the stacked heels of his cowboy boots.

Wager and Ray sat in silence on the aluminum-and-web chairs until Ramey came back out. The necks of three frosty 7Up bottles dangled between his thick fingers.

Ray took a long drink and used the bottle to tip back the bill of his cap, then wiped the cold glass across his forehead. Wager sipped at his.

Ramey set his hat carefully on the veranda rail beside him and took his own deep drink. To form the two braids, his black, glossy hair had been parted tautly in the middle and showed a line of white scalp. After a slightly muffled belch, he asked, "You think somebody killed my cousin?"

"We don't know how he died—that's one of the problems. Do you think somebody wanted him dead?" Wager asked.

The man's heavy shoulder lifted a bit. "Maybe. Maybe not. I don't know. I didn't know much about him. He was my cousin, but he didn't live here with the people."

"Did you see or talk to him any time before his death?"

The man answered with measured solemnity, "It would be hard to talk to him after his death."

Wager heard a slight noise from the tribal policeman beside him; but the younger man, too, was stone-faced. For the first time, Wager had a sense of the distance between them and himself as a non-Indian, a distance magnified by their shared, if masked, laughter. "Any time shortly before his death."

"No. Not shortly. A couple of months ago, maybe, I hired him to drive one of my horse trailers down to Towaoc." He glanced at Ray. "The Four-Corners winter race."

"How'd you do?"

"Pretty good. Won more than I lost."

The tribal policeman didn't seem surprised.

"Did Rubin ever mention any kind of deal he was involved in?" Wager asked.

"Not to me. I heard from some other people that he was working for that FBI man or somebody."

"That's all you heard? Nothing more specific than that?"

"I wasn't interested in hearing anything more. His business was his business, not mine."

"Who did you hear it from?"

The man's thick eyebrows shrugged. "Around. A couple of people told me. Rubin always liked to talk, you know? Always talking about his big plans. Not many people paid much attention to him anymore." He gazed off toward the splintered cliff of red and orange and white rock that formed the sun-washed face of Dark Mesa, a half mile or so away. "We figured that was the white man in him." Then he said, "You tell me you don't know if Rubin was killed by somebody. But you talk like you think he was. Why?"

Wager had to admit that he didn't have much that was concrete, just some circumstantial facts. "Well, he was working for Agent Durkin—he was looking into any ties between the Constitutional Posse and people on the reservation. Trying to get information about the two government men who were shot. And, like Ray says, his body was found a long way from anywhere. How'd he get there, and why? Most important, we have no explanation for the death of an apparently healthy man who did not drink." Wager waited for Ramey to say something, but the heavyset man remained silent. "He was also excited about some recent deal. He said he had something that was finally going to have value, and he met with someone the morning he disappeared—the same morning he was supposed to be on a scheduled trip to Phoenix. Do you have any idea what that might have been about?"

Ramey listened as Wager spoke, his black eyes on Wager's mouth as if he wanted to see each word and to study it. After a while he answered Wager's question with one of his own. "Didn't you talk to his brother, Luther? What did Luther tell you?"

"He didn't tell us much. Just that Rubin had spoken to him and some other people about some kind of important deal coming soon. He said he knew nothing about it, but he thought you might."

Ramey took another long drink from his bottle and gave another belch, more subdued this time, as he looked toward the mesa. "I didn't see Rubin before he died. But he was always talking about his deals. He talked a lot."

"When you did talk to Rubin, did he mention any names? Luther said there could be some white men involved in whatever it was."

"No." He finished the 7Up and set the bottle on the board floor of the veranda. The planks had been painted sky blue a long time ago, but now raw, gray wood showed in many places where sandy boot soles had ground through the color. "When do you think Rubin was killed?"

"It could have been the day he disappeared, the seventeenth. Not much after that."

Ramey nodded slowly, apparently thinking back. "I was in Denver on tribal business that day, me and Julian Cloud. We drove to Denver on the fifteenth and came back on the twenty-third."

Ray finished his pop and set his bottle near Ramey's. "Do you have any idea why Walter Lawrence was killed?"

Again, the man countered with his own question, directed at Wager. "You think him and Rubin were killed by the same man?"

"I have no evidence one way or the other. What about the government workers? Do you have any idea why they might have been killed?"

Ramey Many Coats sat, unmoving, before he spoke. "No idea why. But I think it was white men who killed the government people."

"Why?"

"I think it was maybe a white rancher. They have hard feelings about the government changing their way of life. Now *they're* learning what it is like."

"The Constitutional Posse?"

"Maybe. No Indian would kill those men. Why should he? Those men brought no harm to my people." The strong jaw thrust out. "The white wolves have killed off all the game and now they eat each other."

"Aw, come on, Ramey!"

"I am not an apple like you, Ray Eagle Son." He emphasized the policeman's translated last name, black eyes narrowed slightly as he stared at him. They were about the same age, late twenties, but because of his bulk and the rumbling, measured pace of his speech, Ramey seemed much older. "Maybe the tribal council should think over your contract when it comes up in September. Maybe our people need someone who is more proud of his race."

"Maybe the tribal council needs a member who is Squaw Point Ute and not somebody whose grandfather's father was a Jicarilla Apache!"

"My mother is Squaw Pointe Ute and her mother and hers before her." He slapped his chest. "I am Ute of the Squaw Point tribe and not one of those Southern Utes who do everything the BIA tells them to do and never make no trouble for the white man." He abruptly swung his body to face only Wager. "Rubin Del Ponte maybe had something somebody wanted. That is maybe why he was killed. I don't know what it was, and I don't know who did it. But maybe you should talk to Luther Del Ponte again. Maybe he knows more than he has told you about. That is all I have to say."

THEY HAD BEEN riding in silence for about five minutes when Wager finally muttered, "I feel like we told him more than he told us."

"A Many Coats usually gets the better part of a bargain."

"Any idea why he's siccing us on Luther?"

"No . . . They don't like each other, that's for sure. And I'll bet Ramey knows a lot more than he told us. But just what kind of game he's playing, I don't know."

Wager asked, "You going to keep your job?"

"Not if Ramey has much to say about it, I guess. Given the pay, it'd be no big loss." He sighed away the worry. "I really don't know how I got hired in the first place, except Ramey wasn't ready to stir up any more resentment among the people by putting another relative on the payroll." His dark face lit up with a wide grin, "Probably they were all in jail at the time."

"What'd he mean, he's not an apple?"

"Red on the outside, white on the inside. An Uncle Tonto figure." Ray snorted. "He gets a lot of mileage from playing the stage Indian—I've heard he goes back to Washington and talks about 'forked tongues' and 'great white father' and 'gone with the buffalo.' But they eat it up, Gabe; that's the kind of Indian those white people want to see. And I got to admit he usually comes back with more money for the tribe—and for the Many Coats, of course."

"It's an act?"

Ray considered for a few minutes before answering. "Not exactly. I mean, sure, he gets most of his Indian talk from watching old movies on TV. You know, Jeff Chandler playing Geronimo. But at the same time, he has a right to it. I mean, it's phony, yes, but it's also real because it's the real way a lot of white people see us. Now, if you talked that way, people would say 'Yeah, Gabe's pretending to be an Indian.' But when an Indian talks that way, they say, 'Now there's a real Indian!' " He lifted his cap to let cool air blow across his damp hair. "Some of the kids on the reservations, it's the only mythology they have. They act that way because they think it takes them back to their roots. Others don't know any other way to act around white people because they haven't been given a chance to grow away from that." Another grin. "Frankenstein Indians, I call them. Creatures of the myth!" More seriously he said, "It's kind of sad, though. What it shows is that these kids have no sense of belonging, no sense of self off the reservation except for what the white people think they should be. That's why there's so much resentment against these New Agers who run around pretending to be Indians— it's a further debasement of what little sense of Indianness is left."

Wager, not looking for a lecture, kind of wished he hadn't asked the question and tried to get back to the real topic. "Why do you think Ramey wanted us to know he had an alibi when Rubin died?"

"Yeah, he did, didn't he? Made that real clear." Ray guided the wheels around a bed of soft sand in the road. "Well, he's a Many Coats so he's got a permanently guilty conscience. I don't know, maybe he stands to profit somehow from Rubin's death and wants us to know for sure that he couldn't have killed him."

"We better go back and talk to Luther again."

Ray nodded. "Let's stop off in town first. Let's talk to Isabel and Cynthia, first. You got time?"

"That's what I'm here for."

LUTHER'S MOTHER AND sister lived in one of the military-style houses that were arranged along the curving lanes and fenceless sandy lawns of a transplanted suburbia. A two-room bungalow that looked like all the others in shape and color, it shared the waterless and worn grass of its neighbors. A small strip of petunias and marigolds planted at the house's foundation looked wilted in the midday sun, and waited for the relief of the house's shadow to reach them. Some children's toys were scattered in a sandy play area scratched beside the small concrete landing. Through the open front door came the thin, mechanical laughter of a television show. Ray tapped his fingers against the frame of the screen and then politely gazed away from the dimness inside to wait for an answer; a few moments later, a woman wearing a brightly flowered muumuu came to the door.

"Mrs. Del Ponte? Isabel Sena Del Ponte?"

"Yes? Somebody get hurt?"

"No, nothing like that." Ray introduced himself and Wager. "We'd like to ask about Marshall's son, your stepson. The one who lived off the reservation." That was the way Ray avoided Rubin's name.

"Why?"

"To try and find out what happened to him." That was the way he avoided the word "dead."

"I don't know what I can tell you."

"Neither do we." He smiled. "That's why we're here."

She thought about that, then opened the door. "Come in. You want something to drink? Coffee?"

They both declined, Ray apologizing for interrupting her morning and saying that they wouldn't be staying very long.

She was almost as tall as Wager, and the muumuu draped over a body that, though thickened with age and childbearing, was still lanky. Her hair, streaked with gray, was gathered into a knot at the back of her neck and held with two large wooden pins. She took a coloring book and some crayons off the sofa and gestured for them to sit, then settled herself in a rocking chair that was padded with bright blue cushions. The television in the kitchen was still chattering and Wager could hear the tink of silverware against a dish and the occasional voices of talking children. Her daughter's probably—the one who would be working at the food-stamp office this time of day.

"Can you tell us when you last saw this person?"

"Four weeks ago, maybe five. When we had the big rain."

"End of February," Ray explained to Wager. Then to the woman, "Here?"

"No. I was visiting my son. He came by."

"Do you remember what they talked about?"

She stared at the worn carpet that hid the creaking floor boards, but that wasn't what she saw. "Horses. They always talked about horses and racing. And the sheep, what the spring lambing was going to look like."

Ray caught Wager's eye and made a wry face. Those were universal topics on the reservation; Luther and Ray had talked about them, too.

Wager asked, "Did he say anything about family troubles? About any problems he was having with his wife?"

Interest brought her eyes off the carpet. "Sharon? Were him and Sharon having problems?"

That sort of answered Wager's question, so he sort of answered hers. "I don't know. It's just the kind of thing we have to ask."

"No. He didn't say nothing about Sharon that I remember. Not while I was there, anyway."

"Did he say anything about working for the FBI? Or about learning anything that the FBI might be interested in?"

"Not while I was there, no." Wager was obviously ignorant of Ute ways. "That's something they would talk about in the shade house or in the hogan. Men only. But it was raining, so they had to stay inside and wouldn't talk about things like that."

They sat in silence for a few minutes. On the wall behind the woman hung a flat, brightly painted drum and beneath it two crossed sticks, each of which had something hairy dangling from an end. They didn't look like drumsticks. Prayer sticks, maybe. On another wall was a brightly colored picture of Jesus looking up into a light that came from somewhere outside the picture frame. It was a lot like the one hanging in his mother's living room in Denver.

Wager finally asked, "Was Luther's brother getting an allotment?"

"He was one quarter. He couldn't."

"He said something about his allotment. Said it was finally going to be worth something."

The woman frowned, thinking. "He didn't get no allotment. Maybe he meant his portion—land portion—from his father. But I don't know how he could get anything out of that: He couldn't sell it and he couldn't live on it. He let Luther use it for running sheep." She wanted them to understand: "Luther paid him for the use of it. In sheep. One quarter of each spring lambing went to him for the use of it. Luther didn't really have to pay him nothing, but he did."

Ray asked, "Where is this land?"

"It's a section up Narraguinnep Wash. His father felt like the government was wrong to say his son was not an Indian anymore so he left him a section in his will. His father thought maybe the government would change its mind again, so he wanted to make sure his son had a place on the reservation when it did." She added, "It's a real nice portion."

"Who does it belong to now?" asked Wager.

She shrugged. "Sharon, I reckon. Maybe the children—

Estelle and Blanche. I don't know what the new rules say. Probably the children—they're one eighth." Another shrug. "But they won't get nothing out of it unless the rules change again. They can't sell it and they can't live on it either, unless the rules change."

Ray asked, "How far up Narraguinnep Wash is it?"

"Near the border. Runs into the land of that-man-who-died-from-a-knife."

"That man who died maybe two months ago?"

"Him. Yes."

14

RAY SAT IN the pickup truck's sun-heated cab and did not start the engine right away. Luther's mother had not been able to add anything about either Rubin's death or that of Walter Lawrence, and she had nothing to tell them about the Constitutional Posse or anything else of what she called "white man's politics." After a while the tribal policeman said, "I'd like to talk to some other people before we go see Luther again."

"Why?"

"This land that belonged to Rubin, it's the first I heard about it." The sunglasses swung toward Wager. "Who told you about it?"

Wager repeated what Rosemary Morris had mentioned. "But I don't see what its importance is. It can't be sold or lived on by anyone off the reservation." A thought struck him. "Or is the law going to change? Will Del Ponte's wife be able to sell it?"

"The rules can always change. This new tribal sovereignty plan means the rules probably will change. In fact, that's its purpose: to get rid of the reservations, let the tribes fend for themselves without any more government handouts. Some of the people see it as America's 'Final Solution to the Indian Question.'" He started the vehicle and slowly swung around in the street. "Four hundred years of solutions and still trying. But whether or not it means people off the reservation will be able to sell reservation land to nonresidents is something else. I can't see any of the tribes agreeing to that. I mean, the whole idea of restricting tribal membership to half-bloods was to consolidate the tribe—to give it closer unity. That, and so the royalty payments from gas and coal wouldn't have to be split among so many claimants. And to keep the 'Made by Native Americans' labels from being used by anybody who said they had a drop of Indian blood in them."

Driving slowly, Ray gave himself time to talk and to think. "Native American artists! We used to have all these people moving to Santa Fe and Taos and claiming their great-grandfather had some kind of Indian blood and then setting themselves up as Native American artists. Crap!"

"What's to stop them now?"

"Federal law—truth in packaging, believe it or not. Law now says you can't claim you're making Native American handicrafts unless you're a registered member of a tribe. Pissed off a lot of whites and Hispanics who were running around wearing headbands and feathers and selling their pots and rings and rugs as Indian-made."

Wager steered the man back to what he figured was more important. "So if it's not likely that Sharon Del Ponte can do anything with the land, what's important about having it?"

"If Rubin was killed, it must have been for some reason. And the land is the only thing he had that maybe was worth anything. His truck, sure, but his wife won't get much more than a few thousand out of a used semi." He nodded thoughtfully. "And nobody mentioned his land to me. That's kind of weird—I think maybe people didn't want me to know about it for some reason."

Wager, too, was thinking. "Do mineral rights go with the land?"

"No, they're collective—tribal rights. That way everybody

gets some of the royalties even if the minerals aren't on their portion."

"But that could change?"

"Could. I don't think it's likely, but it could. But I haven't heard of any mineral finds up in Narraguinnep Wash."

"Might the land go to Luther?"

"Depends on Rubin's will, I think. If he made one. If he didn't, the state will probably probate the property to his wife and children rather than to a half brother. Any way you can find out if Rubin had a will?"

"If it's been filed, sure. Should be with the Montezuma County clerk and recorder's office. I can give them a call."

"I think I'll ask around some about this land of Rubin's. Maybe there's something about it being next to Walter Lawrence's place." A moment later Ray mused, "I wonder who got Walter Lawrence's land when he died?"

RAY LET WAGER use one of his office telephones to call the county clerk's office in Cortez. The woman down there said it would take a little while to get the information, could she call him back?

"I'd better call you. I won't be at this number later."

Ray, leafing through the small pile of memos and mail that had come while he was out of the office, looked up when Wager stopped talking. "No luck?"

"She has to go through the court files. Takes a couple of hours, she said." He thanked Ray for the use of his telephone. "Let me know when you go out to talk to Luther. I'd like to go along."

The younger man nodded. "And you let me know what you find out from Cortez." He pointed a finger at Wager, his thumb cocked like a pistol. "And look over your shoulder now and then, OK?"

Wager promised he would and, stomach grumbling about missing lunch, plodded to his car through the weight and glare of the early-afternoon sun.

IF SHARON DEL Ponte was getting tired of seeing Wager, she didn't show it. This time he accepted her offer of coffee—it might fool his stomach for a while—and joined her in the small kitchen with its dark cupboards of imitation wood. A girl eight, maybe nine years old, with dark eyes and sun-bleached hair hung around watching Wager until her mother told her to go outside and see what her sister was up to. "An in-service day at school," she explained to Wager. "Teachers anymore seem to send more time studying how to teach kids than teaching them."

"Yes, ma'am." Wager sipped and complimented her on the coffee. "I understand your husband owned some land over on the reservation."

"I don't know if 'owned' is the word for it. It didn't do us any good; we couldn't use it for anything."

"Can you tell me what happens to it now?"

"What happens to it?" Her pale eyebrows went up. "I don't know. Goes to Luther, I guess. He lives there—he's been using it for his sheep."

"It didn't go to you or your daughters?"

This seemed to be the first time she'd thought of that possibility. "No—I don't think so. Why should it?"

"Well, your daughters are their father's heirs. Property usually gets handed down to the closest relatives. Did your husband leave a will?"

"No, not that I know of." Again, it seemed to be an aspect of his death that she hadn't considered. "Rubin didn't own anything worth putting in a will."

"Do you know what would happen to the property if he didn't leave a will?"

"No. I ain't thought much about that. Like I said, it never was worth anything, so I never really thought of it as belonging to us." She studied Wager's face. "You think that land might belong to the girls? You think I ought to hire a lawyer to see they don't get cheated?"

"I don't know about hiring a lawyer yet. If your husband didn't leave a will, the state will have to get involved."

"How come?"

"Just the way the law reads. Anyone who dies without a will or a trust has to have his property go through probate court. That's in order to make sure any claimants against the estate— anybody he borrowed money from or bought things from on time—gets paid. The court also makes sure that Colorado gets any outstanding taxes and fees."

"I didn't know that."

"Yes, ma'am. They advertise for claimants to the estate for three days and then wait three months to give people a chance to get to court and file. What's left goes to the heirs by a state formula." Wager watched the two children messing around near the swing set. The younger one was gingerly walking up the slide and talking as she held on to the metal sides; the older girl, poking a stick at something in the dirt, was ignoring her. "I noticed that the only telephone number painted on your husband's truck is this one. Did you answer his business calls for him when he wasn't here?"

"Yes. Mostly took messages for him, and he'd call back when he came in."

"So you had a pretty good idea of his schedule?"

"Not a good one, no. A lot of the time I'd know where he was supposed to be, but he was the one who set up his schedule. He wouldn't let me do that. He said he knew best how long a job might take and he'd better be the one to do the schedule." She repeated what she'd already told Rosemary Morris. "Sometimes he'd lose a job because the caller wanted to know right then if Rubin could do it. He couldn't wait for Rubin to get home and call him back."

"Did anyone phone him just before he left on the seventeenth?"

That demanded an effort of memory. "I'm not sure, it was so long ago, now. Let me see if I maybe wrote something down." She went around a small partition that set off the dining area from the kitchen with its wall phone. Wager heard the light scrape of a desk drawer and she came back, the heels of her slippers tapping the linoleum. "I'd keep his messages in a notebook," she explained. "That way I wouldn't forget, and if I was gone or asleep when he got in, he could look at them." She said apologetically, "I don't know if this'll help you any. It ain't much." The notebook had a bright-red paper cover; printed neatly on it in black marker was "Daddy's Message Book." She saw Wager reading it. "I got it for him for Christmas a couple years ago. For the kids to give him for a Christmas present." She stared at it for a second or two before opening it. Wager expected tears, but aside from a slight weariness, her voice did not change. "I reckon it'll be one of the last pages, won't it?" She leafed backward past a few blank sheets. "Here."

Wager turned the booklet so he could read it. Vertical ink lines had been carefully ruled down across the printed blue lines. The first column was headed "Date and Time," the second, "Name and Number," the third, "Message." The last entry was from Bill Nyholt, followed by a phone number and "21 March?" There were a couple of others like that—Wager figured they were ranchers who wanted to set up cattle moves, and Mrs. Del Ponte said he was probably right, she recognized a couple of names. Then a note that said "Mr. Sloan, Lastwell Furniture, ASAP" that was dated March 18. A few more names and numbers were scattered through the week preceding the seventeenth, but the only one Wager recognized was Lou Gregory, dated the sixteenth at 10:30 A. M. and followed by a number.

"Your husband saw all these messages?"

"That's what that little check is there. Means he saw them, but it don't mean he called back. I don't have any way of knowing if he called back—that was his business."

Wager looked over the list once more, copying the names and dates of the calls. "He didn't have a mobile phone?"

"No. Said it would cost too much. He had a CB in his truck, but he didn't use it much that I know of. It was for emergencies and to keep awake with on his long hauls." She shrugged. "It didn't work too good around here anyway."

"Did he have many of those?"

"Long hauls? No. Mostly local. The furniture store job was about his longest. Down to Phoenix—that's that Mr. Sloan. He runs the furniture store up in Grand Junction."

"Did your husband have any income other than his trucking business?"

"No. He owned some of his brother's sheep; that's what he got from him for using that land. But there wasn't much money in it. They sheared the wool every spring, but they didn't sell any for meat."

"Did he ever talk about canceling his run for Mr. Sloan?"

"Canceling it? What for? He was one of Rubin's steady customers."

"According to his log book, that was the trip he had scheduled for the seventeenth and eighteenth. But he never made it."

She looked at Wager, puzzled. "He never said a thing about quitting that job. Or any other. He was always looking for work."

"He met somebody at Mallard's Garage, midmorning of the seventeenth, when he should have been well on his way to Phoenix."

"Uncle Malcolm never said anything about that. Not one word!"

"Any idea at all who he might have been meeting?"

Slowly, she shook her head.

"I think that whoever he met had something to do with his death, Mrs. Del Ponte."

"I don't know who it could have been." She spoke slowly, as well, and her eyes were on Wager, but they saw something else.

"Well," Wager said, draining his cup, "we'll find out sooner or later. We'll find somebody who saw something, and then we'll know." He waited for her to respond in some way, but she was silent, now looking out the window and across the play area toward the distant mountains. "Thanks for the coffee, ma'am. I'll be in touch."

Still silent, she followed him to the door. As he was going down the steps, she asked, "Was it a man or a woman?"

"Who?"

"That person Rubin went to meet. A man or a woman?"

"I don't know. Not yet. Is there somebody you think he might have been meeting?"

Her hand rested on the tiny porcelain knob of the screen door; the skin over its knuckles was white from her grip. "Heidi Herrera. Jesse's wife."

15

THE HERRERA HOUSE, like the Del Pontes', was a manu-
factured home set on a cinder-block foundation and fronted with
a small elevated platform of a porch. About half a mile away
from the Del Pontes', it was placed among old and heavy cottonwoods whose bare branches blocked off the openness of the
desert and, while giving welcome shade in the summer, must
have made the long winter and slow spring even colder and
damper.

Heidi Herrera was not cold and damp. Short and plump,
with a round, warm figure, her gray eyes studied Wager with a
gleam of humor, as if she saw something that he didn't and would
like to tease him about it.

"You're the policeman who talked to my husband earlier?"

"Yes, ma'am."

"I wondered how long it would take you to get here."

"Why's that?"

"Sharon. She told you I had an affair with her husband,
didn't she?"

Wager could be just as blunt. "Did you?"

Her eyes glanced past Wager's shoulder toward the store, a
small, dark rectangle far across the high grass of an unmown
pasture. "Come on in."

He did. The paneling in this house was light-colored, imitation pecan wood dotted with imitation worm holes. It held a dozen or so decorative tapestries of knotted brown twine—rosettes, geometrical designs, tightly woven bands alternating with large loops of dangling string. The room's flat surfaces—paired stereo speakers, coffee table, low bookcase—held pottery tufted with dried weeds and flowers. The vases and pitchers were twisted awkwardly off center, the clay randomly dented here and there; their colors were faded shades of light green and blue and pale yellow that bled into each other like spreading puddles. The effect was one of contortion.

Mrs. Herrera saw him studying one of the vases. "I do a lot of handicraft work," she said. "I sell through a gallery in Cortez."

"It looks real nice," said Wager. He wasn't sure what else to say about it. And he guessed that since it was art, it wasn't all that careless-looking or ugly.

"H Bar H: That's me." She held up the bottom of a pitcher in varying shades of dull pink to show the brand etched into the clay.

Wager sat in the chair she gestured toward and looked around the cramped room. "You work here?"

"Out back. My workshop's out back—wheel and kiln. Are you interested in pottery?" Scraping magazines to one side of the small couch, she sat and curled her plump legs up beneath her and seemed to purr.

"More in you and Rubin Del Ponte."

"Poor Rubin. He just couldn't get over it." She shook her head, gray eyes twinkling brightly. "He thought it was his irresistible charm; he never could understand it was just the time and the place—this godawful place. The egotism of men!"

"You did have an affair with him?"

"Affair, no, a fling yes—a quick weekend. When Sharon went home to visit her mother or something. And Jesse was working in that damned store."

"When was this?"

"Oh, God—a year ago, now. We'd been here almost two years. I didn't want to come here in the first place. I didn't want to leave L.A. But Jesse said, 'Oh, you'll love it,' 'Oh, you can have your own studio,' 'Oh, if it doesn't work out, we can always come back.'" She snorted her contempt for the man or his words, or both. "Sure, we could. We sold our house out there at the bottom of the market and bought here at the top, and paid most of it for that damned store. We're stuck here now. I guess that was when I first realized how really stuck I was." She smiled again. "And Jesse's really not that good in bed, not anymore. Before we got married, he was great, but as soon as he said 'I do,' man, he didn't. You know the joke about how to cure a Jewish princess of nymphomania? If Jesse wasn't Mexican, I'd say he was a Jewish prince, because marriage sure cured him." She stretched a leg to place her bare foot on the table. It was soft-looking, with a high arch and bright red dots of color on the nails of the small toes, as round as grapes. "Maybe he's Sephardic. Weren't those the Spanish Jews? The Sephardics?"

"A year ago and nothing since?"

"One of my old boyfriends told me about them. He was Jewish. God, he had a schlong—and could he use it! I should have married him, except his mother kept calling me a shiksa; never called my by name, just 'the shiksa,' like I was this con-cubine or something. Good enough to be a goy toy for her boy, but not good enough to be his wife." She finally answered, "Yeah, just that one time. It wasn't any grand passion, you know? It was more get-to-know-your-neighbor, like." She shrugged. "And I was really depressed; that was when I realized I wasn't getting out of this hole." A demure smile. "Having an affair's a great cure for depression."

If you don't mind using other people. If you don't mind hurting somebody else's spouse or your kids. If all you think of is yourself. "Rubin didn't want to call it off?"

"It wasn't his to call off."

"When did your husband and Sharon find out about it?"

"When Rubin told her, I suppose. But she's never said anything to me directly. And Jesse doesn't have the guts to ask me anything about it—he knows if he opens his mouth, I'm out of here. I'm making it now with my pottery and textiles—I don't have to take any crap from him!" Another small smile. "Or anyone else."

"Did your husband threaten Rubin?"

"Not to my knowledge. Rubin never said anything about being threatened, either. Like I say, Jesse's smart enough not to ask questions." The edge of contempt was back in her voice.

"Is it possible he and Mrs. Del Ponte were having an affair?"

The woman laughed outright, head back and eyes shut. "Maybe. I really don't care. If it's a get-even fuck she wants, she can have it." The laugh faded, but the smile didn't. "I'm not jealous of Jesse, Mr. Wager. There's not a damn thing left to be jealous of. We don't screw more than once every two or three months anyway, and then he's like a rabbit—a little-bitty hot rabbit. In fact, I wish he and Sharon would get it on—I've got nothing against an open marriage." Stretching an arm along the back of the small sofa, she straightened her back, pressing her full breasts against the cotton blouse. He could not tell whether she was wearing a thin bra or none at all.

"How often do you visit the gallery at Cortez?"

The question surprised her. "Once a week."

"Do you have a lover there?"

"You are a detective, aren't you! Sure, Pat Halverson—he owns the gallery."

"Did Rubin know about him?"

She shrugged. "I don't know. I don't think so. We never talked about it. Anyway," she explained, "I met Pat after I told Rubin to cool it."

"Was Rubin persistent? Did he keep after you?"

"Not very, what, ardently. Oh, he'd drop by now and then—

just to say hello, you know—and hint about a quickie for old times' sake. But he knew it wouldn't do him any good. It was over—I didn't need him anymore and that's what I told him."

"How did he take that?"

"He didn't get upset, if that's what you're asking. I really don't know if he took it home with him and whined to Sharon or not. And I don't care." Her eyes widened into a blink and her mouth made a little round O. "You mean, would Jesse have killed him? Or Sharon? Or me?"

"Is it possible?"

She gently stroked her arms with the fingertips of both hands and then ran her spread palms down her stomach and across her thighs. "Well, certainly I didn't. Why should I? But Sharon or Jesse actually killing him . . . Ooh, wouldn't that be something!"

Wager asked her a few more questions: when she'd last seen Rubin—"Oh, I don't know. Last month sometime; he wasn't around that much"—if she knew he was an FBI informant—"He said he was. Tried to make me think he was some kind of James Bond"—if shortly before his death, he'd mentioned anything about a new scheme or a meeting with anyone—"I didn't see him before he died, but he always did have all sorts of big plans. Trying to impress me."

When he said good-bye at the door, Mrs. Herrera told him her phone number and asked him to keep in touch. "It would really be something, wouldn't it? I mean, if Sharon or Jesse killed him over me!"

WITHOUT A SPECIFIC time of death, there was little use in asking either the cuckold or the widow for their alibis; Wager turned his Plymouth west on State 181, the car's shadow rippling on the often patched tarmac ahead of him. Food. His stomach was telling him that not only was coffee insufficient, it was a dirty trick to play on a poor and unsuspecting organ. They would both be happy to reach the Gypsum Motel, and both disappointed if the kitchen were closed.

At last Wager crested a slight rise and saw, far down the slope of the highway ahead, the scatter of buildings and the few trees that marked the metropolis of Gypsum. The broad, shallow bowl that surrounded the crossroads was starting to gather that dusky look of sunset, though the distant ridge on the horizon behind it was still sharp and bright with glare. As Wager approached the pink glow of the motel's sign, three or four vehicles pulled out of its parking lot, leaving a thin cloud of dust in the quiet air. One of them, a dark sedan, came Wager's way, still accelerating as it flashed past. Its plates, Wager automatically noted, were the same Denver plates he had seen on the Lexus parked at the motel earlier this morning—AZW 3818; the blurred face behind the wheel looked like a white male in his fifties or so—gray hair, clean-shaven, meaty features—but that was about all Wager could make out in the instant of passing. The other vehicles were pickup trucks, two of which headed north on 666. The third took the unpaved county road west and left a tall trail of gray dust hovering behind it.

Wager once more placed his car in front of the picture window of his unit—a nod at security—and stopped off at the bathroom before walking down to the office and restaurant. The kitchen, his stomach was joyful to hear, was open, and Paula was already serving a handful of early diners.

"Verdie says you have a couple of messages, Officer Wager, if you want to stop by the office after supper."

He smiled his thanks and studied a dinner menu that he already knew by heart. A little later he chewed through a thick slice of beef from a cut that probably had provided a few of his previous meals.

Verdie, counting out his change, asked Wager to wait a minute while she got his messages. The first, a little pink form that had spaces for caller, room number, time, and message, was

marked 5:25 and had a single word from Durkin: "Report."
Wager expected the second to be from Sheriff Spurlock and
saying the same thing. But it was from Ray: "Call," followed by
two telephone numbers, one of which Wager recognized as the
office of the tribal police.

After he glanced at them, Verdie said, "I hear you're working for Sheriff Spurlock? Looking into Rubin Del Ponte's death,
that right?"

"Yes, ma'am. Did you know him?"

"Just to say hello to. He stopped by now and then, but not
often. Mostly he was off trucking."

"How about Walter Lawrence or the two government men?
Did you know either of them?"

"No, sir, I didn't."

"Does Mrs. Del Ponte ever stay here?"

"Never has. What for? They live just over in Egnarville,
don't they?"

Wager nodded. "Does she ever stop by for a drink—meet a
friend?"

"Could, I suppose. I wouldn't know her. I knew Rubin, but
I never met her."

"Did Rubin meet anyone here?"

She lifted her chin in thought. "I don't know about meet. He
said hello to whoever he knew. Sat down and had a cup of coffee
with them, sometimes."

"Was there anyone in particular he'd visit with?"

"No. He knew all the ranchers around here. Worked for most
of them at one time or another. Just sat and talked with whoever."

Wager thanked her and folded the messages into his pocket.
The outside air was chill with night, losing its heat quickly at
this altitude; along the walkway, the yellow lights beside each
door made a tunnel of glare that deepened the surrounding darkness and made the small cluster of window lights across the
highway seem even lonelier. Down near his room, blocking his

view of his car, sat an oversized pickup truck backed toward the motel. It had dual wheels in the rear and high, slatted sides around the bed, for carrying livestock.

As Wager drew near and could glance past it at his own car, partially shadowed by the truck, he saw a figure squatting beside his front wheel.

"Hey!" Wager darted toward the shape, but it did not move. "Hey—what—"

A hard thud from something solid caught him on the back of the head and exploded his vision into swirls and blossoms of yellow and orange. He felt his body get hit again, somewhere on the upper back, but there was no pain in that blow, just a lurch that drove him to his knees. Then his face was hit with something and his head snapped back as his mouth and nose went numb and coppery with hurt. Hands grabbed his weakly flailing arms and twisted them up behind his back. A heavy punch drove into his stomach and knocked the wind from his lungs with a flash of sharp, hot pain.

". . . you hear me? You hear me?"

". . . unh . . ."

"I said, you get your som-bitchin' ass out of here now! You leave now—tonight—or by God, you are a dead man!" The voice was a hot whiskey smell at his ear.

Another hard, solid punch to his ribs, but it didn't hurt as much because he was still gulping and struggling to suck air into his shocked lungs.

Somewhere he heard another voice mutter something and his arms were let go of, but it didn't do any good. His legs, empty of strength, buckled to jam a knee in the gravel and he tried to fold his arms up before his head hit the ground, but he could not lift them. Another smacking explosion shattered the dark of his clenched eyes, and he heard more than felt the rush of falling a long, long way.

16

HOW LONG WAGER lay there, he didn't know. What he
did know was that he was cold. That was the first thing he felt:
the cold. It filled the world around him like icy water and he
had a dream-vision of a figure that twisted awkwardly and somehow hung suspended in a lightless void of cold space. The figure
looked like him, and he watched it slowly drain of body heat as
a wind blew steadily across its flesh from some unseen glacier.
The cold made the body tremble in bone-racked spasms that
brought a slowly waking sense of recognition: It really was him,
Gabe, lying there shuddering, with an arm bent uncomfortably
beneath his body and something rough and equally uncomfortable pressing sharply up against the hurting skin of his face,
and he made some kind of noise as he struggled to blink his eyes
open.

The stab of yellow light grated like hot sand into his eyes
and he closed them again, but he knew where he was now:
facedown in the gravel of the parking lot beside his own car. He
heard another groan, clearly his own, and became aware of his
arm folded and pinched of blood beneath his torso. Another
heavy spasm of trembling shook his body and, stiffly, awkwardly, he grunted himself on to his side. A rolling ache moved
across his skull, starting at the back of his head and slamming
against his brow to make him wince and catch his breath. His

face felt swollen and numb and like a foreign shape to his clumsily probing fingers. Grunting once more, he pulled himself up by the car's door handle, his arm needling with the pulse of blood, and the muscles of his back cramping and clutching with cold. The pickup truck was gone and only his car and four or five others sat in the cold night wind, empty and scattered along the row of doors lit by their orange-tinted walk lights. He felt other things now: a sharp stab of pain in one of his ribs when he inhaled shallowly, the rub of the night wind across his stinging flesh, the throb of his head, his nose clogged with swelling and blood that began to drain into his throat and make him cough. The coughing told him that others of his ribs ached and that the muscles of his stomach hurt, too, and he stumbled across the walkway to his door, fumbling the key in the lock and leaning on the handle as it swung open.

He was shaking harder now, perhaps from shock as well as the cold; the heat of the room made the iciness of his flesh seem even deeper, down to the core of his being. Stripping off his bloodied denim jacket and shirt, his jeans flecked with dark-red drops and scrapes of grime, he clumsily turned on the shower to let the bathroom fill with steam as he pressed his clothes into the cold water of the sink. Mechanically, not really sure why he was doing it except as something that had to be done, focusing all his strength on the task, he drained the first two or three bowls of their darkly stained water and then let the clothes soak. Then he could let himself soak in hot water, feeling his body's taut muscle and sinew begin to relax. The deep tremors grew less frequent and bone-rattling, and the bite of the water on his abraded flesh gradually turned into the throb of bruises.

He didn't think his rib was broken—it still hurt when he deeply inhaled the steamy air, but its sharpness had faded, which told him it was probably a bone bruise or a minor crack instead of the splintered end of a rib sawing into flesh. His swollen nose had a new bump that burned like fire and said *broken* when he touched it; he held his breath and tried not to howl as he pushed down hard with his thumbs to realign the ragged stubs of bone and cartilage; he felt something deep inside his skull snap into place with a loud grating noise that made the roots of his teeth ache. Tears of pain ran from his clenched eyes and the bleeding started again; he watched in dull numbness as it washed down his body and swirled into the drain for a while. When he dared touch his nose again, it was sore and swollen, but the sensitive bump was gone. Now he could feel the tenderness in the hinges of his jaw, and the tip of his tongue ran across a sharp, rough edge of lower front tooth where a chip had been knocked off. It was sharp enough to cut the bottom of his tongue, and he tasted fresh blood from that and tried to keep his tongue away from it. But, of course, his damned tongue was curious and kept probing at that unfamiliar change in its world.

Slowly, Wager worked his torso and shoulders and arms, stretching and loosening the muscles in the flow of hot water. It had been a good ambush—give the bastards credit. It was the kind an experienced game hunter would set up—Wager, remembering the slashed tires of two days ago, had focused all his attention on the figure kneeling at his wheels; the assailant simply waited out of sight, hidden behind the high walls of the truck, and hit the back of Wager's head as he blindly and stupidly lunged for the bait. Liquored up. There had been the smell of whiskey on the muttered curses at his ear. A goddamned dead man if he stayed. And he hadn't gotten a good look at either of them. Two—at least two—one to hold and one to hit, but after that first slug to the back of his head, Wager hadn't been able to see anything clearly, and he couldn't say for certain how many there had been, let alone what they looked like.

The heat of the shower began to ebb, and Wager, skin wrinkled from soaking and the traces of blood finally gone from the water, turned off the squeaky faucets and gingerly patted himself dry. He could use some antiseptic here and there—his knee where the gravel had cut through his pants and into his skin, and his arm, which, for some reason, had a deep scrape. Defensive wound, maybe—maybe, hell, that's what it was; a homicide detective could spot defensive wounds, even on his own arms. Finally, he wiped a circle in the steamy mirror and looked at his face.

It was his. Except for the nose, already welted and swollen dark with subcutaneous blood across the bridge and spreading under his eyes. That fleshy lump belonged to a much bigger man. But, in general, his face didn't look nearly as bad as it felt. Lips beneath the shaggy mustache a bit puffy and split here and there with crusted blood, and a red swelling on his sharp cheekbone that would turn blue by tomorrow. And there was the chipped lower tooth that his tongue kept poking at, the front of it lifted off halfway down and its surface now slanting back to a slightly shorter rim of knifelike sharpness. A few light lines in the enamel showed cracks that went down into the gum; a dentist would have to do some work on that, but it looked as though it could be saved. He hoped it could—he'd had that tooth for a long time and was downright attached to it. Those on either side of the chipped one were sore, too, to the pressure of his finger, but they didn't seem loose and no blood showed at their gum lines. All in all, not too bad; he'd had worse. Whoever those cowboys were, they knew how to hit in a fight, but not how to hit to cripple a victim. Certainly not enough to drive him off. In fact, just enough to really make him mad. Just deeply, coldly, calmly pissed off.

The two pink message slips lay tossed on his bed with the rest of the stuff from his pockets. He dialed one number first but there was no response. Apparently the tribal police office did not have a twenty-four-hour duty watch or an answering machine, so he tried the second number. It was answered after one ring. "Hello?"

"Ray? Wager. I got your message."

"Man, I tried to raise you on your radio, but I guess mine won't reach that far. I found out something that might be interesting. Then again, it might not, I don't know. Anyway, Walter Lawrence's land reverted to the tribal holdings. He didn't have any direct heirs, and tribal law says that any portions without direct heirs living on the reservation revert back to communal lands if the owner dies intestate."

"It doesn't go through state probate?"

"No. The reservation comes under federal jurisdiction, which supersedes a state's laws. And in this case, the tribal law governs."

Wager forced himself to think about that. "Does that mean anyone can buy the land now? Somebody off the reservation, say?"

"I suppose they could if the tribal council wants to sell. But I don't think that's likely; council members would really get a lot of heat from the tribe if they started selling off the reservation to outsiders. What it means, in effect, is that the tribal council will keep the land in the collective holding and operate it for the benefit of the tribe, supposedly. My guess is they're more likely to reallot it to some other tribal member, probably a relative who needs land, or swap it for somebody else's reservation property that's maybe not as good. But by law it's theirs, the tribal council's, to do with as they please."

"That would apply to Rubin's land, too, if he didn't leave a will?"

"I don't see why not. What'd you find out from the county clerk?"

"She hasn't called me back yet. I'll have to try in the morning."

"You catch a cold?"

"What?"

"You sound stuffed up. Sounds like you caught a cold."

"Stuffy nose." He told the tribal policeman about the tangled love life of the Del Pontes and Herreras.

"So Herrera and Sharon Del Ponte have something going?"
"I'm not sure. Herrera's wife didn't know for sure, either.
Didn't really care." Wager, squinting through the throb of his
sore head, formulated the thought. "It might be they just talk to
each other—Sharon Del Ponte got pretty angry at being linked
to Herrera, and there's no reason for her to get defensive about
it. Not now, anyway." Thinking about it, in fact, publicly taking
Herrera from his wife could be a means of revenge for Del
Ponte's widow, but she hadn't done that. "She didn't know anything about the disposition of Rubin's land. Thought it would go
to Luther. Said she didn't know of any will or trust, either."

"Still, there could be a motive there."

Wager started to nod and caught himself before it hurt more.
"True."

They briefly talked over things they both already knew, the
way people do when they share an interest in something and get
along pretty well. When Ray hung up, Wager dialed Agent
Durkin.

This time the telephone rang half a dozen times and Wager,
feeling relief, was just about to hang up when the FBI man
answered with a groggy mumble.

"This is Wager. I got your message to call."

"Yeah. Jesus, what's it—after midnight?"

"A little bit. I've been busy."

"Yeah . . ." There was a rubbing sound, as if the man were
scrubbing at the flesh of his face with a dry hand. "All right,
what's your report?"

Wager told him.

"That doesn't tie into the Constitutional Posse, Wager. In
fact, it implicates a different motive altogether."

"It's what the facts say, Durkin. Theory comes after the facts
are gathered, not before. Remember?"

"Yeah, well, the facts I'm interested in gathering concern
the killings in federal jurisdiction. I don't see that Del

Ponte's love triangle has a damn thing to do with that!"

"You wanted me to report, that's my report." He had said
nothing of Ray's theory about the value of Rubin's land. For one
thing, the reservation land didn't seem to have any value for
anyone; for another, Wager didn't want Ray taken away from
him. And that's what Durkin would do if he thought Ray could
provide an avenue through Rubin or Walter Lawrence to anyone
who might be linked to the reservation murders—Durkin would
order Ray to work exclusively with him, cutting Wager off from
his access to the reservation on the grounds of protecting the
security of Durkin's own investigation. "What do you have to
report to me?"

"What?"

"Your report. What's your report? I'm supposed to be the
liaison between you and Sheriff Spurlock, so what do you have
that I can tell him?"

A silence. Then a muffled sigh. "The FBI lab reports have
come back and those three bombs were made of C-4—that's a
military explosive. Plastic compound. The lab's ninety-nine
percent certain that the chemical makeup was the same for all
of them. It was an older batch distributed to several National
Guard engineering units, including some in Colorado, Wyo-
ming, New Mexico, and Utah." He mumbled something about
the need for a law requiring manufacturers to put traceable
chemicals, taggables, in high explosives.

"The explosives were used for military training?"

"That's right."

Which meant that someone had access to phe munitions as
well as the expertise in using them, and Wager guessed that
Durkin had thought of that, too; he was just becomingly modest
about that information. "What names did you come up with?"

"What? What do you mean?"

"You did ask Washington to fax a roster of members in those
regional engineering units, didn't you?"

Another brief silence. "Yeah." Then, grudgingly, "The 138th Engineering Battalion up in Grand Junction has over a hundred members. Maybe ten or so are from around here."

"Read them off."

He wasn't happy about that, either, but he did. Wager wrote and asked about the spellings. He recognized six of the names: Gregory Hunter, the county highway worker who found Del Ponte; Bradley Nichols; Pete Stine; Henry Many Coats, whose last name rang a bell; Louis Cloud, another Ute last name; and Howard Morris, Sheriff Spurlock's deputy.

"Two of those are Constitutional Posse members, Nichols and Stine," said Wager.

"Oh, yeah? That's interesting."

"And Morris is Spurlock's deputy for this section of the county, which is where Nichols and Stine have their ranches."

"Christ!"

Even through the heavy throb in his skull, Wager could almost see the FBI man's thoughts: With Spurlock's deputy a possible suspect in a federal crime, the entire sheriff's office was tainted. The orders from Durkin's regional director about cooperation with the local police agency might now be reversed—no more "liaison" with Wager and Spurlock—and Durkin's authority to pursue the investigation off the reservation expanded. Perhaps Wager should not have identified those names for the FBI man, but he would have found out in time. And besides, Durkin was a cop, too; liaison meant sharing the information. Maybe now Durkin would recognize that Wager was playing reasonably straight, and his cooperation with Wager would move from reluctant obedience toward a more effective willingness. "Have you talked to the battalion commander? Checked his demolitions inventory?"

"Not yet; the information from Washington came in too late. But I have an appointment with him tomorrow."

"Up in Grand Junction?"

"That's right."

"You'll let me know what he says, right?"

"Yeah. Sure thing. And—ah—thanks for calling."

WAGER WAS MUCH sorer the next morning. He had felt the hurt increasing in the night when, restless, he had tossed from one ache to another, half awake from the effort of trying to breathe through his swollen nose. But when he sat up and twisted to shut off the motel's clock radio, his breath caught and he almost groaned aloud at the wrenching pain of his ribs and shoulder. The hinges of his jaw were even tenderer, as was his tongue where the damned thing kept moving over to find that sharp tooth, and in the bathroom mirror the bruises and swelling made his face look like a third-rate boxer's after a first-rate fight. All in all, it was the kind of start to the day that he could do without.

As he entered the empty restaurant, the waitress apparently shared his opinion. "Oh, my Lord! What happened, Officer Wager?"

"I'm beginning to think somebody doesn't like me, Paula. How about some coffee?"

"Yessir." Frowning, she half ran to the hot plate and, with an insulated pitcher and a rattling cup and saucer, followed him to a table. Her soft voice held a note of anxiety. "Is this because of your investigation?"

He nodded, gingerly inhaling the fragrant steam whose warmth and moisture soothed the damaged tissue in his nose. Seemed as if everyone had heard about his investigation, even people he had met as recently as last night. "Did you know Rubin Del Ponte?"

"Not too well. He was kind of a cousin, through my dad. His mom's somebody married my dad's somebody on the reservation a long time ago. I never did understand exactly who. Have you found out something about his death?"

More cousins. Wager figured the whole world was cousins if you went back far enough. Too bad people didn't act like they were all related. Or maybe they did, but in a family that was held together by mutual hatreds and jealousies instead of shared love. "Not much yet, but I intend to. Did you know Mrs. Del Ponte, too?"

"Sharon? I met her a couple of times. She used to come to the Bear Dances when they were first married."

"The what?"

"Bear Dance—that's the big spring festival on the reservation. Every Ute tribe has its Bear Dance once a year. It tells about how the Utes and the bears are friends and celebrates the bears waking up in the spring. Depending on which reservation it's on, it lasts three or four days. It's a big party and all the relatives and friends of the tribe come from all over. They eat a lot and watch the dancers and horse races and play hand games and gamble. That's where I met her."

"Have you ever seen her here?"

"At the motel? No—why?"

"Just wondering. Verdie tells me that Rubin came by occasionally."

She nodded, glancing at a family of travelers entering the restaurant: sleepy-looking man, two school-age boys poking and pushing each other irritably, wife trying to hush the whining of the youngest.

"Was there anyone special he met with? Anyone he seemed to be looking for?"

"Not that I recall. He was friendly with just about everybody, though."

"Especially the week before he died, did he seem to meet with someone or wait for someone?"

"I can't really remember . . ." Her attention was drawn by the tourists, who were glancing her way, hesitant about which table to seat themselves at. "Excuse me, Mr. Wager. I got to work. If I think of something, I'll tell you."

He thanked her and returned to his coffee, trying to keep its scalding heat away from the splits in his lips, his raw tongue, his broken tooth.

THE MONTEZUMA COUNTY clerk and recorder's office opened at eight; Gabe, speaking carefully around the little piece of chewing gum he used as a cap over his broken tooth, placed his call shortly after. The woman said, "Oh, yes, Officer Wager. No, I found his death records, but I don't have any record of a will being filed for that person, so it seems he died intestate. But I didn't find anything on the docket for probate action, either. Now if his property was in joint ownership, say, with his wife, it wouldn't go through probate. So I'm not sure what to tell you."

"It wouldn't be handled up in La Sal County, would it?"

"No, they don't have a county court. If there was probate, it would go through the court here, though the three-day notice to creditors would appear in the La Sal paper. My guess is his property was either in joint ownership, or for some reason the paperwork just hasn't been completed yet. I'll keep looking."

"He owned some land on the Squaw Point Reservation. I understood that would not come under the state's jurisdiction, is that right?"

"Is he an Indian? If he's an Indian, his will would likely be handled in federal court in Denver. Maybe that's why there's no record of it here."

Wager explained about Del Ponte's one-quarter status.

"Oh. No, then that would be state jurisdiction. All his property that wasn't restricted to the reservation, anyway."

"So that reservation land would stay in the tribe?"

"If he was intestate or didn't have close relatives living there, that's right."

"What about a half brother living there? Would the land go to him?"

"I don't know, Officer Wager. You're talking reservation law there, and that gets pretty complicated because it's a mixture of tribal and federal laws. And each tribal council has its own way of doing things."

"Is there anyone who could tell me? A tribal lawyer, perhaps?"

"Yes—that's a good idea! You ought to talk to Everett Snyder. He represents the Ute Mountain tribe, so it's likely he could tell you. His office is in Cortez. Would you like his number?"

"Yes, thanks." He dialed the tribal lawyer's number.

A clerk's voice answered briskly. "Snyder, Silvers and Slaby." Wager told the young-sounding man who he was and what he wanted. A few moments later, an older male voice asked, "Officer Wager?"

He explained again.

"I see. Well, I don't represent the Squaw Mountain tribe, so I can only answer in general terms. But the procedure is fairly uniform on all Ute reservations: Absent a will or trust, the property would probably go to the closest member of the family residing on the reservation. Each tribal council has slightly different rules governing the ownership of real properties for their respective reservations. However, the principle in general on all reservations is to maintain Native-American ownership of any and all reservation lands, water rights, mineral rights, and other property titles whether entailed through individually registered members of the tribe or through collective ownership of the tribe in the corporate person of the tribal council. In this case, I assume that ownership would be transferred either to the half brother or to the tribal council as collectively owned property. Have you talked to any of the tribal council yet to see what they have ruled?"

"Not yet."

"That's where you should start." The voice said the interview was over—as an officer of the court, the lawyer was bound
to help the police in a case; as a lawyer, his time was too valuable
for much pro bono work. And he hadn't said anything Wager
hadn't already surmised. He thanked the voice and called Ray's
office number.

17

RAY WAS OUT. The young woman said she would leave a message for him, and Wager dialed another number. He had better luck with this one.

"Been wondering what you've got up to, Wager." Sheriff Spurlock's rumbling voice sounded as if it came from the bottom of an empty barrel. Which, given his physique, was close to true. Wager told him what Durkin had said about the C-4 explosives.

"Distributed to a local National Guard unit? He's sure of that?"

"The chemical analysis identified it, he said. Ninety-nine percent certain—good enough for courtroom use, anyway." The line was silent, so Wager added, "Here are some names of people who belong to the engineering battalion up in Grand Junction." He read the list of ten names.

"Uh-huh." The sound was noncommittal.

"You want to talk to Morris or should I?"

"Wait a minute, Wager. You ain't saying my deputy had a damn thing to do with those bombings!"

"What I say's not important; it's what Durkin thinks. If Morris wasn't your deputy, wouldn't you want to talk to him?"

"Damnit, Wager—!"

"I'd want to talk to Nichols, Stine, Hunter, Many Coats, Cloud, and the other five, too; but I figure Morris might be the most cooperative and the one to start with."

"Damn . . . !" Then, "You at that motel? In Gypsum?"

"Yes."

"Stay there. Me and Morris will be there in about an hour."

It was closer to forty-five minutes. Morris arrived first, looking grim and tight around the mouth, then surprised when he saw Wager's face. "What in the world happened?"

Wager told him, then had to go through it again when the sheriff arrived about five minutes later. Spurlock studied the bruises on Wager's face. "I take it you didn't get a look at them or you'd have them on an APB by now."

Wager verified that. "I think they were driving a dark, dual-axle pickup with cattle rails on the bed."

"Fits a lot of vehicles around here," said Spurlock. "And in every other county and over in Utah as well." He wagged a meaty finger at Paula for a cup of coffee, sighed deeply, and leaned his elbows on the creaking table. "What's that on your tooth?"

"Chewing gum. Keeps my tongue off it."

"Oh. Well, I ought to give you protection of some kind."

"I can handle it."

"Don't much look like it. But then, I don't have anybody to assign to you anyway. What about getting someone else from Denver or the CBI to come out? I'd feel a hell of a lot better knowing somebody was watching your back."

"I'll be all right." He turned to Morris, who had been sipping his coffee and gazing silently through the plate glass of the restaurant window. "Did Sheriff Spurlock tell you why we're meeting?"

"No—just said to be here."

Wager explained about the C-4. "Who handles demolitions in the battalion?"

"We all do, one time or another. It's part of the combat engineering training program: Build things up, blow things down."

"How easy would it be to steal some C-4 and caps from the battalion supply room?"

"I guess it could be done. God knows, other stuff gets stolen easy enough."

Spurlock sighed and refilled his cup, draining the small pitcher. "Howie, somebody had to've stole it from a National Guard unit. It has the same chemical signature as the C-4 issued to the regional engineering battalions, and that includes your unit. Most likely, somebody took it and either used it themselves or handed it on to somebody else to use. You got any idea who in your battalion might have done that?"

Morris, narrow face sallow and whiskers already dark despite a morning shave, eyed the sheriff. "You think it was me?"

"No, damnit, I don't think it was you. If I thought it was you, I wouldn't be here drinking coffee with you, I'd have your butt in my office under oath. But I do think Wager, here, is right. It could well be one of those weekend heroes you soldier with. Now maybe it wasn't you—and I'm not saying it was—but you do train with these people, and you been training with them for quite a few years. Do you have any idea who wanted to do it and who had the opportunity to do it?"

The deputy rubbed at his eyes with the tips of narrow fingers. "I couldn't say for sure, Sheriff."

"Howie, you're my deputy and by God, I expect the truth from you. Nothing but, and nothing held back! And I tell you this: The FBI's going to question all of you. Every name on this list is a suspect. If this thing drags out, Durkin and a flock of other agents are going to come in here and stomp around and question these people: All their relations, their employers, employees, their friends, their fellow church members, anybody who might know them and anybody who might have a grudge—they're going to rip through this county like a goddamn tornado, turning up as much dirt on every name on this list as they can, upsetting people, causing suspicion, trying to turn neighbor against neighbor to shake out every rumor and whisper. And there's not a thing I can do to stop them because it was a federal crime to steal the stuff and a hell of a lot worse one to use it. These are our people, Howie, our neighbors, and a lot of them's our relatives—brothers, sisters, children, cousins, you name it. Now I think we ought to do what we can to keep an inquisition like that away from them. So now, goddamnit, I want you to tell me who of these people most likely stole that C-4!"

"I ought to quit this job." The man set his empty cup on the saucer with a loud clatter. "Just up and quit the goddamn thing—Rosie don't like the goddamn hours, don't like living how she has to with me gone all the time. And now this. By God, Sheriff, it just ain't worth it!"

"Who, Howie?"

"Move to California. Hell, there ought to be plenty of room out there by now."

"Tell me, Howie."

His jaw made the odd chewing motion that Wager had seen before. Then he finally spoke. "Maybe Bradley Nichols. But I don't know for sure. He was the platoon sergeant in charge of an exercise last November—exercise in the demolition of a reinforced structure. A couple of old concrete silos somebody wanted to get rid of, and the battalion commander got the OK to blow them up in return for us hauling off the rubble. Nichols had the demolitions platoon: He set up the problem and signed for the C-4. I remember Karl Yeager—he's the supply sergeant—joking about how much demolition Nichols requisitioned. Said he had enough to make face powder out of those silos."

"Did he turn any back in, or did he use it all?"

"I don't know. But we haven't had any demo exercises since then. It's been some bridge and road building, communications problems, equipment maintenance to get ready for the summer field exercises. And some flood-control training in case of the spring runoff." His voice fell. "Nichols makes no secret of his feelings about the BLM, and I don't know who else had a better opportunity. But I also don't know if Yeager's had any stolen from supply since then, either."

Spurlock edged his cup to the side of the table so Paula, appearing with her steaming pot, could refill it. He told Wager, "You better let me handle this—I want to talk to Nichols without getting him riled up." He watched Paula top off his cup. "He'll be more likely to talk to me than to you."

"You sure you want to be the one to ask him questions?"

The sheriff eyed Wager over his coffee cup. "Meaning you think I won't ask him any hard ones?"

"Meaning I don't need his vote next election."

"Well, Officer Wager, I think you mean that kindly. I think. But I figure if I do my job, the votes will take care of themselves."

"Fine with me. But you ought to know that Durkin's going to be talking to the supply sergeant sometime today—he'll probably say something about Nichols being the last one to be issued demolitions."

"Yeah. I better see him right off."

"Tell me, Morris, was it possible that Del Ponte learned about the C-4?"

"Now damnit, Wager—"

The deputy shrugged. "I don't think so. He had nothing to do with the National Guard unit. And I don't know anybody who'd tell him anything about it—everybody knew who he was working for."

"What about any enemies Nichols might have? Somebody who might want to get him in trouble?"

Both Spurlock and Morris looked at him. "Bradley's stepped on some toes." The deputy spoke slowly, thinking. "He's got a mean mouth sometimes and don't mind using it. But only the people in the Guard unit would be likely to know about the C-4, and there's none of them Nichols has any real problems with, I don't think."

Still, Del Ponte could have received the information in a roundabout manner. And suppose he had tried to use it to blackmail Nichols? "Was Gordon Hunter part of Nichols's demolition platoon?"

Morris shook his head. "He's in motor transport. A driver."

"Are he and Nichols good buddies?"

"I've never seen them together much. At Guard meetings, Hunter's usually driving or doing vehicle maintenance. Why?"

"He found Del Ponte's body. Maybe he knew where to look, maybe not."

"Well, let's not go chasing all over hell and gone when we got enough to worry about right here, Wager. I'll talk to Nichols and see what he has to say. And the both of you keep quiet about this."

Back in his room, Wager once more tried the tribal police number. This time he was put through. "Ray, have you found out anything about who gets Rubin's land?"

"It all depends on whether there's a will or a trust somewhere. Was one filed?"

"No. Was Sharon Del Ponte listed as part owner of the land?"

"Nope. Tribal records show just Rubin's name. Without a will, it looks like it goes to Luther. He's the closest registered relative, and that's what the tribal law says: Intestate property goes to the closest relative who's registered. A registered relative who no longer lives on the reservation has first claim but has to come back and live on the property. If he doesn't, it goes to the next closest relative who lives there." That called for explanation. "That's a new tribal law that went into effect after Rubin inherited his land, but it wouldn't have applied to him anyway; you can still leave your land to someone off the reservation if they're named in your will."

"Have you talked to Luther yet?"

"Haven't had a chance. Probably not until tomorrow. You want to come along when I do?"

"I sure do."

WAGER SHOULD HAVE gone out and interviewed Gordon Hunter—he had planned to, despite Sheriff Spurlock's caution against casting too wide a net. But his head still hurt—was worse, in fact, maybe from all the coffee he'd drunk to cut through the haze—and breakfast rode uneasily in his touchy stomach. Symptom of concussion, maybe. He felt as if he had been hit hard enough and often enough last night to be concussed. He was sleepy, too, which was another sign, and he still felt too groggy and disconnected to trust himself behind a steering wheel for very long. So he settled at the small writing table in his motel room to wait for his system to get over the effects of the beating. He jotted notes to himself, fragments of things he remembered and bits of ideas those things generated, and he forced his mind to be focused and alert to the differing possibilities and relationships of the case. But his eyelids kept closing and a rushing sound kept filling his ears until he jerked awake over words that scrawled into illegibility. Finally, sometime before noon, he gave up and stumbled toward the bed and was asleep before he hit its surface.

When the rattle of his telephone pulled him from the depths of a numb sleep, the unshaded window was gray with dim light. He muttered hello and glanced at the glowing numbers of the clock: 6:45.

"Gabe? Did I wake you?" Liz's voice. "What are you doing sleeping so early?"

Early? He stared at the clock's numbers. Early meant it was evening, right? "I—ah—I was up late."

"Oh." Then, "Are you all right? You sound funny."

He felt funny, too. A lot of the soreness of his body had congealed into stiffness from lying so long without moving, and the sharp ache of his head had been replaced by a cottony, punchy feeling that told him he wasn't thinking too clearly—

concussion for sure. "Yeah, fine, I'm just . . . Is it morning or evening?"

"Evening! Are you sure you're all right?"

"I'm OK, Liz. How about you? You doing all right?"

The line was silent for a few seconds. "You don't at all sound like you're OK."

He made an effort to seem perky and happy. "I really am fine. Just waking up." Or trying to—the surging pull of drowsiness had subsided but not gone away, and he vaguely remembered something about the dangers of a concussion slipping into a coma. But he did feel better than he had when he'd fallen asleep—the nausea was gone, the headache less. All he needed was a little more sleep. "What's going on?"

"I wanted to tell you that Evelyn Litvak has filed for a change in venue. She's asking for some neutral site for the hearing."

"Good idea." Something . . . what was it? He groped through the fuzziness, then ran down the almost illegible notes and came up with it. "If she doesn't get the change in venue, tell hev to ask for a continuance—try to delay the hearing for a couple of weeks."

"Why?"

"I can't give you any details yet—I haven't come up with much evidence. But her ex might be involved in this case I'm working on."

"Oh? A felony charge?"

"Would be, if the suspicion proves true."

"When will you find out?"

"I don't know, Liz. Things are still pretty muddled." Both inside and outside his head.

"Do you have anything at all she can take to the judge to support her request for a continuance?"

There would be something wrong with that and he concentrated hard to figure out what. "Not right now, no. I wouldn't want Litvak or his buddy to learn anything about my investigation yet. But it shouldn't be more than a few days."

Another pause. When Liz's voice came back, it was sharper. "It's Evelyn's child, Gabe. Her daughter. The hearing is scheduled for Monday unless the change in venue is granted. And even if it is, the date for the new venue might not be changed—they'll look for a docket that's not crowded."

What was today? What the hell day was it? "I'll call you as soon as I can, Liz. If my suspect slips out of this because he hears about it through Litvak, there won't be any conviction, anyway."

That made sense to him, which, given his state of mind, wasn't saying much. It didn't convince Liz. "The court will demand a reason for issuing a continuance."

"Tell her to get sick—have her grandmother die. Liz, until the evidence is gathered, I can't take the chance of tipping my hand to anyone, including Litvak."

"You can't take a chance on a case, but you're asking Evelyn to take a chance on losing her daughter?"

Put that way, it sounded pretty bad. "All right, suppose she can't get a change of venue or a continuance, suppose the child is awarded to her husband, if he's convicted of a felony, she can sue to get her daughter back."

"After how long? And after how much damage to that child? And suppose he's not convicted? Your case is not more important than a child's welfare!"

"The child's welfare might depend on this case, Liz. Or it might not—the guy could be innocent. I don't know yet."

She interrupted him. "It's a gamble with a child's life."

He kept talking as if she hadn't spoken. It was a little trick of his that really irritated her, but between the returning intensity of his headache and the struggle to find words in a woolly brain, he was careless. "What I do know is that three people have been killed, that a close friend of Litvak might—just might—be involved, and that if he is, I do not want him warned off."

"Three people killed?"

"Yes. Probably four, and some bombings as well. But it's not clear yet. Nothing's clear yet. If my suspect is arrested and charged and Litvak is named as an accomplice, the court should grant an automatic continuance pending the outcome of his trial. I will do what I can as fast as I can to see if the facts call for that. But I won't endanger my case by tipping my hand to Litvak too soon."

"Three homicides and bombings—good lord, that man can't be allowed near that girl!" When she spoke again, her voice had lost its combativeness. "All right. I'll tell her to try for a delay. And I'll have her tell the judge that you can't talk about an ongoing case, but that her husband may be involved."

"Not even that—the judge would have to pass it on to Litvak's lawyer. She'll have to come up with some other reason to ask for a continuance. I know it's a gamble, but it has to be that way to protect the case."

"You really don't want me to say anything about it."

"Nothing."

She shifted topics to get away from an outcome that didn't satisfy her. Her tone told Wager that although she acquiesced, she wasn't convinced. But she was not going to waste any more time or energy on that issue right now. "Here's something else, then. You wanted me to talk to Evelyn about her husband and his friends, remember?"

Not clearly, but he said, "Yes."

"Well, apparently he's been coming to Denver regularly on business. Evelyn said he's been to visit their daughter several times in the last month, and at first she thought it was just so it would look good to the judge in the hearing. But the last time he told her about some deal he's involved in. He said it was going to make him so rich he'd be able to do things for his daughter that Evelyn could only dream about."

"That doesn't mean the court would award him custody."

"No. But it's enough to worry Evelyn even more—which, of course, he wanted to do. That's why what you tell me about his involvement in your case is so important. For Evelyn's sake."

"It's not 'involvement,' Liz. It's only possible involvement—and a damn slender thread to hang any hopes on."

When he didn't say anything more, she continued, "Anyway, whatever he's up to 'involves' a meeting with McGraw, of all people. The last time he was here, he told Evelyn that he was going to lunch with some fat cat investors, and the name he mentioned was Weldon McGraw."

"He's fat?"

"I don't see how he can be skinny—not the way he must feed under the table."

Wager tried to see some sense in that. It connected with nothing, but he noted it on his paper memory anyway. "Could you find out a little more about that?"

"I'll see."

"And check out a license number for me? Or ask Max Axton to run it?"

"Sure."

He read the letters and numbers from his sheet of jottings. The party-and-plate inquiry could, of course, be run through Spurlock's office, but the sheriff might want to know why and Wager wasn't certain he wanted the man to know everything he was doing. Especially since the sheriff had shown tender concern for Nichols's feelings. "It's a new Lexus. I'd like the name and address of the registered owner."

"Is it important? You want me to get right back to you on it?"

"When you can. It's more curiosity, right now."

The faintly crackling line was silent for a long moment. "Gabe? You sound as if you're ready to pass out. Are you sure you're all right?" Concern had replaced anger.

"Just sleepy, Liz. I was banging around pretty late last night and got up early this morning. It's nothing a little sleep won't take care of."

"I'd give you a back rub if you were here."

"That would be great!" He could almost feel the warmth of her small, strong hands gently digging into the taut muscles of his neck and shoulders. He enjoyed rubbing his fingertips deep into the yielding flesh of her back, too. It was an intimacy they hadn't shared in a long time, something that had been almost forgotten, sacrificed to the competing demands of their busy schedules. But he realized now how much he missed it. "I'd like to rub you, too." And that led to oblique statements of what each of them would like, and somewhere in the soft exchanges of how they felt he vaguely remembered saying good night and hanging up, and then falling immediately into darkness.

18

WHEN HE OPENED his eyes, the unshaded window had the same tint of grayness as when he'd fallen asleep. But the clock said 5:52. Wager, feeling turgid from too much immobility, clicked on the radio to lie half awake and listen to the nasal voice of the local announcer run through stock and grain prices and finally declare the end of the morning farm report. Morning. He'd slept without waking through the night—he hoped it was only one night—and, stiffly, he hauled himself to the shower to steam some life and alertness into his flesh and mind.

Starving, he felt saliva squirt into his mouth at the thought of eggs and hash browns and hot, juicy sausages, and his hand quivered weakly as he carefully scraped off his two-day growth of whiskers. The television had replaced the radio, and he heard a hearty voice tell the world good morning, it was seven-thirty, Thursday, April 6, and here were the stories News Center Nine was following. Thursday . . . He paused, razor held just off his soapy chin and stared without seeing himself in the steamy mirror. Liz—he'd talked to Liz and made a promise . . . Monday court date, that was it: Evelyn Litvak's daughter. See if Litvak was involved in any way in the bombings and killings. And now he'd lost a day—an entire day gone. A lost day of his life because of those two yahoos, and that made him angrier than being hurt.

The marks across his nose and under his eyes were still

there, as ugly as sin and a lot less fun. The purple blotches had begun to change around the edges to that dark red tone of old bruise, and some of the lighter ones were turning brown and yellow now. Looked like a damned Gila monster and felt just about as hungry as one. But he did seem to be a lot better: only slight twinges in his torso, which should work out with movement. And most important, he was clearheaded. Food would make him feel even better. Eggs. Over easy. Hash browns. Spicy sausages, link or patty, either one—a hearty cholesterol boost to clog the arteries, washed down with a pot of strong black coffee to raise the blood pressure. . . .

Wager was wiping up a remaining trace of egg yolk with the last corner of his toast when Paula stopped by the table to check his coffee. "Your poor face looks so sore!"

"Looks worse than it feels, Paula. Really." Even his tongue was better. It had grown used to the change in the surrounding teeth and no longer poked itself against the sharp edge.

There were no other diners and the girl glanced over her shoulder toward the doorway to the lounge and the cash register beyond. "Yesterday, you and the sheriff were talking about Mr. Litvak?"

Wager nodded.

"Well, that reminded me—you remember you asked me about Rubin? If he'd met with anybody in particular before he died?"

He nodded again.

"He and Mr. Litvak spent some time one afternoon, with that man from Denver. I don't know his name, but they were talking about something important, it looked like. You know, their heads all close together and no jokes or storytelling—all business."

"When was this, Paula?"

"Maybe a week or two before Rubin died. I don't remember the exact day, I'm sorry."

"That's all right. Just the three of them?"

"Yes."

"Who was the other man? The one from Denver?"

"I've never heard his name. He's been here a few times—drives a really nice new car, a Lexus, with Denver plates. That's why I think he's from Denver." She bobbed her head at the plate-glass windows open to the parking lot and the stretch of empty highway and the equally empty range beyond. "He usually parks just out there, that's how I know what he drives."

"Can you remember anything at all about their conversation?"

"No, sir. It was pretty busy and I didn't visit their table much—they just had coffee and ice tea. I wouldn't've remembered it at all except for what you and the sheriff said yesterday."

"Does Verdie know him?" Wager remembered the several times Paula had stood silent and unnoticed while he and Morris talked.

"I don't know." But it was clear that she was uneasy at the idea of Wager talking to the older woman about it.

"Well, if he comes in again and I'm around, let me know, OK?"

"Yessir, but I don't know if he'll be back too soon. He was here again just a couple of days ago."

"Who'd he meet?"

"Mr. Litvak and Mr. Hegendorf and another rancher that I've seen a couple of times, but I don't know his name."

"When was this?"

"Day before yesterday. Late afternoon."

And that Lexus Wager passed as he was approaching the motel must have held the man. "Tell you what," Wager said, jotting Sheriff Spurlock's number on the back of one of his DPD business cards. "If I'm not around when you see him again, leave a message for me at this number. And thanks, Paula."

She nodded but didn't move; Wager guessed that she had more on her mind.

"Something else you remember, Paula?"

"Not remember, no. But . . . do you know Denver real well?"

"That's where I work, usually. I'm a cop there."

"Could you—I mean if maybe I went there, could you sort of talk to somebody about a waitressing job for me?"

"Well, I suppose I could, sure. But you want to think very carefully before making a move like that, Paula. Denver's a big city—and not a very friendly one, sometimes." Certainly not the way Wager experienced it. "Especially for a girl who doesn't know anyone there."

"I'd know you. I mean, I wouldn't be hanging around you, not that, but if I needed help or something, I'd be able to call you, wouldn't I? You're a policeman, you said."

"Well, yeah. But it could be dangerous, too." He stopped himself from giving her a cop's jaundiced view of life in the city. "Not everywhere, but there is danger there."

"There is here, too," she said. She started to add something but the sound of voices in the lobby caught her ear and she turned to leave.

"Paula?"

"Yessir?"

"Thanks for the warning the other night. When you called me."

She froze for an instant, biting her lower lip. Then she nodded quickly and before Wager could ask anything else, hurried away with her head bent over the pot of coffee.

Verdie wasn't at the cash register when Wager finished his meal. He left a bill to cover his breakfast and a generous tip and headed for the telephone in his room.

The toe of Wager's shoe tapped the rug with impatience as he waited for an answer to the call he had to make but didn't really want to. Durkin's voice finally came on: crisp, efficient, brusque. "Where the hell have you been, Wager? I tried two or three times to call you yesterday. You wanted to know what I found out, remember?"

"Right, sorry, I was out of reach. What'd the National Guard people say?"

"No thefts. All of their C-4 is accounted for. They keep it in a secure underground magazine that only the supply sergeant and the battalion commander have access to. And they run a signed, monthly inventory on all munitions as well as the weapons in the armory."

"And Nichols was the last one to be issued any?"

Durkin's tone revealed a mix of surprise and irritation. "If you already know this, Wager, why the hell are you asking me?"

"I got it from a different source—think of it as corroboration and be happy. Did Nichols turn any back in?"

"Not that I was told of. Why?"

"I heard that, at the time, the supply sergeant thought Nichols had requisitioned an excessive amount."

". . . He didn't tell me that . . ."

There could be a couple of reasons for the supply sergeant's silence: It didn't seem important to the man, he simply forgot about it, he didn't want to get a friend in trouble. Or himself, if Nichols was the type to get even. And from the little Wager had learned about the man, he was. "You might check with Sergeant Yeager—see if he remembers."

"Yeah. I will. Nichols is a member of the Constitutional Posse, you said."

"One of its leaders, from what I hear. Along with a good friend of his, Stanley Litvak. They see a lot of each other; my guess is that if Nichols is up to something, Litvak at least knows about it."

"I see . . ."

"Plan on talking to them?"

"You bet I do. I'll be in touch, Wager. Thanks."

And thank you, Special Agent Durkin. That line of inquiry would be very helpful: It would keep Nichols's eyes away from Wager, give the FBI man something to do, and—if dropping Litvak's name worked out—might even make Liz happy.

He finished brushing his teeth and was almost out the door when his telephone rattled and Liz's rushed voice said, "Good morning! How are you feeling?"

"Fine—really. Good sleep, good breakfast. And I was just thinking about you."

"Pleasant, I hope."

"Thinking of something that would make you happy."

"I'd like to hear more about that! But it'll have to wait—meeting in ten. But I wanted to tell you what I found out: That license plate? It belongs to a car owned by Ronald Pyne. He's that wheeler-dealer Weldon McGraw likes to do favors for. The Riverfront Project man?"

"I remember. But why—"

"I thought you'd want to know. So I asked Weldon about him—why he's running around the western slope. And of course Weldon couldn't help a little puff about his intimate knowledge of his wealthy friends and their deals. Pyne owns a ranch somewhere out there. He bought it a couple of years ago, and McGraw says he's planning on developing it. Has asked McGraw to come in with him—provided, is my guess, McGraw can deliver on the Riverfront Project."

"Develop it how?"

"McGraw wasn't too specific about that. Resort hotel, recreation stuff. Some kind of vacation village, I think."

"Do you know what ranch?"

"He said it was the Flying W. It's somewhere in La Sal County, but he didn't know exactly where."

Wager gazed off at the county map he held in his mind. "I know where that ranch is. But Weldon better not count his money yet—there's not much out there for recreation unless you like scrub range and high desert."

"He said Pyne has been out there a number of times, doing

research and talking to county residents about the plan. Have you read or heard anything locally?"

"No."

"OK—that's all I have—got to run!"

She hung up before he could thank her.

RAY QWANA'TUA, TOO, had tried to call Wager yesterday; he had planned to drive out to Luther's place in the afternoon and Wager had said he wanted to go along. But Wager must have slept through the telephone's ringing at his bedside, though he only told Ray that he had been out, so the tribal policeman had put off his visit until he could reach Wager. Now, as they rattled along the bumpy track toward Narraguinnep Wash, Ray, who had finally gotten over his shock at Wager's bruised face, listened as he described Rubin's tangled love life.

"What's the sheriff think of all that?" Ray asked.

"I haven't told him all of it."

The tribal policeman tapped a finger on the steering wheel. "Maybe he already found out about Rubin and what's-her-name, Herrera's wife. Maybe it was bad enough his niece married an Indian, but then that Indian started cheating on her."

Wager didn't see it that way, but he'd learned long ago that a lot of things weren't always the way he saw them. "Sharon said he and Rubin got along all right."

"Spurlock got along with an Indian?"

Wager shrugged. "That's what she said, and I haven't found anything different. And Rubin was an Indian who was family."

Another tap on the steering wheel. "Yeah, that's so. And I don't really know Spurlock all that well, just what I hear about him on the rez from people he's arrested for drunkenness. Not your least biased testimony, I guess." Then, "Maybe we should go back to the test by smoke."

"What's that?" asked Wager.

"Ute marriage test—a boy and girl who want to get married have to sit all day in a teepee filled with smoke. Hot, hard to breathe, stings the eyes, itch with sweat—just sit there for a whole day with only water to drink. If they don't get on each other's nerves, then the marriage is OK; if they start bitching at each other, it's off." He lifted his cap and resettled it on his glossy black hair. "Hell of a lot cheaper than a divorce, I think. Lot less trouble, too."

Wager couldn't argue with that; he'd only tried the expensive option. But it crossed his mind that Liz could get through the test OK; in fact, she'd probably make it a point to do better than Wager. "They still do that? The Utes on the reservations?"

"Some might, I suppose. But I haven't heard of it in a long while." He guided the bucking steering wheel across a ledge of exposed rock. "No television inside the teepee, so probably not. Say, did Don Henderson get in touch with you? He called me yesterday, said he'd been trying to reach you."

The BLM man who had picked Wager up at the airport. "No. Did he say what he wanted?"

Ray shook his head. "Didn't sound too excited, though. Just said thanks and hung up."

If it was vital, Henderson could always leave a message for Wager at the sheriff's office and the dispatcher would pass it on. He squinted against the late-morning glare as the vehicle rocked and lurched toward the distant and isolated split-level home. The last time they had arrived, they'd sat patiently in the truck until a figure had come out of the house to welcome them. This time it was a woman, Luther's wife, to judge by her age; and like the man's mother, she, too, had her hair gathered into a knot at the back of her neck and anchored by two long wooden pins. But instead of an ankle-length, baggy dress, she wore Levi's, a flannel shirt, and tennis shoes. A heavy silver-and-turquoise necklace hung around her neck, and turquoise rings glinted on both hands. She greeted Ray with a Ute phrase that

Wager couldn't quite hear, and Ray replied something just as quietly. Her name was Cerise and he introduced Wager as a Colorado lawman. Then he asked if Luther was around.

"No. He's out with the sheep." She lifted her chin toward some vague point on the eastern horizon. "Left a few days ago, be out maybe a week more. You got to see him right away?"

Ray made a so-so gesture and glanced in the direction she had indicated. "Is he up the wash? Toward the land of his half brother who had bad luck?"

She nodded. "Could be near Knife Springs, maybe."

"Knife Springs? Is that on Luther's land?"

"No. On the other one's. His brother's. Up by Siva'atu Mesa. You know that place?"

"I've never been there. You think I can find it OK?"

Her black eyes shifted to the truck's door, to the ground as she thought. "There's other places got water right now, so I don't know if that's where he is. But Knife Springs's the only place up that way got water all year, so it's the only place with trees. Just go along the wash to Siva'atu Mesa and then look for the trees; I think you can find it OK. But you got to go around." Her arm made a wide circle in the air. "Off the reservation, if you want to drive there. From here you got to have a horse. You going there now?"

Ray thought it over. "That's a long way to go. Maybe you can tell me what I want to know—save us the trip."

She waited for the question.

"Luther's mother said she heard his half brother say his land portion was going to be worth something now. I'd like to know what he meant by that."

Wager watched closely, but the woman's expression did not change. Her wide face still aimed at the ground, her black hair glistened in the sun. "He was real happy about something, I remember. But a lot of times he was just full of hot air, so I didn't pay much attention."

Ray waited until he was certain she had said all she was going to say. "Luther owns the land now, I understand. It went to him as the closest relative on the reservation. Is that right?"

"I don't know. He hasn't told me much about all that. But Knife Springs is on that land. He wouldn't take sheep up there if it wasn't his to use no more."

Another long pause. "What about the land farther up the wash? The land that belonged to another man who had bad luck."

She shook her head again. "Sometimes Luther talked with him about sheep, I think. But that man didn't like people and stayed by himself, so I don't know much about him."

"Ramey Many Coats told me that Luther knows a lot about his half brother's bad luck."

The woman's full lips made a tiny sound and a bit of spittle flew towards the ground. "Ramey Many Coats! You can't believe nothing that man says—unless he says he wants something. You can believe that because he always wants more." She looked up suddenly. "He was the one wanted Ru—Luther's brother's land! I remember, now: just after Christmas. They were talking about maybe selling the land to Ramey Many Coats. Luther's brother said it wasn't worth nothing to him and he could use the money. Luther didn't think it was a good idea because it meant getting rid of Knife Springs. He said it might be better to keep it in the family, you know, because land will stay, but money will go. But Luther said it was up to him, his brother, because it was his land given to him by their father. Luther said even if he didn't like the idea of selling the land, it was up to his brother. But then his brother decided not to sell it just yet. I don't know why, for sure. Maybe just because Ramey Many Coats wanted it so bad."

"Why did he want it so bad?"

She shrugged. "You got to ask Luther that."

Wager leaned forward. "Did Ramey Many Coats want to buy the other man's land, too?"

Her eyes, almost black, stared at him for a long moment, wide with thought. Then she spoke as much to herself as to Wager. "I think maybe that was really why they didn't sell. I think I remember now Luther telling his brother that if Ramey wanted so much land, there had to be some reason for it. He didn't say so, but I think now he was maybe talking about that other man's land, too."

Her answers to the rest of their questions were "I don't know" and "You got to ask Luther that." Ray finally thanked the woman and politely declined the offer of something to drink. As he started to turn the truck around, he muttered to Wager, "I'm thirsty as hell, but that invitation was just out of politeness. If she'd really wanted us to visit, she'd have asked us in right away. Besides, I think we better talk to Luther." Reflexively, he jerked the wheel, startling Wager and lurching the truck to avoid the broad, grainy mound of a large anthill. "Indian grave," he explained with some embarrassment. "Utes tell their kids that ants build their nests where an Indian is buried, so you don't step there. I guess driving over one would be the same thing."

It made sense to Wager; food was scarce out here, and ants had to eat, too. "So Utes didn't stake their prisoners down across an anthill?"

"And disturb the dead below it? No way, man. Really bad karma! You're talking Comanche or Arapaho—they're the mean Indians." He wagged his head. "Still are—so you don't want to let any of them get a look at that hair of yours. Might make those suckers revert."

"Yeah, well, they'd have to catch me first."

Ray laughed. "Judging by your nose, that's not hard to do."

THEY HAD TO recross the desert, but the trip did not seem as long as the ride out. For one thing, they were discussing the possible meanings of what Cerise Del Ponte had told them; for another, Wager was familiar with the track now, and a known road was always shorter than an unknown one. But once they reached the pavement and had cleared Squaw Point Village, Ray pushed the pickup over seventy as they headed for the junction of 181 and 666, a loop of highways and dirt road that would circle around to Knife Springs and Luther Del Ponte.

"What made you ask Cerise about Walter Lawrence's land?"

Wager had figured Ray would get around to that sooner or later, and he had been thinking about it himself. But he didn't have a clear answer. "I'm not sure. You've suspected that that land might be a motive for Rubin's death—that it was the only property he owned that might be worth anything. Now some ideas are starting to fall together a little." He couldn't tell the tribal policeman clearly what it was his thoughts groped toward because he wasn't that clear on it himself. But the only alternative to Rubin's love triangle as a hazy motive for his death was Rubin's property as an equally hazy motive. "You have any idea why Ramey's after all that land?"

The pockmarks in Ray's cheeks grew shallow and then deep with shadow as he shook his head slightly. "Tribal Council's been talking about putting up a gambling casino. That's the big thing on reservations now: casinos for the white man to leave his money in. Call it a new way to scalp him."

Wager considered that. "Would they need a state-wide referendum to do it?"

"No. Reservation has sovereignty to do it, and it's under the federal Indian Gaming Act of 1988. If the tribal council votes it in, it's in."

Wager wanted to be certain. "Right now, the Squaw Point Council could build a casino without any approval from the state of Colorado?"

"Could do it tomorrow. Like I say, they've been talking about it since the other two reservations put in their casinos four or five years ago. The only kind of state control is over what kind of gambling."

"How?"

"Well, right now, the state gaming commission says the reservations can only have the same kind of gambling that's allowed in Central City, Blackhawk, and Cripple Creek. Those are the only places in Colorado with legalized gambling. On the Southern Ute and the Ute Mountain reservation, that means slot machines, keno, and low-stakes poker and blackjack. Those are state of Colorado restrictions, but that could change if the Indian Gaming Act is amended by Congress."

"Is that being considered?"

"There's a senate bill to take the state regulatory agencies out of it. That would leave reservation gambling under the sole authority of the Interior secretary in Washington."

"So the tribes could then offer any kind of gambling?"

"Just like Vegas. But you have to remember, all three reservations are a long way from Denver, Salt Lake City, and any other population center. The other Indian casinos make some good money, especially on weekends and in the summer when the tourists come in. But they're no way near to making Las Vegas run scared. Here—on the Squaw Point Reservation— they might get a lot of people from Grand Junction, maybe take away some of the players from the three gambling towns in Colorado; but we don't have a major tourist attraction the way Mesa Verde is for the Ute Mountain Reservation. And we don't have the major highways the Southern Ute Reservation does. In fact, we're a long way from any major highway. Not many people are going to drive so far to lose money at roulette when they can get to Vegas faster and cheaper by flying." The bill of Ray's cap wagged back and forth. "I think it's a dumb idea—Ramey and his family will pour the tribe's money into building the thing, then lose it all because no one's going to come out this far just to gamble."

"Didn't you tell me that the Flying W ranch is just across the reservation line from both Rubin's and Lawrence's land?"

"Yeah. Why?"

Wager told him what he'd learned from Liz earlier.

"Development? Out there? Why the hell would anybody build out there?" The truck lost speed as Ray's foot relaxed. He stared down the ribbon of asphalt toward something Wager couldn't see. After coasting a mile or so, the speed picked up again. "But if it's true, that could be why they were killed, both Rubin and Lawrence. And it maybe says why Ramey Many Coats wanted us to know he had an alibi for when Rubin was killed, if someday he ends up with Rubin's land. But I can't see any kind of retirement or recreation community being set in a place like that. There's nothing there! And I don't see that it has a damn thing to do with the deaths of the two white men."

"Me either. Maybe it doesn't." He explained about the C-4 explosives. "Nichols's name came up there." He asked, "You know Henry Many Coats?"

"Henry? Sure—Ramey's older brother. Why?"

"He's a member of the National Guard unit that was probably the source of the C-4. Him and Louis Cloud. Are they close friends?"

Ray's tapping finger moved to the bill of his uniform cap. "Not close, no. But the Clouds generally go along with the Many Coats in tribal business—hell, just about everybody does, sooner or later. But I guess the Clouds are closer to being side-kicks; the Many Coats know they can count on the Clouds to vote with them on everything, and the Clouds know the Many Coats will toss a few crumbs their way when the goodies are handed out." Ray thought for a few minutes. "But why would they bomb government vehicles? That's Constitutional Posse stuff—or somebody like them."

Wager nodded. "Yeah." Still, something felt like it was

there, just beyond his reaching fingers, just past the edge of his vision.

Ray, too, was apparently trying to work something out of the tangle of possibilities. "Harder than hell to cross Narraguinnep Wash from the Flying W to Rubin's or Walter Lawrence's land. Have to put a bridge over it somewhere—expensive, man. Need all the infrastructure for a town: electricity, water, streets. An airport, even. Highway, too—there's no paved road leading to the Flying W." He wagged his head again. "A major casino with unlimited stakes' gambling . . . I don't know . . ."

Neither did Wager. But even if he couldn'p clearly grasp or see whatever it was, something was there.

19

THE TWO-RUT ROAD leading to Narraguinnep Wash
sliced through the sagebrush and cedars of a high plateau, then
tilted sharply as it followed a ledge that sloped down the face of
a rock-and-sand wall about twenty feet high. It ended in the
untracked gravel and dirt of the wash's wide bed, a twisting
avenue of wind-sculpted sand bars and ragged clumps of willow
and tamarisk saplings that would, when rain or runoff brought
water, form islands of brush nodding in the fast and muddy
current. Crossing the plateau above, Ray had pointed out the
occasional weathered stake or survey plate that marked corners
of BLM land, the Flying W ranch property, and, finally, the
Squaw Point Reservation. Now he pointed at a red-and-orange
rock formation that rose like a bony finger above the southern
lip of the wash. "Over there's what the white men call Needle
Rock. That's where they found that USGS geologist a couple of
months ago. The one who took so long to die."

Wager studied the spot. "Any idea why he was out this way?"

Ray shook his head. "No. It's about here that the BLM land
meets the reservation, but what he was doing there, I don't know.
You got to ask Agent Durkin that."

He had, but the FBI man hadn't known either. "Is that where
Lawrence's or Rubin's land is?"

"I'm not sure where the boundary is. The geologist was found on BLM land, but I'd have to look at a survey map to know just where the lines are. Lawrence didn't have any need to mark the boundary with a fence—he'd know from living here where his land ended and Rubin's or the Flying W or BLM land began. Luther can probably tell us—he's out here with his sheep a lot."

They followed the bed of the wash as it twisted generally west, running from behind them out of the higher ground and the mountains on the eastern side of the county, and growing gradually deeper as side gullies formed cracks and fissures that would funnel in more water. "You can't see it, but Luther's place is about eight air miles from here. We had to drive about sixty miles around."

"Where's the Flying W ranch house?"

Ray gestured toward the right. "On the other side of that ridge. Probably two or three miles."

"I'd like to drop by there."

"If you want. But we can't drive out of the wash anymore. Have to go back a couple of miles above where we came in and pick up a ranch road that comes down to the wash."

The sandy bed writhed and twisted between its gradually deepening banks toward the foot of a long mesa that began to fill the southern horizon. "That's Siva'atu Mesa—Goat Mesa. That's where Knife Springs is. The water collects up on top and seeps down, I guess. Or maybe it's where the water table comes to the surface. Lawrence's portion has a couple of small springs, maybe fed by the mesa's eastern seepage. But I guess they're not year-round like Knife Springs. We should see the trees in a bit—I hope. Be awful embarrassing for an Indian to get lost on his own reservation."

"Are we on Rubin's portion yet?"

"Could be. But we'll have to ask Luther."

They ground on in four-wheel drive through the ridges and beds of soft sand, picking up speed where the shelves of firmer gravel or shoulders of water-smoothed rock lifted out of the pink grit, slowing again when the wheels sank and churned. Behind them hung a thin haze of dust, and the baking heat that bounced off the bed and walls of the wash was intensified by the lack of wind in the sheltered gully.

Ray let out a little sigh of relief. "There we are. And there's the herd up under the mesa. Luther should be around somewhere—probably he's watching us right now."

Ahead, where the sandy bed swung close under the towering red-and-orange rock wall of the mesa, a narrow strip of bare cottonwood branches painted a gray band above the ragged lip of the wash. Ray angled toward a gap where the sandy bank crumbled into a wide V and thickly growing reeds and grass marked an entering watercourse. It turned to flow down the sandy wash and brought life to a tangled line of leafed-out brush and tamarisk that curved out of sight with the twisting gully. They ground upward a bit, and Ray stopped the truck on a shoulder of hard earth above the floor of the wash and tapped the horn. Then the two men got out to stretch their legs and wait.

Higher up the bank and in the tangle of cottonwood trunks, Wager could make out a sagging fence of wire and sticks and a small corral that held a horse who looked back warily at the truck. Above the trees on the steeply sloped talus that rose up to the rock face of the mesa, a flock of sheep grazed, yellow-brown dots that moved slowly from one scattered tuft of grass to another. The soft clank of a bell came, muted and distant, the only sound under the vastness of sky and high mesa wall. Then Luther, without seeming to move, appeared beside the small stream.

"OK," said Ray. "He sees us. Let's go."

Wager followed as the tribal policeman picked his way between cactus and yucca spears up the rocky bluff, the sun hot on his shoulders and head.

Luther, face impassive in the shadow of his hat, greeted them.

"Cerise told us you might be here," said Ray. "Looks like a good place for the sheep."

"Pretty good." They stood in silence for a few moments, watching the animals graze, looking at the horse and corral, at the shade house tucked under the trees. The cottonwoods were tall with thick, deeply furrowed bark and stubby limbs. A lot of them had been broken at one time or another, and the ragged gray of dead wood poked out here and there. They were old trees that had stubbornly survived in a harsh climate, but against the towering face of cliff behind them they looked dwarfed and fragile. "You come a long way."

"Well, we've got some things we need to talk to you about. Couldn't wait."

"OK."

He turned and led them into the welcome coolness of the grove. The wind in the new leaves of the underbrush made a sound that matched the steady, bright ripple of the creek. A bird twittered among the reeds down in the wash.

"This is nice," Wager said.

Lutler nodded, his thick glasses reflecting the mottled light. "Peaceful. No kids with the television on all the time."

"Need one hell of an extension cord if they wanted to have one," Ray said and laughed.

"Sometimes I bring one or two of them out here, just so they'll know what it's like without it," said Luther. "But after a while they want to go back. Get bored, you know."

Ray nodded as they squatted on cool, soft sand. A light breeze brought the faint, acrid smell of animal urine from the corral, but Wager welcomed it for drying his sweaty face and neck.

"We have to ask some questions, Luther. We have to know some things about your brother, about some other people."

"OK. You want a cigarette?"

This time Wager followed Ray's example and took one,

keeping it unlit in his hand while Luther held a match to his own.

"All this is the land your father gave to your brother, right?"

He nodded, his thick glasses sliding a bit down his nose.

"And I hear that Ramey Many Coats wanted to buy this land from your brother. And the land east of here."

Another nod.

"Why, Luther?"

The man took his time lighting his cigarette. "Ramey wants everything he can get. He's a Many Coats."

"I hear the tribal council is thinking of selling him the land east of here—the land that belonged to that man."

"It don't surprise me none."

"It surprises me, Luther. So I've been thinking a lot about it. Ramey will buy that man's land, but he doesn't run sheep. He will buy that man's land, but there's only enough water for sheep and not enough to farm. He will buy that man's land, but to get here, he has to drive sixty, seventy miles around Siva'atu Mesa and Narraguinnep Wash. He will buy that man's land, but there's closer and better land he could buy down near Waini Suuvu Mesa. So I'm surprised: Why does he buy that land?"

The man protected his mouth by drawing deeply on the cigarette, then holding the smoke down for a long time. When it came out, it was almost colorless. But he said nothing.

Wager listened to the song of a cricket somewhere in the sun-heated grass beyond the trees; an insect zinged between the seated men and was gone. He felt his knees start to tighten from his crossed legs. Ray, not looking at anyone, dribbled sand through his fingers for a long time before going on. "I hear big things may happen on the Flying W ranch over there." His head nodded toward the far side of the wash. "You hear anything about that?"

Luther's shoulders rose and fell with a deep sigh. "I heard a little about it. Not much."

"And I hear the tribal council is thinking of finally putting up that casino for gambling."

The brim of Luther's hat tilted slightly. "They been talking about that for a long time."

"Is this where they're going to put it up, Luther? Up on the land east of here? The land Ramey Many Coats wants to buy?"

His voice was even quieter and Wager had to strain to hear. "I don't know. Maybe so. You ask Ramey."

"Where will they get the water?"

The man's black eyes flicked up at Ray and then dropped back to the sand somewhere in front of his folded knees.

"Knife Springs is good water. Year-round water. Maybe your brother wanted to sell them his portion because they wanted to put their casino near this water." Ray waited. When the man remained silent, he went on. "Maybe he was going to sell this land and maybe somebody didn't want him to." Another long pause. "Maybe he was killed because of that, Luther."

"I don't know. I have to go to my sheep now." He pressed the half-smoked cigarette in the sand and stood to shove his glasses up on his nose with his thumb. It was a gesture that for some reason made Wager think of what Luther must have looked like as a little boy wearing glasses.

Ray stood, too. "OK. Sheep have to be taken care of. But if that's what happened, I think Rubin Del Ponte's ghost is very unhappy. If that's what happened to Rubin Del Ponte, I think his ghost will bring bad luck to whoever killed him."

"You leave!" Fear at the sound of the dead man's name made Luther's voice squeaky. "I don't want you here no more—you leave now!"

On the way back, Wager asked, "When did you learn about the council selling Walter Lawrence's land to Ramey?"

Ray's smile was not one of humor. "I haven't." He tossed away the cigarette Luther had given him. "It was just a guess from what you told me. But I think I better find out."

20

A MILE OR so after climbing the north bank of Narraguinnep Wash, they topped the crest of a low bridge and swung left
to jolt down into a wide, shallow bowl that tipped gently toward
the west. It was thirty miles, perhaps, from horizon to horizon.
Inside the bowl, the scrub desert sloped toward its lowest point,
where a cluster of tiny buildings marked a distant ranch. A
fringe of leafless trees made a little square smudge at one spot,
hiding the main house from view, but most of the outbuildings
sat shadeless in the sun and unguarded from any direction
against the wind. It struck Wager that this place was similar to
some of those isolated ranches he had flown over on his way
from Denver to Cortez—a collection of forlorn buildings surrounded by a patch of hoof-worn dirt and the focus of wavering
cattle trails that converged from out of the surrounding miles of
empty sagebrush.

Dotting the vast depression and scattered widely apart were
grazing cows, their dark-red backs showing above the gray-blue
sage. To Wager's right, on the northwest horizon, the tips of the
La Sal mountain range in Utah showed snow-covered and sharp
above the flat rim of the bowl. Ahead, beyond the ranch, the
world seemed to drop away into a distance that was unbroken
by anything except heat waves. At other points of the compass,
mesas and buttes formed distant landmarks, and on their left,

looking even bigger than it had when they were at its base, stood the split and weathered wall of Siva'atu Mesa.

"Where is Knife Springs from here?" Wager asked.

Ray glanced toward the rock face. "Over there, two, maybe three miles. It's down there, under that point."

Wager wasn't sure which point Ray meant—there seemed to be a dozen of them rippling along the palisade of rock, all looking about the same—but that wasn't what was important. "It's not that far away, is it?"

"Not if they can put a bridge over the wash. If the tribal casino went in at Knife Springs, and the condos were on that high ground on this side of the wash, they'd be even closer together—four, five hundred yards, with a bridge."

Wager watched the red-and-orange spires and ledges swing slowly past on the other side of the now invisible Narraguinnep Wash. The only eye-catching features on this side of the wash were the ranch and a string of skinny telephone poles that strode across the desert and out of sight over the eastern ridge behind them.

"I guess I'm just not a visionary kind of guy," said Wager. "I can't see condos, a golf course, and five thousand people filling up this place."

Ray shook his head, mirrored glasses reflecting the line of the horizon and the empty blue sky above it. "This is high desert, all right. Good for nothing but cows, and not more than two or three of them on a square mile." As he guided the truck along the dips and bumps of the two-rut road, he told Wager about the ranch manager, a bachelor named Archibeque who, with an occasional ranch hand or two, had been working the place for almost thirty years. "They call him 'Happy,' but I don't know if that's because he is or because he's lived by himself for too long." And about the founding of the ranch in the last century by a Mormon who settled it and died struggling against the empty land. His descendants hung on until they could take it no more, then sold out to an absentee owner, an Englishman, in the early 1900s. "It's changed hands three or four times since then: never has made much money, I figure. The only reason the place is here is because the Mormon wanted to be left alone with his wives, and he found enough water to allow that." He lifted a finger from the steering wheel to point toward the tiny windmill whose spinning vanes winked with sunlight. "I'll bet this whole bowl drains into some aquifer or underground pool. See how the ranch sits in the lowest spot? Maybe there used to be a spring or a sink in there." The man's cap brim bobbed to his left and he intently studied something in that distance. "But there's another windmill a few miles down that way on higher land. Along with a stock tank." He slowed the truck to a halt and stared more closely at something that Wager could not see. "And those cedars— look how they make a kind of wide strip coming across the bowl from the southwest."

With the tribal policeman pointing it out, Wager could note a pattern in the almost black dots of round, stubby trees. They grew hundreds of yards apart, as Ray said, separated by the clumps of gray sage. The cedars started below the western ridge that the truck faced and made a wide band that curved across the site of the ranch house. Then, even farther apart and some- where on the southeast rise behind them, the growth of trees ended. "I see it. But I'm not sure what I'm looking at."

"Maybe there's an underground river runs through here. Or a water table. Something holding enough water, anyway, to keep feeding those trees over a couple of hundred years." He put the truck in gear and started rolling again. "If there is, you might see a golf course out here, Gabe."

It took another half hour of driving—ten, twelve miles—to reach the ranch gate, a pair of tall poles capped with a crossbar. A Flying W welded in rusty iron dangled from the middle of the bar. The tires rumbled briefly on a cattle guard of rails, and Ray pulled to a halt in the shade from the line of the ill-tended and naked Lombardies that surrounded the ranch house.

It was square, built of large blocks of sandstone that lifted to a second story. A shallow roof capped it, and flat dormers with small windows showed a third level cramped under the rusting sheets of galvanized tin. A deep veranda, shaded by its own unpainted and rust-scarred tin roof, ran around the three sides they could see. A yellow dog, leaning back on its haunches with its tail between its legs, barked excitedly from a corner of the steps. Ray got out of the truck, slamming its door loudly, and Wager followed. "White folks expect you to knock on the door," Ray said. "They pretend they don't hear anything until you knock."

Barking even more frantically, the dog retreated into the shadow under the veranda, darting forward with a growl toward their ankles as they went up the porch stairs. Ray feinted an arm at it and it ran off to hide behind the TV dish angled in a corner of the yard. "Sneaky one. Not as bad as some Indian dogs I know, but sneaky enough." He rapped loudly on the frame, the rusty screen door chattering a reply.

After a minute or two, they heard the thud of heels and a tall stoop-shouldered man whose whiskery face seemed to sag with worry appeared out of the dimness of the room. "Do for you folks?"

"Hello, Happy. Remember me? Ray, the Indian cop?"

The man squinted. "Sure! You ever find them rustlers?"

Ray had told Wager about last year's excitement: a cattle truck that had made three trips and stolen about thirty head from open range on the BLM land—some from the reservation, some from the Flying W. "Not a thing; probably never will."

"Yeah," he said slowly, thinking it over. "Bastards." His eyes widened suddenly. "They doing it again? That why you're here?"

"Nope." He introduced Wager. "We'd like to ask some

questions about the new owners. If they've told you anything about their plans for the place."

"Not much, they ain't. But come on in, anyway." He held open the screen door and wagged a hand at the sagging couch and two worn armchairs placed in a semicircle to face a blank television set. The room was generally clean but, except for the beat-up furniture showing occasional spurts of stuffing, almost bare. It didn't have much color, either, and the feel of the space was brown. Against the front wall and under a curtainless window leaned a small, scarred bookcase holding two shelves of worn and splayed paperback books; Wager could see part of the title on one curling cover: "—ers of the —rple Sage." Set out from an interior wall stood a large oil stove, cold now, on a square of cracked and faded linoleum. Its chimney pipe disappeared into an asbestos grommet set into what looked like a bricked-up fireplace. "I got some coffee on. Folks want some coffee?"

Both men declined and Happy looked even sadder. "It's good coffee. I make real good coffee."

"Well, I guess I could use a cup," said Ray. Wager shook his head again; if he'd wanted coffee he'd have accepted it the first time.

The stoop-shouldered man came back with a heavy mug for Ray and one for himself. "Sure I can't get you one?"

"No. Thanks. I'm fine."

Ray sipped at his cup and Wager saw the muscle of his jaw tighten as he swallowed. "That's . . . real coffee all right, Happy."

The sad face lightened a bit. "The boys likes it. Says it gets them up and going in the mornings."

"Yep." Ray nodded agreement and gingerly set the mug on the wooden floor beside his chair. "We hear the new owner's thinking of doing some development out here."

"Don't know much about that. He ain't thinking about running cows much longer, that's for sure. Told me he wants to sell off the herd." The man's eyes glanced around the cheerless room. "It's a real nice place, but it ain't good for much else. Guess it won't be good for much of anything, he sells off the herd."

Wager asked, "The new owner's name is Ronald Pyne?"

"Mr. Pyne, yep. Don't know what his first name is—he never told me that."

"Has he been out recently to look at the place?"

"Not recently, no. Came out, let's see, sometime between Thanksgiving and Christmas. Cold enough to freeze the balls off a brass monkey, so he didn't stay long. Mostly sat by the stove and studied his maps and walked around looking out the windows." He drained his mug. "Don't know what he was looking at."

"When does he want to sell the herd?"

"Ain't said. If it was me, I'd tell him end of summer. Get their weight up and then sell them off." He explained, "Everybody's already bought their spring yearlings—ain't no market for cattle right now."

"He didn't say anything to you about his plans for the ranch?"

"Nope. He talked with the other fella mostly. They looked at maps and the other fella wrote some stuff down, and they looked out the windows and after a while they got in their truck and went on off. Now—" Happy nodded to himself, "he did say they'd be doing some drilling here and there on the property."

"For water?"

"Didn't say what for."

Wager leaned forward. "Have they drilled yet?"

"Did some a while back. What was it . . . late last year, I believe."

Ray asked, "Did he say he'd keep you on?"

"He said there'd be work for me, but he didn't say what kind. Tell you the truth, Ray, I don't know what kind of work I'd be good for without the cattle."

"Who was this other person?" Wager asked.

Happy wagged his head. "I can't remember; we wasn't introduced. My Pyne called him something, but I can't remember what."

"Was he a rancher from around here?"

"No. Wasn't no rancher. Some kind of geologist, I think. Talked about what kind of soil we got and fault lines and rock layers and what all. On the kitchen table he spread out a whole bunch of aerial photographs he kept showing to Mr. Pyne."

"Could his name have been Buck? Buck Holtzer?"

"Could've been, yeah. I think that sounds like what Mr. Pyne called him. 'Buck.' Something like that, anyway."

Wager studied the face with its deep lines that made the flesh seem to sag in teardrop shapes under his eyes, beside his mouth, even off his bristly chin. It was hard to tell if he was responding to Wager's suggestion or if the man really remembered it. But there should be ways to find out who Holtzer, a freelance geologist, might have worked for besides the USGS.

"What have you heard about the killings, Happy?" asked Ray.

"What killings?"

He told the man about the four deaths.

His head wagged in surprise. "First I heard about any of that! I don't get no newspaper, and the boys mostly watches the TV at night. I got enough to keep busy without worrying about what's going on everyplace else. First I heard of it."

He offered more coffee, which Ray quickly declined; and as the truck jolted its way back along the faint ruts through the sagebrush, the tribal policeman tried to stifle a loud and sour belch. "Gawd, that coffee! Happy said it gets the ranch hands up and going in the mornings."

"Hell yes—they're trying to get away from it."

21

RAY LET WAGER use his office. "I'm going over to the tribal center, Gabe. I'll let you know if I find out anything." Wager's first call was to Henderson; the man had tried to reach him, and now Wager had a question for the BLM agent. A recording of the Oklahoma voice told all and sundry to leave any messages and he would call back as soon as possible. So Wager took him at his word. The next call was to Sheriff Spurlock.

"Yeah, I talked to Nichols. At first he said he turned in the unused sticks of C-4. I told him Sergeant Yeager didn't have any record of it, and then he said he must've used it on that silo, that it was a long time ago and he didn't remember for sure, but that he sure as hell didn't take any of that crap home and anybody says he did is a liar. That didn't surprise me, of course, but I think it worried him to be asked about it. Which I suppose don't surprise me either, if he took the stuff."

"Did he have an alibi for the times of the explosions?"

"Not for the first couple. Said he was working his spread. Maybe he was, maybe he wasn't—be hard to prove either way. But he was in Rapid City, South Dakota, when the last bomb went off."

That might rule out Nichols, but it didn't rule out an accomplice. "Do you know if he's one of the people investing in the Flying W development?" Wager explained about Ronald Pyne and his plans for the ranch. "I understand his buddy Litvak met with Pyne off and on over the last few months."

"How in hell'd you dig that up? I don't know. What I do know is Stan's been running real lean on that ranch of his lately. All the ranchers in the county are short on credit and long on debt, price of beef being what it is and costs of operating going up. I didn't think he had any cash money to invest in anything."

"He's recently married, right?"

"Yeah—second marriage for both of them. Maybe it's her third: gal named Bonnie Reimer. Seems a real nice gal. Why?"

"I heard she brought some money to the marriage. Maybe that's what he's investing."

The sheriff was silent for a long moment. "Damn, you sure hear a lot of things and you sure got a twisted mind, Wager." Another silence. "But I don't see how that has anything to do with the bombings and killings."

"Me either. I'm just trying to find out who's up to what and why."

A shorter silence. "OK—I'm not sure who to ask, but I'll try to find out."

The third call was long distance but he got only Liz's answering machine. He left his message and two or three ways she might be able to reach him, then turned to leaf through the advertising pages of the local telephone directory. It was a magazine-sized publication that covered La Sal and two other counties, as well as the reservation. "Mr. Haydn? This is Officer Wager. I talked to you four or five days ago regarding the death of Rubin Del Ponte."

The man said he remembered, and Wager asked if he had been contacted about doing any drilling on the Flying W ranch. "Yeah—I was contacted. Done it, too."

"When was this, Mr. Haydn?"

"Oh, hell, let's see—first week or so of December, I think it was. I didn't want to do it, I tell you that! Colder'n hell out

there and no place to hide from the wind. But that new owner—
what's his name—said he wanted it right now and he was willing
to pay my winter rates."

"What kind of drilling?"

"Water—that's the only kind I do. He wanted some test
holes dug, so I dug 'em."

"Did you find water?"

"Sure—it was there. There were a couple of dusters and dry
holes, but the rest of them had a pretty good flow. Exactly how
much and how long it's going to last, nobody can say for sure—I
don't care what these fancy hydrologists claim. And there might
be some question about who it belongs to, too. But I guess that
fella's got his lawyers working on that."

"Who it belongs to?"

"It was a subterranean water course. Comes in from the
southeast side of the ranch, somewhere under Narraguinnep
Wash, is my guess. Probably starts out on the reservation—
that's the high ground south of the ranch. I told him that and
that it could mean all sorts of legal questions about who owns
what portions of it, but he didn't seem too worried. Just wanted
to know if it was there and how much. Hell, water flows toward
money, and if he's got the money, he'll get the water."

"Did he have a hydrologist working for him?"

"Yeah—same fella got killed not too long after. Working for
the government. What was his name . . . Holtzer. That's it,
Holtzer Surveying."

"Did Holtzer say anything to you about what they were after?"

"Not to me, no. Just told me where to drill and visited the
sites a couple of times. Mostly just wanted the site reports—
depth, soil samples, flow, pressure." Haydn snorted. "Too damn
cold out there for a fancy desk engineer to hang around."

"Do you remember the locations of those sites?"

"Oh, yeah. Got them in my records somewhere. Why?"

"Could you give me a copy if I came by?"

"I reckon," he answered. "Wasn't asked to keep them secret, anyway. Sometimes people want the drilling records confidential, and I'll do that if a customer wants. But he didn't."

Wager didn't bother to explain the power of a deuces tecum subpoena regardless of what a customer might want. He just thanked the man. Then, before hanging up, thought to ask, "Did Rubin Del Ponte work with you on that job?"

"Well, yeah. Matter of fact, he did. It was so cold I needed to bring out heaters for the rig—he trucked them and some fuel out for me."

"Did he seem interested in the job?"

"Not too much. But he knew what I was drilling for and where. I don't know what else he would want to know."

"He went to each site?"

"Had to—to move the heater units and butane tanks."

Wager was staring out the office window when Ray came back. "I guessed right, Gabe."

It took a second or two for the man's words to register. "About what?"

"The tribal council selling Walter Lawrence's land. Ramey Many Coats put money down on it in late February, less than two weeks after Lawrence's death."

"Lawrence didn't have any relatives with a claim on it?"

"Not living on the reservation. And from what I guess, the council didn't make much effort to locate any relatives off it."

"I wonder if Ramey has an alibi for that death, too."

"He'll find one, I bet."

Wager told the Indian policeman about Haydn Drilling Service.

"And he identified Holtzer?"

Nodding, Wager glanced at the notes he had been scratching on a pad headed "Squaw Mountain Tribal Police" and bearing a feather-decorated Indian shield and crossed lances colored red and yellow.

Ray caught the glance. "Red and yellow, those are the Ute war-paint colors. Somebody before me designed that. I'd rather have blue. Means peace. Could use some peace around here."

"Del Ponte worked for Haydn on that job."

The tribal policeman stared at Wager for a long moment. Then he ticked off the names of the victims on his fingers. "Buck Holtzer. Walter Lawrence, now Rubin. All three tied to the Flying W project. But where does Larry Kershaw come in?"

Wager started to say he didn't know when the telephone rang. Ray answered, then held it across the desk. "For you."

It was Don Henderson returning Wager's call. "You wanted to know what Holtzer was doing when he was killed? I know what he wasn't doing—he wasn't sent out there by USGS. His job for them was erosion measurement over on the BLM land west of the reservation. They wanted to get some winter base readings in the canyons to measure spring runoff. They didn't have any surveys up north, near Needle Rock, where he was killed."

"Isn't that BLM land, too?"

"Yeah, a lot of it is. He might've been found on government land, but he wasn't on government time."

Haydn had said nothing about drilling outside Flying W boundaries. "Any idea why he'd be there on his own?"

"No, but I'm on my way up to Grand Junction. Maybe I can drop by and talk to his widow, see if she has any idea. Maybe she'll let me look through the papers from his office."

"You need a subpoena? I can get you one."

"I don't think so, Gabe. I'll tell her it might have a bearing on who killed him. I'm sure she'll let me."

After the BLM agent hung up, Wager shared his message with Ray. "Can you show me where Needle Rock is on your map?"

Ray turned to the acetate-covered wall map and began tracing his finger down a corridor of contour lines that Wager figured was Narraguinnep Wash. "The white name for it's 'Needle Rock.' We call it something else."

"What?"

"What did it look like to you?"

Wager thought back, remembering the round, weathered spire aiming its blunt tip at the sky. "Oh."

"Here it is." He held his finger on a small, packed circle of contour lines.

Tiny black print spelled "Needle Rock," and south of it were a dozen or so points off Goat Mesa, each given a name: Saffron Point, Thompson Point, Kanab Point, Knife Point . . . "This is the BLM boundary, here?" Wager pointed to a black line whose long dashes were separated by dots of ink.

"Yep. Needle Rock's just inside BLM land. This would be the Flying W Property on this side of the wash, and the reservation starts here."

"Walter Lawrence's land. Now Ramey Many Coats's."

"Now Ramey Many Coats's."

"Holtzer was found, what, a quarter mile inside the line?"

"A little less. It was here, on this side of the Needle."

"Was the body moved?"

"Nobody seemed to think so. He was found at his truck—its motor had a bullet in it, too. If you're asking whether he could have walked across the line, been shot on the reservation, and made it back to his truck before he died, yeah, he could've. I was asked to look for bloodstains, but I didn't find any. It was a gut wound that bled mostly internally, and he had on a down vest and parka that absorbed what leaked out."

Wager nodded, still studying the map.

Ray rubbed a thumb along his pocked jaw. "It seems to me we're getting close to a 'why,' Gabe."

It felt that way to him, too, but they still didn't have a "who."

"I'd like to talk to Henry Many Coats and Louis Cloud—they're in the same National Guard unit as Nichols."

Ray took his cap from a point of the deer antlers that served as a coat and hat rack. "Let's do that."

WAGER EXPECTED ANOTHER long ride, but it was a short walk instead. Both men were in the comfortable air-conditioned lounge of the tribal building and neither was anxious to talk to Wager about Nichols or the C-4.

"I wasn't on that detail," said Henry Many Coats. He had his older brother's stocky build, but his features were sharper, making him look younger than his twenty-two years. He sat deep in the leather armchair and held a Pepsi can on his lap in laced fingers, as if challenging Wager to pull him out. "So I tell you what I told that FBI man, I don't know what C-4 Sergeant Nichols used or didn't use."

"You've talked to Agent Durkin?"

"That's why we're here. He called my brother, Ramey, and said he wanted to see us this morning, so we come here." Slowly, Henry raised his can and drank, black eyes never moving from Wager's face. "Maybe you ought to ask him, that FBI man. He talked real tough—I bet he's got all the answers by now."

Wager nodded. "He probably does, and I probably will. Did you talk to Nichols about things the tribal council's planning?"

"What for? Tribal business is our business. Not a white man's. Any white man's."

"But he knew the council was planning on putting up a gambling casino?" If Ray could make guesses, so could Wager.

"The council's been talking about that a long time. It's even been in the newspapers."

"Did Nichols ever talk to you about the Flying W ranch?"

"No."

"What about any of his friends?"

"Whose?"

"Nichols. Did any of Nichols's friends talk to you about the Flying W. Say, Stan Litvak?"

"I don't know. Can't remember."

Was that answer too quick? Wager tried to read the young man's expression, his posture, any indication of wariness. But he could see only dislike. "Did anyone ever ask you anything about the casino? Where or when it might be built?"

A quiver of uneasiness, now, which told Wager more than the youth's words. "Not that I remember. I don't know. We talk sometimes. Can't do much else when you got a midnight-to-four duty watch."

"Was Nichols interested to learn that Ramey had bought Walter Lawrence's land?"

The defiance returned. "Why don't you ask Sergeant Nichols about that? Or that FBI man with all the answers."

Wager turned to Louis Cloud. He, too, had a young-looking face, but his was round, the full cheeks smoothing out his prominent cheekbones. "Were you on the demolition team?"

"No." Like their elder relatives, this Cloud apparently followed this Many Coats's lead.

"Did Nichols or Litvak ever ask you about the tribe's plans for the casino?"

"Don't remember." His eyes wandered back to the large-screen television set. The room was crowded with padded chairs and game tables, lamps and standing ashtrays. But the young men were the only ones enjoying its dim coolness.

"Did you ever hear either one of them mention Rubin Del Ponte's name?"

"No."

"What about Ronald Pyne?"

"No."

"Did either of you go to Litvak's wedding?"

That question puzzled both of them and their answers sounded less defensive. "No."

Wager wagged his head at Ray, who smiled widely and said, "Thank you both, gentlemen. You've been a big help."

Outside, in the heat, Ray said, "They don't want to say anything to cops. Can't win them all." A snort. "But we probably got as much as Durkin did."

"Would they lie in court?"

"If it came to that, I don't think so—not if it involved white man's business. They'd want none of that." He lifted his hat to let the wind cool his hair. "Why?"

Wager shook his head. "Just looking down the road."

HE WAS STILL looking down the road when he stopped off at B. J. Haydn's ranch to pick up a copy of the well-site coordinates. They were described in relation to distance and angle from surveyed benchmarks rather than by longitude or latitude, and Wager would need a USGS topo map of the area to locate the sites. Sheriff Spurlock might be able to help him with that, and on the way up State 181 from Egnarville, Wager tried his radio. The dispatcher told Wager that the sheriff was out of the office but that she could relay a message. He told her what he needed.

"We've got maps of that area, Officer Wager. You want to swing by here, I can have one for you."

He glanced at his watch and pressed on the gas pedal. "See you in about an hour."

SPURLOCK WAS BACK in his office by the time Wager arrived. "What you need a map of the Flying W for?"

Spreading the topographical map across the small folding table in the alcove he had been assigned, Wager told Spurlock about the drilling, what the drilling might mean, and Rubin.

"They drilled along here—just inside the eastern boundary of the ranch."

"Just off Narraguinnep Wash—I see. And this here's Rubin's land, and Walter Lawrence's is here?"

"Generally. And here's where they found Holtzer."

Spurlock didn't say anything, just made a grunting noise. Wager traced farther down the jagged pattern of contour lines that marked the face of Goat Mesa. This map did not name the points, but close between two sharp clusters of brown elevation lines was a blue squiggle that came out of a notch in the face of Goat Mesa and fed into Narraguinnep Wash. It was labeled "Spring," but had no other name—apparently the mapmakers hadn't talked to the Utes who lived there. It was the only permanent spring in the area and was surrounded by a splotch of green ink to indicate trees. It had to be Knife Springs. "Was Lawrence's land. Ramey Many Coats bought it, and this is Luther's land, now."

Spurlock grunted again and looked at the paper Wager had received from Haydn. Then he went back to his office and reappeared with a small plastic protractor, the kind schoolchildren were required to have. He searched the map for a benchmark corresponding to the elevation that identified it in Haydn's notes. Measuring the back angle from the black X on the map, he marked off the distance by means of the map's scale. "They drilled in a line just off the BLM land and the reservation—starting up here above Lawrence's property and then down past Rubin's, and turning back, here, toward the ranch house." He looked at Wager. "These along here were dry, but the rest looks like they found water. Most likely all the same water table, which means a hell of a lot of litigation over water rights. Could drag out for years."

"The Utes can claim the subterranean water?"

"Given the crazy water laws in this state, anybody on neighboring land could probably claim it. But the Indians would have a real good case, being upstream—especially if they could show that using the underground water would affect their natural springs."

"Like Knife Springs."

"Yep. Can't dam water or take water that makes a man's well or spring run dry." He added, "Not without a good lawyer, anyway."

"Unless the landowners sell the rights."

"Yeah. Unless." The sheriff wiped both thick hands down the front of his swelling shirtfront. "Three deaths linked up with maybe some kind of motive—you done good work, Wager. I mean that. I don't know where it's got us or how it ties into anything else, but there sure as hell seems to be something here."

As Ray had said, motive was there. But whose motive? Right now, it looked like Luther Del Ponte and Ramey Many Coats profited from two of the killings. But who profited from Holtzer's? And from Kershaw's?

"Did you find out anything about Litvak's new wife?"

Spurlock looked up from the map. "Not much. She comes from over on the eastern slope. Colorado Springs, I think. Not many people here know her."

"How did Litvak meet her?"

"I been told it was up at the Lazy J outfit. They run a fancy dude ranch and fishing camp—Litvak was doing some wrangling for them and met her a couple of summers ago." A wag of his head. "That's about all anybody around here knows. Everybody says they seem real happy together." He rubbed his eyes. "That man Durkin's started talking to people about that C-4. Howie told me he got a call this morning from Durkin. Asking all sorts of questions and not sounding like he believed any of the answers. Even threatened to bring Howie before a federal grand jury! I hope that man don't stir up people any worse than they are. All we need's a federal agent hauling people off for questioning, threatening them, making them feel like Washington's a bigger enemy, even, than before. God only knows what'll happen if he gets folks riled enough."

"He's supposed to keep a low profile. That's one of the reasons I was sent out here."

"Yeah, well, the man's got power. And he likes to use it. I wish to God the FBI would test people for common sense before they go handing out badges." Spurlock had an idea. "Why don't you remind him why you're out here? Make him back off until you finish up your job? I'm not just whistling Dixie about the way folks around here feel, Wager. Durkin starts throwing his weight around, somebody's going to shove back, and then people are likely to get hurt."

The sheriff was right. Dislike of federal agents simmered among a lot of people in the county, heated by stories and rumors of government abuse of power elsewhere. It wasn't impossible that, given the Constitutional Posse telling each other scare stories—and in turn scaring Durkin—that a Waco or Ruby Ridge assault could erupt in La Sal County. "Have you talked to him?"

"You think he'd hear anything I said?"

Wager nodded agreement. "There's no guarantee he'll listen to me, either. But I'll try. Do you know if he's talked to Nichols yet?"

"Probably. I don't know. Maybe he's saving him for last— but you can bet your month's paycheck that some of the people he's talked to have already let Bradley know about it."

"Officer Wager—you got a long-distance telephone call." The woman who looked like a golf ball on a tee leaned into the small room. Spurlock told Wager to take it on the extension in his office.

"Gabe! This is about the third place I've tried—I left messages at your motel and at the tribal police number, so don't pay any attention to them." Liz's voice sounded both excited and worried. "That woman you asked me about? Stanley Litvak's new wife?

She's the ex of Woody Riemer! Don't you know who he is?"

"No."

"One of Exxon's big executives. He had an affair two or three years ago with Mai Sorensen. She was that newscaster on Channel Five in Colorado Springs. Remember?"

"No. But you're telling me his wife sued for divorce and got a good settlement out of it?"

"She had Marvin Eben for her lawyer."

That was a name Wager did recognize—three times over: the firm of Eben, Eben, and Eben, whose motto was, "You get Eben, we'll get even." Not many of the people Wager dealt with could afford their fees, but he'd heard of their reputation for big wins. "She was happy with her settlement?"

"Her lawyer said at the time that it was 'satisfactory.' And she's refused all interviews since then, so I guess she was paid enough to keep her mouth shut." Liz's next comment showed why she was worried and why she'd tried so hard to locate Wager. "With that much money, they'll be able to provide very well for Evelyn's daughter, Gabe. The court will have to consider that."

"It may not be Litvak's to spend—if the woman's smart, she'll have a prenuptial agreement."

"Perhaps. Perhaps she put most of it in a trust for herself and any children she may have in case her marriage to Litvak doesn't work out. That's the kind of thing her lawyers would think of. But I'll bet Litvak had her money in mind when he told Evelyn he was going to be rich! Do you have anything on him yet? The hearing's only three days from now."

Durkin had done his part—if unknowingly. "Tell her that a close associate of Litvak is under investigation by the FBI about the theft of explosives from a National Guard unit." He stretched it a bit. "And that Litvak may be an accomplice."

"Oh, wonderful!"

Litvak probably wouldn't think so. "The guy might not be

guilty, Liz—he's not the primary suspect." That as much to caution her as for Spurlock's worried frown. "Here's the local FBI agent's name—and write this down: Douglas D. Durkin. And here's his phone number in case Evelyn's lawyer wants to talk to him." Wager spelled the name and read the number from his notebook. "He's the one investigating the theft. It's not much, but it might be enough for the judge to grant a continuance until the FBI investigation's over."

"Wonderful!" Then, "But what about your investigation? What will this do to that?"

"I'll give me a little more time. Did you find out anything about the investors in the Flying W?"

"Oh, I almost forgot—yes. I told McGraw I was very interested in investing, but I wanted to know who else was in on it besides him. He was pretty coy about it—apparently he's one of several smaller investors and didn't want to come off like just another frog in the pond. But they're hungry to raise a lot of money as soon as possible, so he mentioned some of the big names. Hang on, I've got the list right here." The line hissed. "All right, here's what Weldon gave me: George M. Turner, Richard Maxfield, Lester Windecker, Jack Daily, Robert Cameron. Turner's a big wheel in United Airlines and Maxfield is one of the DIA land speculators who made a fortune from the new airport and apparently wants to make another one—they both play golf with Pyne, and Weldon wanted me to know who his buddies are. I don't know any of the others. Do you want me to ask around?"

"See if Bradley Nichols is one of the smaller fish." He spelled the name.

"I'll try—I know Turner from the Stapleton Airport committee. He's a pretty decent guy."

"Try hard, Liz. It might be important. And be sure to give Evelyn the word on her ex and the FBI today."

Spurlock spoke even before Wager had set the telephone on

its cradle. "Why'd you bring Stan's name into Durkin's investigation, Wager?"

"Durkin is already looking at anybody Nichols has ever talked to. You know that. And if he has some outside lawyers interested in what he's doing—for whatever reason—he might think twice about how he does it. At the very least, they'll be taking up some of his time."

The sheriff, though he nodded, wasn't convinced.

22

IT WAS EARLY afternoon when Wager's tires stirred up dust from the gravel in front of his motel. Since breakfast, he had been doing a lot of driving and not much eating, so he felt stiff and hungry as he walked to his room before heading for the restaurant. The message light on the telephone beside the bed blinked a bright red, and he pushed the number for the office. Verdie answered after about three rings. "One message is just a telephone number, no name, but she called two times: once this morning and then about an hour ago." She read it off and Wager recognized it as Liz's office. "The other's from a Mr. Henderson. Here's his number."

Wager called the BLM agent first.

"I don't know how much I got from Holtzer's wife, Gabe. She had no reason to keep paying rent on his office and threw away a lot of stuff when she cleaned it out. What she did keep were any legal documents and tax records. You know, pay slips, expenses, contracts, receipts for operating overhead, that kind of thing. Anyway, Holtzer received four payments from the Flying W Development Corporation, starting in November. The last one was a couple of weeks before he was killed, dated 3 January for what looked like 'hydrology analysis.' His handwriting was hard to read, but I think that's what it said."

"Any government work in January?"

"Not in his account book. He had pay slips for that—kept them separate from his freelance work. Probably because the tax and FICA and Medicare were withheld. Anyway, he did most of his government erosion surveys in November and December. Nothing for January."

"Any other private jobs near the time of his death?"

"Nothing I could find in his records. Looked like the Flying W was it."

Wager thought that over. "Do you know if he ever worked for the Ute tribal council on the reservation?"

"Matter of fact, he did, but it was over a year ago—last February or March, I think. I saw an entry, but I didn't write down the date. I should have made copies of all those papers, I guess. What I did make copies of is a couple of legal documents that might interest you."

He waited, apparently for the sake of drama, until Wager asked, "What?"

"Holtzer seems to've had a lawyer draw up a couple of contracts. I won't read all the whereases, but what it boils down to is him providing his professional services and consultation in return for twenty-five percent of the future net income from any and all marketed water. They were both made out for signature, but only one was signed. One was for Walter Lawrence, the other—the signed and witnessed one—was for Rubin Del Ponte."

"Who witnessed it?"

"A notary public in Grand Junction."

"So Holtzer was Del Ponte's partner?"

"That's about it. He would provide the technical knowledge of how much water they should contract to sell and for what price, as well as the development and cost of the delivery systems. Del Ponte was the owner. No money up front—all for future income only if and when the water should be marketed—and then a percentage after expenses instead of out of the gross.

All in all, it was a pretty fair contract. A hell of a lot better, I bet, than anything the Flying W would have wanted to offer."

"Was Holtzer's income a good one?"

"You mean for last year? Didn't look too good—his taxable income was a little over twenty-five thousand. Most of that was from the USGS, but since he was a contract agent, he didn't get any of the benefits. His wife's a secretary for a building company up in Grand Junction, but she can't be making all that much, not on hourly. And with three kids . . ." Henderson asked, "Why? That something that might be important?"

"I'm not sure," said Wager. "I'm just trying to make some sense of all of this."

"Well, he cut himself in on one water deal. And tried for another one with Lawrence. That's clear enough. I guess somebody on the Flying W side could've got pissed off and killed him for going over to the Indians, but that seems kind of extreme."

Murder was always extreme—or should be. "What's the date of the contracts?"

"Only one's dated, the signed one—Del Ponte's. Twenty-two January, this year."

One, maybe two days before Holtzer was killed. Wager asked Henderson to make copies of the documents for him. "Thanks, Don. That's a big help."

"More to you than to me, it sounds like. But you're welcome."

Liz herself answered on the first ring. "Oh, good—I was afraid you'd think my last message was the old one. Turner had a list of all the investors in Ronald Pyne's ranch—there aren't that many. Bradley Nichols's name was on it. And so was Stan Litvak's."

"Both?" That figured—they were buddies in everything else.

"That's right. And it's probably what Litvak meant when he told Evelyn he would have plenty of money to spend on their daughter. It wasn't his new wife's money he had in mind, but this deal. Is it important?"

"I don't know yet."

"Will it help Evelyn?"

Wager didn't know that, either, but he said he sure hoped so. Mostly because the other worries he had were increasingly sharper than the approaching custody battle of Liz's friend, but he didn't add that.

After Liz hung up, Wager's train of thought was led back to familiar ground, and he wished he had asked Luther Del Ponte a few more questions. But maybe there were different roads to the same place. He ran through the Egnarville section of the small telephone book and dialed Sharon Del Ponte's number, identifying himself when the woman answered. "Did your husband ever talk about a geologist or mention the name Buck Holtzer?"

The line made a faint hiss as the woman thought.

Wager nudged. "He may have been doing some business with him. Or waiting to get a report from him. Or perhaps planned to meet with him and maybe Luther . . . Probably sometime last December or January . . ."

"I'm not real sure. I think he was going to meet somebody like that a while back. I didn't pay much attention, but I heard him talking to Luther on the telephone about a job he was working on for somebody who was doing some kind of drilling survey. But I can't remember any names—like I said, it was a while back."

"When, Mrs. Del Ponte?"

Another long silence. "Late last year maybe? Sometime around Christmas, anyway. But I can't remember if it was before or after."

"Did he say anything at that time about Ramey Many Coats?"

"No . . . But he could've. Him and Luther always talked about the reservation. But I don't remember them talking about Ramey."

Wager thanked the woman and started to hang up, but she

had a question for him. "Have you told Uncle Malcolm anything about Rubin and—you know—Heidi Herrera?"

"No."

"I wish you wouldn't. Not unless you really have to." She explained. "It wasn't right of Rubin, but he's dead now, so it don't make any difference anymore. And that woman's a slut anyway, and I'd just as soon Uncle Malcolm didn't think of Rubin that way. You know."

Wager guessed that he did know. "I have no reason to tell him, Mrs. Del Ponte."

A FEW OF the noon diners were still lingering over coffee, and layered cigarette smoke made a haze over a couple of the tables at the far end of the dining room. Paula smiled with shy excitement as Wager took a table beside one of the windows.

"I finally told Verdie I was thinking of moving to Denver."

"What'd she say?"

"She says she doesn't want to see me go. But she thinks it would be good for me and I ought to do it while I'm young enough. She says to just give her a couple of weeks' notice and to write to her. She says she'll write to anybody I want a job with and tell them how good I am."

"What about your folks? How do they feel about it?"

She shook her head. "They're worried at the idea. But my grandma says there's nothing for me here except working for Verdie and marrying some cowboy, and then giving my pay-check to him instead of keeping it for myself. She says I should do it. Especially," the young woman looked down at her order book and made a scratching motion with her pencil, "especially since I know somebody now who can kind of help me there." Quickly, she went on, "I don't mean like a grandfather or some-thing—just somebody who could tell me where it would be best to live and I could call if I needed help or something. I told them

you were a policeman there and you lived there all your life."
She became businesslike. "Can I take your order now?"

A grandfather? "What? Oh—ah, the chicken-fried steak.
Coffee."

She was gone before he could say anything more.

Well, his own grandfather would have been in his fifties
when Wager joined the Marine Corps, so he guessed that from
Paula's view he might look that old, even if he wasn't. It was a
realization that brought with it the quiver of something lost,
which, he guessed, was sort of what women meant by their "bio-
logical clock." But the tick of Wager's clock was a muted one,
and you couldn't stop time; as one of his uncles always said,
time takes things from you or takes you from them, and that's
all there is to it. As for Paula coming to Denver, it wouldn't be
as if Wager were adopting the girl. And if she was as determined
to go as it seemed, she would go whether he thought it was a
good idea or not, or whether he offered any help or not. So he
might as well do what little he could. Besides—and most important—he owed the girl: She had tried to do him a favor.

He was mopping up some gravy that had crawled out of its
little cup of mashed potatoes when Paula came by with a refill
of coffee. "Paula, tell me: Who did you overhear making threats
against me?"

The muted aura of happiness and excitement she had shown
when he first came in faded.

"You called me and warned me about being attacked. I need
to know who it was."

"I . . . I'd just as soon not say, Officer Wager. It's not like I
listen to what people are talking about—I'm not trying to eaves-
drop. They just keep talking a lot of times like I'm not there."

"I'm not going to let anyone know who told me. The reason
I'm asking is it might help me solve Rubin's murder."

"He really was murdered, wasn't he? I mean, it wasn't an
accident, was it?"

"I can't prove it yet, but I think he was." He held out his cup for her glass coffeepot. "Whatever you tell me, I will keep secret. But I need information—any little kind, and some of it might not even seem important. So I'd like to know: Who did you hear threatening me?"

She still hesitated, but Wager could not tell whether it was from fear or a community distrust of outsiders.

"Was it Bradley Nichols?"

A quick nod.

"When he was here with that man from Denver?"

"No. A couple days after. Him and Dave Turney and Stan Litvak. And one of the Many Coats. They were talking about you causing trouble and Bradley Nichols said they ought to give you more trouble than you could handle."

"A Many Coats? Which one?"

"I don't know, there's so many of them. But they're mostly all built with that squat look. You know, their heads are kind of too big and their bodies are real short and thick."

"Could it have been Ramey?"

"I couldn't say for sure. It was a Many Coats, is all."

"What kind of trouble was I causing?"

"I don't know. Asking questions, I suppose. Maybe finding things out that they didn't want found out."

That's what detectives did, all right. "Did anyone else say anything?"

"Stan Litvak just said it was a good idea, and that's all I heard."

Wager nodded his thanks and the girl left quickly.

He was almost through with his coffee when Verdie poked her head around the door looking for him. "Got a message for you, Officer Wager. He said it was important."

"Coming."

He read the slip of paper as he paid his bill. Then he went to his room to make the call. "Ray? What's the problem?"

"Cerise Del Ponte came into the office about an hour ago. I'm not sure what's going on, Gabe, but somebody's up to something. Anyway, Luther came home in a sweat this afternoon and grabbed what he could carry, then headed down Narraguinnep Wash. He said he was going to the Navajo reservation for some big medicine. Said if he didn't come back, he wanted her to have Rubin's land. If he didn't come back, it was hers, he said, and he wrote out a piece of paper naming her as owner in case he died. He said she shouldn't let anybody buy it or steal it from her. Said she should keep it no matter what and then hauled his tail out of there in a cloud of dust and a hearty 'Heigh-ho Silver'."

"Did he say who'd want the land?"

"No. And she was too surprised and didn't think to ask."

"You think we have him worried? Scared him by naming his dead brother?"

"That could be it—he might have been visited by Rubin's ghost." It didn't sound to Wager as if Ray were joking. "But something else happened, too: A few hours after Luther left, a white man came by, asking for him."

"Did she recognize him?"

"No. A stranger to her, but he seemed to know Luther all right. Asked how the kids were doing, knew the names of a couple of them, that kind of thing. So, Cerise told him that Luther had gone to see his medicine man and she didn't know when he'd be back. The man said OK and left. Then she got a call from Ramey Many Coats who said he had some money to give Luther—said Luther really wanted it and he—Ramey—had promised it as soon as possible. Did she know where Luther's medicine man lived? Cerise figured Luther needed it to pay the medicine man, so she told Ramey Luther had gone down to the one on Montgomery Creek, and Ramey said thanks and hung up. Then Cerise began wondering if she should have told Ramey anything, and that got her more worried and upset, so she drove in to see me. At first I thought it was our talk about Rubin that scared Luther, but now I'm not sure."

"Why?"

"It's about two hours by fast horse from Knife Springs to Luther's house, and it took us three hours to drive around. Which is about how long it was before the white man showed up behind Luther. I figure Luther might have seen that white man driving down the Wash toward the Springs and high-tailed it for home. It doesn't make much sense, but it's possible Luther's running from him and not from Rubin's ghost."

"Where's Cerise now?"

"I just now sent her over to her mother's house, but I think you'd better talk to her."

That's just what Wager was thinking. "I'm on my way."

23

THE LOWERING SUN caused Wager to squint as he drove the last miles toward the wall-like silhouette of Dark Mesa and the village at its foot. But it wasn't only the glare that brought a frown. Events were moving into some kinds of patterns now, and a few of those patterns seemed to make some sense while others made no sense at all. With all of them, the reasons for killing one or another of the victims either multiplied or remained obscure. The rule of thumb that Wager and a lot of other cops used in most cases told him to go after the suspect who ran, and that's what he'd do here. But if Luther had reason to kill his brother and perhaps even Holtzer because he had a contract with Rubin, Wager didn't see any cause for him murdering the other two men. Which, of course, meant the probability of other perpetrators. The frown that deepened Wager's squint came from trying to link the best motives and opportunities with the various names drifting through his thoughts.

Ray met him in the shade of the building's front door and walked with him to the tribal police office. "Durkin just called. He wanted to know if I'd seen Nichols. And he wants you to call him right away."

"Nichols is missing?"

"Looks that way. Durkin took a sniffer dog and a search warrant out to Nichols's ranch just after noon. Nichols wasn't there, but the dog turned up some sticks of C-4 in a corner of the barn and Durkin put out an arrest warrant for him. But nobody seems to know where he is, so Durkin wants you to call."

Wager did.

"I thought you were supposed to coordinate things, Wager. I by God call the sheriff for some help in locating a wanted fugitive and he as much as tells me to kiss his ass. Now that I need it, where in hell's all this cooperation you keep talking about?"

"I can't coordinate if I don't know what's going on, Durkin, and I just heard from Officer Qwana'tua about Nichols. Did you tell Sheriff Spurlock you were going to run a search of Nichols's ranch?"

"No, I did not. Nor am I required to."

"Was that because you didn't trust him not to warn Nichols?"

"Well, no—! It was . . . you have to move fast on these things, and I didn't have time. You know what it means to preserve evidence in a search!"

Wager knew what it was to lie, too, and he caught that defensive note in Durkin's voice. "Any reason why Sheriff Spurlock shouldn't assume you didn't trust him?"

"Wager, goddamnit, I am not the one who's derelict in my duty here! I'm a by God federal officer and I order you—that's an order—to assist in the location and apprehension of Bradley Nichols, who is a wanted fugitive from justice!"

"Do you have any idea what a damn fool you sound like?" The noise on the other end of the line became a squawk and Wager had to raise his voice over it. "I'm willing to help you, Durkin, and I can. But you're going to have to help me, too."

"What!"

"You give Sheriff Spurlock your word that you will not mount any more operations or exercise any more warrants in his jurisdiction unless you inform him first and request and heed his advice in dealing with the local population."

"What?"

"Otherwise you are out there by yourself, Durkin. And you

will not have any local agencies to hide behind if some of the county's hotheads feel like shooting to defend their liberties."

"Wager, you—"

"You can give me your word on that, and I'll pass it on to Spurlock. And then I'll ask him to help you with Nichols. But without something from you, I'm not going to get a damned thing out of him."

The line was silent. "Let me speak to Officer Qwana'tua."

Wager handed over the telephone to the tribal policeman, who grunted a few times in response to whatever the FBI agent was saying. Then Ray handed the telephone back to Wager. "He wants to talk to you again."

"OK, Wager. You tell Spurlock I'll work with him. In his jurisdiction only. But I expect help in locating Nichols. And you tell him he calls me—I by God am not going to call that man first."

Wager thought that was a small price and made his call, hoping Spurlock would think so, too.

"Durkin wants what?"

"In return for your help, here's what he agrees to." Wager told the sheriff about the bargain.

"That som'bitch ran a search warrant in my jurisdiction, Wager! Went out and raided the home of a member of the goddamn Constitutional Posse and stirred up the whole goddamn bunch worse than a hatful of hornets! I got a call from Morris, who saw Pete Stine and half a dozen others going down the goddamn highway in a parade of pickup trucks and rifles!"

"He found the C-4, Sheriff. It was there. In Nichols's barn."

"He what? He found it?"

"Buried in a corner of the barn. Dog sniffed it up."

"Oh, goddamn."

"Think Morris can get that word to Pete Stine and the rest of the Posse members? It might cool them off to learn that Nichols is guilty."

A deep sigh.

"And you can promise Stine and the others that the FBI won't pull any tricks—that the FBI has agreed to work through your office for any and all operations in the county, and that they can come to you with any questions or worries they have about FBI activities."

"You think Durkin means that?"

"All you have to do is call him."

"It's worth a try. Hell, it's the only thing I got for a try."

Wager hung up the telephone and stared for a long moment at the office wall without seeing it. He hoped it would work. "Coffee," he said to Ray. "I need a cup of coffee."

"It's not as good as Happy's, but here you are."

Wager took a long swallow. "What did Durkin tell you?"

"Said I was a federal employee, that I was to report directly to him, and that I wasn't to work with you anymore, forthwith. I think he was trying to save face—figured he could stomp around in his own sandbox, since he couldn't stomp around in Spurlock's anymore."

"What are you going to do?"

Ray's eyebrows lifted. "I'm not a federal employee—I'm an employee of the sovereign state of the Squaw Mountain Ute Reservation. And we've got a case to finish."

That was what Wager wanted to hear. He drained his cup. "Have you talked with Ramey yet?"

"No. Why?"

"How did he know Luther had gone to see a medicine man?"

"Aw, crap!" The younger man looked embarrassed. "The white man told him. I should've thought of that." Then, "But what would this white man and Ramey want with Luther?"

Wager brought him up to date about Holtzer's contract for a share of Rubin's water and what Paula had said about Ramey meeting with the new owner of the Flying W.

"Ramey met with Ronald Pyne after you got here? Just a couple of days ago?"

"And Ramey knew I was looking into Rubin's death." As, it seemed, everyone else in the county did, too; but Wager didn't bother telling the tribal policeman about the threat Paula had overheard—Ray had already seen the results of that.

"But I still don't see why anyone would go after Luther."

"I don't know for certain. But it looks like we have two people running: one who planted some bombs, the other who claims Rubin's land." Wager told Ray what he had been formulating on the drive to the reservation. "My guess is Luther had a deal with either Ramey or Pyne or both. Maybe Luther killed Rubin or helped someone else kill him so he could claim the land. Then maybe he got greedy and raised the price of the water—Rubin must have told him about Holtzer's contract and what the water might be worth. Or even what it might be worth not to file a lawsuit that could tie up the Flying W development for years. But in some way, Luther and Ramey both have to be involved with the Flying W. Things just don't make sense without that. And, if Luther is, then my guess is that either Luther didn't deliver something to someone, or he knows something that someone doesn't want him talking about."

"That someone's the white man?"

"Nobody knows where Nichols is. If he went out to Knife Springs, he wouldn't know yet about Durkin's raid on his ranch. So maybe he's not running from Durkin, but running after Luther."

"Where does Ramey come in?"

"I figure he smelled money and pushed his way in. Maybe through killing Lawrence, certainly through buying his land from the tribe. So he got a foot in the door through Lawrence. But Knife Springs is a better water source. The problem is, it belongs to Luther, now. So how's Ramey going to get it? Luther has relatives living on the reservation who would have first claim if he dies. But what if Luther could be frightened enough to sign over the land to Ramey—scared enough that Nichols or somebody was going to kill him, and that the only way to get out alive would be to take what Ramey offered for the land. Then Ramey would have both portions. The Many Coats would own all the water Pyne needs to buy, plus the land the casino is going to be built on with tribal money."

"He could make Pyne pay through the nose."

"Well, Pyne might back out if it gets too expensive. That would screw up his and his investors' plans to get rich, as well as Ramey's own investment in Walter Lawrence's land and make it worth zilch again. But Ramey sure would be able to bargain for a much sweeter deal than if Pyne or Nichols already had some kind of claim to the water—say, through a deal with Luther."

Ray dragged his thumb along the bumpy flesh of his jaw. "So Ramey figures maybe Luther can be scared into selling the land to him—warns Luther than Nichols is out to kill him, and the only way to prevent it is to get rid of the land. But Luther doesn't sell. Instead, when he sees Nichols, he runs and he also makes his wife promise never to sell—that's what that was all about! So Nichols tells Ramey what happened, and Ramey calls Cerise to find out where the medicine man lives. And then he tells Nichols—who goes after Luther to make him live up to the deal they'd offered Rubin." The tribal policeman nodded to himself. "And if Nichols does happen to kill Luther for whatever reason, Ramey can make—will make—the offer to Cerise. And she'll probably be easier to handle than Luther, especially if her husband's just been murdered. He could even scare her by saying he caused Luther's death with his medicine, and in a way he'd be right." Ray stared at the map on the wall as if it were a television screen. "And even if that little plan doesn't work, Ramey's no worse off than before. It doesn't answer all the questions, and I don't see where Kershaw comes in, but it makes a lot more sense than it did before."

"It also makes it pretty important that we find Luther while he can still talk."

CERISE DEL PONTE had told them that in the past Luther had used a Navajo medicine man of the Begay clan. "Henry Begay. He lives somewhere over here near Hovenweep, on Montezuma Creek." Ray's finger on the map had followed the boundary lines where the northern edge of the Navajo reservation lapped up into the southeast corner of Utah, almost to the Hovenweep National Monument.

"This is where Luther's headed?"

Ray shrugged. "It's where Henry Begay lives."

And that was why Wager now sat rocking and swaying on the more gentle of the two ponies Ray had led down the ramp from the police trailer when the fragmenting track finally grew too rough for the truck's four-wheel drive. A helicopter would have been quicker and a lot more comfortable. But it wasn't in Wager's budget, and the only one available to Ray was the one all the federal agencies chartered when they needed it. It was also the one Durkin would know about if Ray did request it. Besides, Ray had said, and grinned, it felt good to get out of that truck and back in the saddle again. Wager had not grinned back.

The sun faded into a dying smear of red off to their right. Against the clear green of the evening horizon loomed the black silhouettes of buttes and broken ridges, and it was becoming increasingly difficult to see the dips and hollows of the earth as the light gradually settled into a single gray shade. But the ponies did not stumble often, and Wager hung on in trust of his animal's hooves and Ray's knowledge of where they were headed.

Once, early on, Wager had asked Ray if he was sure the widely scattered sign he was following was Luther's and the tribal policeman had shaken his head. "Nope. Who do you think

I am, Tonto?" Then the wide smile lit up his face. "But anybody headed for Hovenweep country has to come this way. Land's too cut up to go any other way." He gestured vaguely to both sides. "Some humongous canyons to wander around in. No, we might not be following every step of his trail, but there's no other way to take a horse from here to there."

"Why didn't he drive?"

"Maybe he was afraid Nichols could drive faster or that truck of his couldn't make it. Or that he might meet Nichols coming back to the rez as he was leaving. Besides, there're only three roads in this whole corner of the Navajo reservation and they all link up. Wouldn't be hard to look for someone who had to stay on those roads."

"Do you think Nichols might have come this way, too?"

"Not without a horse, and I haven't seen but one set of fresh tracks. My guess is he's driving. It's a long way around, too. Either up through Monticello and down 191 to Bluff, or over on 666 toward Cortez and then back up to Aneth. Either way, the trip takes a whole afternoon to get somewhere ahead of Luther."

They rode until it was almost black, then Ray swung out of the saddle and took a long drink from one of the large, cloth-covered canteens slung from his saddle. "We better camp now. Cold camp. Be light enough again, six, seven hours."

A cold camp, Wager found out, meant no campfire; Ray didn't want to take the chance of Luther discovering that they had followed him. It also meant being cold, and Wager buttoned the neck of his denim jacket and turned its collar up against a wind that had shifted from a warm, upslope direction to bring a bone-deep chill from the icy glitter of the stars. Ray gave the horses a light drink and hobbled them to forage while Wager kneaded a little water into his foil pouch of dried vegetable and beef whatever, and heated it over the hissing blue flame of a dim gas burner. It wasn't good, but at least there wasn't much of it, and even the ground—hard and lumpy through the thin mattress pad—felt better than the barrel-sized saddle that had begun to torture his legs by pushing them into bowed arcs. Now, Wager thought as he quickly drifted into sleep, he knew why cowboys walked the way they did.

AFTER A WHILE, you stopped trying to find a way to keep your knees and hips from hurting or to ease the raw hotness of the saddle chafing against your spine. What you did was let your mind sort of go out into the sun-whitened rock and sand in a feeling that was almost like sleeping with your eyes open. The gait of the horse made a gentle lurch that swayed your body and kept one tiny part of you anchored to the hurt, but the rest could float away above the banks and cliffs of red sand, above the increasingly deep arroyos and gullies that tortured the land, until you could almost see yourself somewhere in the glare below: a tiny figure whose shadow made a tight pattern of black that rippled across the brush and gravel and spines of bone-white slickrock.

Wager ceased to wonder about where he was or how long it had taken to get here. Time was like the surrounding desert, something that went on forever, that had its own being, and into which he and Ray were intruders. The rhythmic creak of leather, the steady slosh of canteens that were fast growing empty, the plopping of hooves—muffled by loose sand or ringing against bare rock—formed the only sounds and helped in their monotony to push his spirit self even farther from its body. And always the sun, like a weight that grew familiar but never easier. Pressing steadily against flesh, against cloth, weighing on his eyes and even the air he breathed so that a breeze, when it came, was only heat from another direction.

"There's water up there."

Ray's voice pulled Wager back from wherever his mind had drifted. "What?"

"Water—we're almost at Yogovu Springs. That's what we call it, anyway. The Navajos call it something else."

"OK."

"Almost" was part of that ill-defined thing called time and Wager wasn't sure how much had gone by, but after a while Ray guided his horse toward a crack in the baking sand and Wager felt his own horse's pace quicken. Then it became choppy as they left the surface and twisted down through ledges of stone and gravel and scree into the slit of smooth-walled rock and a blessed shade that lifted the weight of the sun from his shoulders. His horse snorted, tugging against the reins, and Wager ducked beneath the bulges and shelves of sandstone that pressed in from the sides of the twisting corridor. The sandy floor tilted down more steeply and Wager could no longer see the sky; the light bounced indirectly so that shadows disappeared and illumination seemed to come off the walls that brushed his knees, that closed in behind him, that glided open in front. A cool dampness tickled his sense of smell and a moment later the passage twisted tightly to end at a giant pothole of steep walls and distant, open sky. The floor of the hole was almost covered by a pool of water. It lay clear and still, tinged by a gently sloping beach of coarse gravel and stones tufted here and there with wiry grass. The upper end of the slope ended at polished stone walls that reached a hundred or more feet straight up and were banded in varying shades of red, and were coated here and there by vast sheets of black oxidation. The lower end tilted into water so clear that it was hard to tell which rocks were under the surface and which were above.

The horses lunged forward to thrust their sucking muzzles into the pond before Ray, allowing them a few quick gulps, hauled their heads back.

Wager felt the dryness of his mouth as he listened to the horses drink.

"Look there." Ray pointed toward something on the bank about five feet away.

Wager made out freshly scraped sand and dislodged rocks at the fringe of the pond. "Luther?"

"Has to be. One horse and not too long ago—the ground's still a little bit damp. Figure six, maybe eight hours, max."

Ray dug into a saddlebag for something that looked like a kind of pump and dropped the end of its clear plastic hose into the pool, away from the horses. "Filter—even Indians get giardiasis."

Ray gave the horses a series of slow drinks while Wager pumped water through the filter and into the canteens. Then they left the distant circle of sky and headed back up the crevice to the desert above.

At dusk, they paused on the lip of a series of benches that stepped down and away toward a vast bowl of purple darkness. Far on its other side, beyond the rim of the earth, the dying sunlight flared a deep, final red.

"If he builds a fire, we should be able to see it."

"How close are we to Montezuma Creek?"

"It's down that way. All this drains off toward the San Juan River, and that goes a hundred or so miles over to the Colorado. Some pretty wild country in there. The Navajo reservation starts just down there. See those lights?"

Wager could make out a tiny white cluster of glowing specks that seemed to quiver and dance in the heat still rising from the earth. "Is that the town of Montezuma Creek?"

"Naw, we're a long way from there. That's the Hatch Trading Post, just inside the reservation boundary. Luther'll be more over there, where it's dark. There's a state highway there— Luther'll have to cross it. Probably tonight, just to be safe."

"Do we keep going in the dark?"

Ray glanced at him, his expression blurred by the thickening twilight. "He'll reach Henry Begay's place tomorrow afternoon. I'd like to catch up with him before he does. You up to it?"

"Whatever it takes."

"Let's go a little longer, then." Wager thought he heard a faint note of approval in the man's voice.

They were going again before dawn, Ray shaking Wager's shoulder to pull him out of an exhausted and dreamless sleep and into the chill gray light. The small tin pot of water boiled quickly over the thin glow of the burner and he and Ray stirred powdered coffee into their cups to wash down the breakfast of dried eggs and ham and to warm their cold fingers around the heated aluminum.

"I suppose I should charge you for eating up the office vacation supplies," said Ray. "But it tastes so bad you probably want the tribal police to pay you."

"Tastes better than some of the things I cook. And there aren't many dishes to wash."

Ray, flattening the small mound of empty food packets and packing them into a plastic trash bag, shook his head. "You must be some awful cook."

By the time their shadows had shrunk to half their original length, they had crossed the empty lanes of a lonely highway and dropped down another series of rocky benches toward the swirl of canyons and gullies and the miles of piñon-dotted mounds and humps of rock that had spent the last million years resisting erosion.

"I think that's him."

Wager pulled himself back from the distance. "Where?"

Ray, his uniform cap pulled low over his eyes to filter out the glare, pointed toward a broad triangle of level and brush-choked sand. It was bordered on two sides by gullies and washes that dropped steeply into the beginnings of canyons. The far side of the small plateau ended at the foot of a reef that stood as erect as a rooster's comb and ran for a couple of miles, a cracked and ragged barrier of almost maroon sandstone.

Wager peered through the distance and finally saw that one

of the dark specks he'd thought was merely another squat piñon or cedar tree was slowly moving. It was too far away to distinguish man from horse, but with recognition Wager could make out the shape of a man's shoulders and head above the bulk of the animal he straddled. "You're sure that's Luther?"

Ray nodded. "His horse. A pinto." He glanced at Wager. "And that small tattoo on his left hand, you can't miss that."

Wager strained harder; he couldn't even make out the man's arms. "How can you . . . ?" Then, "Oh—that's a joke."

"I thought it was kind of funny."

Wager's lips lifted in a brief smile. "How long before we reach him?"

"Couple hours, if he don't see us."

They had been riding for half that time when Ray's small radio crackled faintly from a saddlebag. He pulled up to fish it out and aim the antenna toward the northeast. Wager tried to stifle a groan as he hauled himself out of the saddle and unscrewed a canteen cap.

A pinched voice sounded loud in the desert silence. "Qwana'tua? Come in—this is Durkin. Qwana'tua?"

"Go ahead, Durkin."

"Suspect apprehended. Repeat: suspect apprehended. Search is cancelled."

Ray glanced at Wager, who shrugged and said, "Nichols?"

"Is that Nichols? You arrested him?"

"Affirmative. Suspect was apprehended at Grand Junction and is now in custody. Consider the case closed—return to base for further instructions."

Both Ray and Wager studied the slowly moving figure in the distance. "That's good news for Luther," said Wager.

Ray nodded. Then he reached into the saddlebag and pulled out a map. He held the paper near the microphone and crackled it. "You're breaking up—say again all after 'affirmative.' "

The thin voice repeated itself, louder.

Ray held the radio at arm's length, rattling the paper harder. "I can't . . . you . . . breaking up . . . over." He turned it off and dropped it back in the leather pouch.

"His case may be closed and Luther may be safe. But we still need to talk to him."

Wager grunted and hauled himself back into the saddle.

GRADUALLY, THE GLIMPSES of the man ahead became clearer to Wager, and after an hour or so he could make out the checked cloth of his flannel shirt, the high dome of his black hat, the patterns on the pinto horse. Wager did not see Luther look back their way, but for a while the man stayed the same distance and even seemed to increase it a little. Ray goaded his horse into a quicker walk. Wager's own horse stepped faster, the jolting stride uncomfortable to Wager and Wager's stiff riding uncomfortable to the horse.

"He knows we're behind him," said Ray.

"Why doesn't he run?"

"Hey, where can he run to?"

Wager looked at the world surrounding them: a chaos of twisting gullies and washes, of red-and-white mounds and reefs and buttes that rose from those unnamed and contorted crevices, hundreds of square miles of heat-paled sky over an empty tumult marked only by an occasional crooked telephone pole. He figured Ray was joking again. Well, he was young. Wager could not remember telling jokes when he had been younger—as a matter of fact, he couldn't remember laughing very much, either, even before he'd joined Homicide. But Ray's life was a different one, and he saw the world differently, too. Maybe he even saw it as a better place than Wager did. If so, that would probably change in time, but that wasn't Wager's worry. Luther and the man hunting him were Wager's worry. Fortunately, Ray was able to do well what he did—be a tribal cop—and he knew this tortured landscape far better than Wager. Those skills and that knowledge would help Wager get his job done, and that was the only thing that counted.

They began closing in again. Ray followed lines of convergence that shortened the distance every time the rough ground forced Luther to change direction. At the end of a half hour or so, they were close enough for Wager to see the man's saddlebags and a scabbard that showed a rifle butt rising just in front of the man's left knee. Finally the man guided his horse down into one of the larger gullies and out of sight among thrusts of rock and tangles of brush and cedar clumps. When Ray and Wager followed down the slope of slickrock, their horses' hooves clattering loudly in the silence, they saw Luther's riderless horse grazing on a small patch of weeds. The man himself sat smoking in the shade of a larger tree, waiting for them.

24

RAY GREETED THE man in Ute. Luther lifted his hat to wipe a wide palm across his sweaty forehead and nodded back to both of them before resettling the hat in the groove it had pressed in his straight black hair.

"You been following me a long time."

The tribal policeman swung down from his creaking saddle, and Wager followed stiffly. "Couple days."

The horses snorted their own greetings and ambled over near the pinto to help it crop the tough weeds.

Luther reached under one of his braids to lift his package of cigarettes out of his shirt pocket in an offer; Ray took one to hold in his palm. Wager shook his head. Ray, too, squatted; Wager didn't. Standing felt good, and it felt good to move his legs without having a horse between them. He was also more comfortable being between Luther and that rifle holstered on the pinto's saddle.

"You going to see Henry Begay, Cerise tells me."

"Got to."

Ray nodded, dragging his fingers through the powdery sand between his scarred boots. "His place is just over there, isn't it?" Ray tilted his chin down the draw to where it opened into a distant view of the next lower shelf of earth.

"A few miles. Maybe ten." A wag of his head. "Real close . . . real close."

Overhead, somewhere beyond the heat haze that made the sky a silvery blue, Wager heard the tiny, hollow roar of a high-flying jet liner. Headed for Los Angeles probably. Maybe from Denver, maybe from somewhere farther east. No contrail, so he couldn't tell exactly where it crossed the sky. When it was gone, he heard the distant twitter of some bird from one of the narrower gullies that fed the wash, and an occasional sigh of wind through the stiff needles of the cedar that shaded them.

"Be better if you tell us about it, Luther. Henry Begay won't be able to help you much if you don't speak from your heart."

Another gentle surge of wind along the ragged walls of the wash seemed to carry a slightly different sound, so faint that Wager wasn't sure he really heard it. It was an insect of some kind: distant and small. An almost metallic whining that reminded Wager of a tiny engine straining to pull up a hard hill, and he wondered how far they were from any of the faint two-wheel tracks that picked their way through the writhing watercourses that scarred the land. Then the wind faded and the sound was gone.

Ray tried again. "Ramey Many Coats has some strong medicine, all right. He knows how to hex people. If you got him after you, you're going to need Henry Begay, all right."

Luther, squinting, pulled the smoke of his cigarette into his lungs. The brim of his hat dipped once in a nod.

"But, Luther, I tell you this—sometimes a lot of people hex themselves. I had a cousin once, he hexed himself. Tried to blame it on a witch, but the witch didn't know anything about it." Another slow dribble of sand from between his fingers into a growing mound. Luther waited for Ray to go on. "He went to two or three medicine men, paid a lot of money. Didn't do no good."

"The witch was stronger."

"No. The witch didn't know anything about it, not until after it was all over. Didn't have any reason to hex my cousin, either, because he hadn't done anything to the witch."

"Sometimes they don't need a reason."

"This one didn't need a reason because my cousin did it to himself. Made his own bad luck. You want to know how?"

"I guess you're going to tell me anyway."

It was Ray's turn to nod. "What he did was kill a man. That wasn't so bad because he was drunk, so it was kind of an accident. You know: didn't mean to do it, it just happened. But he hexed himself when he woke up sober and saw the man lying there and took the man's money. It was a lot of money. Didn't give it to the man's wife or kids. Nothing to make amends, you know, just took it. Bought himself a new car, bunch of other stuff. Thought he could get away with it."

"You catch him?"

"Not me. Happened a long time before I became a cop. No, my cousin started having real bad luck, so he went to this medicine man and said some witch had hexed him. But he didn't tell him about killing the man and taking his money. So the singing was no good. Tried everything. No good. Sold his new car to pay for a new medicine man. Still no good. Sold his horses. Sold his house and land. Didn't tell the new medicine man the real reason, just that he was hexed. No good. Sold everything. No good. Left his wife and kids, went to L.A.—figured if he left the reservation the hex wouldn't follow him. No good. Lots of bad luck out there—drunk, jail, begging down in Pershing Square. Everything. No good." Ray smoothed out the mound of fine, pink sand and started another one. It looked like a small anthill.

"What happened to your cousin?"

"He came back, what was left of him, and told the family of the man he had killed and what he had done. They killed him."

Wager figured that that was one way to stop the bad luck. But apparently Luther saw more in the story than Wager did.

"He let them kill him?"

"He was happy they did. First time he was happy since he took the man's money."

Luther carefully stubbed out his cigarette against the scarred instep of his boot.

"Henry Begay's not going to help you, Luther. He can't. Only you can, and you can only do it by telling me what happened to that white man who hunted the water under your brother's land."

The man sat still, eyes hidden from Wager by the wide brim of his black hat. Ray waited. The staccato pulse of an insect buzzed from somewhere among the cedar's branches.

When Luther finally spoke, his voice sounded tired and defeated. Wager figured that was how the man felt, too, because now he said the names of the dead as if he no longer cared whether they were listening, to be called back with their bad luck. "Walter Lawrence killed that white man who hunted water. This is what he told me. That white man wanted Walter Lawrence to sign a paper letting him sell the water under his land. Said he could make a lot of money for Walter, but he had to have twenty-five percent of it for himself."

Ray waited until he was certain Luther had stopped talking. "The same kind of paper he signed with Rubin?"

A nod.

"Why did Walter Lawrence kill him? Why didn't he just tell the man no?"

"He didn't mean to. He wanted him off his land so he wouldn't come back, so he shot at him to scare him away, but he missed. Hit the man. The man ran all the way back to his car and Walter was afraid he would go to the police, so he shot the car, too. Then Walter ran away." Luther tried to explain it. "Walter told me he knew the man would take his land. That's what white men with papers like that did, they got you to sign and then stole your land, he said. And he figured that with all the new laws coming to the reservation the white man would get away with it. The man kept saying sign, and Walter kept saying no. Then the man came back one day and told him that Rubin had signed a paper like that. Walter knew that if one Indian signed away his land, the white man would make the rest of them do it—it would just take him a little more time, is all. So he got scared and shot at the man." Luther cleared his throat, dry after so much talking.

Ray sat for a while in silence, thinking over what Luther had said. "So who killed Walter Lawrence?"

From where he stood, Wager could hear the man sigh. "My brother."

"Rubin?"

Luther nodded. "Him and Ramey Many Coats."

"The two of them killed him?"

Another nod. "After that man-who-hunted-water was killed, another white man told Rubin that his land wasn't worth nothing unless they had Walter Lawrence's land, too. Said Rubin had the water but Walter Lawrence's land was the only good place to build the casino on—they could bring in a road real easy and put a bridge across Narraguinnep Wash there. Said they couldn't do that on Rubin's land because something was wrong with the sand around Narraguinnep Wash where he was, and anyway he was blocked off by Yogovu Mesa. Rubin went to Ramey Many Coats to see about borrowing enough money to buy out Walter Lawrence." He stopped, and Ray waited. He began again. "Ramey said he would buy it himself so he wouldn't have to worry about Rubin paying the money back. That was OK because it would still make Rubin's land worth a lot of money. So they both went out to see Walter Lawrence and talk about buying the land. Got him drunk and brought him into Dark Mesa Village to sign papers, but Walter Lawrence kept saying no. He was drunk, but he wouldn't sign nothing for nobody even when he was drunk. He started walking home and Ramey Many Coats told Rubin that Walter Lawrence better sell. He better sell soon or the white man who bought the Flying W ranch would go away and nobody would have anything."

When Luther remained silent this time, Ray asked, "Did Rubin go and stab Walter?"

"Yes. Ramey Many Coats told him maybe that would be the best thing, so Rubin did it."

Wager found a rock in the shade of the cedar and settled on it.

"And who killed Rubin?"

Wager expected the answer to come slowly, but the man simply shrugged and answered. "Me." He added, "That's why I got to see Henry Begay."

"How?"

"Stabbed him. At Knife Springs—stabbed him. Pretty funny."

No one laughed unless it was that distant insect whose chuckling buzz tugged at a corner of Wager's awareness.

"You wanted his land."

It seemed important to Luther to make things clear. "No. I didn't want him to sell the land—he rode out to the springs to tell me he had decided to sell the land. Said this white man would give him fifty thousand dollars cash money to sell the land to Ramey Many Coats."

After a pause, Ray asked, "Why didn't Ramey just buy it himself?"

"Rubin didn't want to sell to Ramey—Ramey wanted the land for next to nothing—a couple of thousand. He told Rubin that he didn't have any more cash money because he'd just bought Walter Lawrence's land. And he told Rubin that if he didn't sell to him cheap, he'd tell the police who killed Walter Lawrence. Rubin said that if Ramey told the police that, he'd fix it so nobody got the water and nobody got rich—no casino, no development, no nothing. So then this white man promised Rubin that much money to sell; he said he couldn't buy any reservation land but that Ramey could and he had already put a lot of money in the project and didn't want to lose it. So he promised Rubin fifty thousand cash if he would sell to Ramey Many Coats."

Wager asked, "This white man, was it Bradley Nichols? Or a man named Ronald Pyne?"

"No. Another white man."

When Luther remained silent, Ray asked, "And Rubin told you he was going to sell out?"

Luther wagged his head slowly. "That's what he came to tell me. Said he talked to this white man that morning. Showed me a letter that told about the fifty thousand and that Ramey Many Coats would own the land. Ramey Many Coats had already put his name on the line. Rubin wanted me to know before he put his name on it. Told me he would give me ten thousand dollars to make up for losing Knife Springs for my sheep."

Wager asked, "What about the other contract? The one he signed with the geologist to sell just the water?"

Luther's long braids bobbed when he shrugged. "That man was dead now."

Holtzer could no longer fulfill his part of the bargain, that was for sure. "Do you know the white man's name?"

"Yes." A long sigh whistling through his nose and the name mumbled so quietly that Wager almost didn't hear it. "Stan Litvak."

"Litvak?" Wager tried to fit that piece into the puzzle. "Did Rubin meet Litvak at Mallard's Garage?"

"I don't know."

Probably. That must have been the business important enough to make Rubin delay his start for Phoenix. Probably figured he could make up the time by driving all night. And Rubin left Mallard's Garage in Litvak's car. "How did Rubin get out to Knife Springs?"

"Borrowed a horse from Ramey Many Coats. Rode out to show me that paper." Another long pause. "That land, it was our daddy's. Daddy gave it to Rubin to make sure Rubin could stay a member of the tribe, but now Rubin wanted to sell it. It was the wrong thing to do and I told him that and we fought. We fought like brothers, real bad. I killed him with this knife." His fingers tapped his boot top, hidden beneath the sheath of his denim pants leg.

They listened to the whisper of the wind as a gust died away. After a while, Ray asked, "But now you plan to sell the land?"

"No. I was just going to sell the water. Like Rubin was going to do at first. Keep enough for my sheep, keep the land. Just sell some of the water. Ramey Many Coats said the tribal council would let me do this. He knew I would never sell the land to him."

"You're working with Ramey Many Coats now?"

"Kind of. Without his land, my water wouldn't sell; without my water, Ramey couldn't get no casino. I had to. But Ramey's got strong medicine, so I wanted to ask Henry Begay about that, too."

Wager said, "Somebody came to your house asking for you. Was that Litvak?"

Luther gazed off down the wash and nodded. "Must be. I told him I needed more than fifty thousand and I would keep the land, too. I told him I wanted a hundred thousand, now, or no water." He explained, "Ramey Many Coats said the white men have that much money and I better ask for that much." His thick fingers gently brushed to safety a gleaming black beetle poised on thin, nervous legs in the sand between his boots. "Litvak got mad, said I was a goddamn thief. Goddamn Indian. Said I better do what Rubin promised and sell the land to Ramey for fifty thousand dollars and do it real soon or he would shoot me dead."

Ray finally spoke. "Ramey told you to ask for more money?"

"Said it would cost a lot to make the tribal council say it was OK to sell the water off the reservation. That I would have to give them a lot of good gifts and that if I didn't ask Litvak for more, I wouldn't have nothing left."

Wager asked, "What about the other government man, the one who was shot a couple weeks ago: Larry Kershaw. Who shot him?"

"I don't know. Wasn't me."

And no reason to lie, now, if it was. "Who told you Litvak was coming for you?"

"Ramey. Rode out to Knife Springs to tell me. Said Litvak couldn't wait no more because he was running out of time. Said he stood to lose all his money and even his ranch unless I sold the land to Ramey now. Said if I didn't, Litvak was going to kill me and then offer the fifty thousand to Cerise and get her to sign the paper. Ramey wanted me to sign right then, but I didn't."

Wager said, "You moved Rubin's body to the highway?"

The tall crown of the black hat bobbed. "Used his horse. Took all night." Wager could hardly hear his next words. "My brother."

"You and Rubin fought, and you killed him while you were fighting," said Ray. "Maybe you can get off with manslaughter instead of murder. Spend a lot less time in jail."

Luther shrugged again, his voice flat and hopeless. "We fought hard—real blood fight. Maybe he would've killed me if I didn't kill him first. But all the same, I wanted to kill him. I meant to kill him." And again, softly, "My brother."

Ray mixed a muffled grunt of sympathy with a long sigh. "But you waited here for us," he said. "You turned yourself in to us and you've confessed to killing Rubin. That will help you."

"It wasn't you."

"What wasn't?"

"Not you I'm waiting for. Him." The domed crown of the hat tilted down the wash. "He's coming. Litvak. I been hearing his truck coming up the wash." A shrug. "It's the Many Coats's hex."

"How close—" But Wager's words were sliced by the sizzling noise of a giant insect and then the sand beside Luther exploded under a solid, heavy punch. Wager flung himself sideways off the rock, his eyes registering Luther's blank face as the still sitting man looked up toward the far side of the wash and the popping explosion that was felt as much as heard. Then a second solid thunk and Luther flew up and back, thrown by the force of a round while Ray, flat on his stomach and writhing like a lizard, crawled frantically toward the shelter of an outcropping.

The horses, tossing and neighing, cantered sideways with their eyes wide and ringed with white, to stare, frightened, at the sprawled men, unsure whether to flee. Wager, rolling now, twisting to make a difficult target, flailed toward the trailing reins of Luther's pinto to grab them and lunge against the warm hide of the skittering and snorting animal. He yanked the rifle from its scabbard, then dove into the shadow of the cedar as another burst of sand flung stinging grains against his cheek; he rolled behind the cover of the cedar's thick and flaking trunk.

"There—" Ray pulled quickly back behind his spur of rock as a bullet rang hot and close through the air. Wager followed his gesture and saw a thin puff of smoke blur the line of rock and sky near a spur of layered white stone. He thumbed the safety off and balanced the stubby rifle, holding the front blade square and level in the notch of the rear sight, concentrating on the flat tip of the front blade more than the target as he gently squeezed the unfamiliar trigger—holding his impatience for the kick of the rifle, steadying his breath and trying not to think about how long the trigger pull was taking—but focusing on the blade and holding the sight picture and steady on the pull . . . steady. . . . The rifle bucked, but Wager didn't hear it; he was already levering the next round into the chamber and settling back against the solid earth, his elbow under the weapon's barrel and his finger tightening again as he breathed out, slowly in— hold the sight picture . . . Again the kick and a third time. The splat of an incoming round followed by the muffled punch of the rifle up on the ridge—the bullet was close, its shattered metal jacket screaming off behind him, leaving the tangy, chemical smell of scorched copper. Litvak had him sighted in now. Off to his left Wager was aware of movement: Ray grappling with the horses to get them under control and tied out of sight. Luther had started making noises and crawling blindly somewhere, but Wager concentrated on the target. Steady breathing, sight picture, rhythmic, gentle pull on the trigger with only the tip of his forefinger—just like the firing line, just like in Vietnam, and hold that sight picture—a movement slightly off his front sight. A round smacked through the cedar's branches inches above his head, spraying thick twigs and a slower rain of tree needles, and Wager, with a shift of his torso, adjusted his sights. The weapon's kick surprised him in the right way, now that he had the feel of its trigger, and this time he could see a trace of something, cloth maybe: and the front sight crystallized in his gaze, black and razor sharp in outline and balanced in the rear notch, and the rifle surprised him again.

"You got him!"

His eye watering with the strain of intense sighting, Wager blinked. He stared across at the far side of the wash. He watched for movement near the outcropping, listened for sound, waited. The stock of the rifle lay an inch from his ready cheek. A fly buzzed somewhere.

"You got him," Ray said again. "I saw him drop."

"How's Luther?"

The short, quick crunch of boots running through sand behind Wager. "Lung shot. I don't know how long he'll live." A muffled grunt and a soft sound of dragging as Ray pulled the wounded man into the shade beside Wager. "Cover me," and the tribal policeman was sprinting across the wash, dodging erratically as he ran crouched toward the shelter of broken rock tumbled down from around the white spur. Wager, the rifle aimed at the target, watched the sweat-stained back of Ray's denim shirt pause against a boulder, then dart out of sight, flicker above the large rock, disappear again. A minute or two later, Ray stood against the skyline and waved an arm. His voice carried across the emptiness of the wash. "He's down!"

25

THEY USED LITVAK'S pickup truck to carry the wounded men. Wager drove. Luther, gray with death but maybe still breathing, lay jammed and still in the cab's small jump seat. Litvak, his ankles cuffed together and his searched, empty pockets dangling inside out, sat in the passenger seat with his eyes closed, sweating with pain and grunting as the truck lurched and jolted slowly across rock and ledge. His scratched face was streaked with dried blood, and his tongue, when it wiped across his chapped lips, was coated sticky white with thirst. A strip of horse blanket wrapped his shoulder and arm and held in place the soggy compress Ray had found in his emergency kit. In front of the truck on horseback, the tribal policeman guided Wager across the country and led two horses behind him as they wound down and out of the broken country that was the face of the plateau they had left. Ahead lay an expanse of brown, brush-filled desert that formed the next wide plateau below. Beyond that wide shelf Wager could glimpse part of yet another, lower plateau. The grinding whine of the four-wheel drive sounded like a giant insect.

At the foot of the thrusting buttresses of gray-and-yellow earth, where gullies spewed their sand in alluvial fans onto the next level, Ray reined in his horses and pulled the transmitter out of a saddlebag. "Might be able to reach somebody from here." Wager rested wearily against the hot steering wheel and watched the man speak into the battery-powered radio. Beside him, Litvak grunted and twisted against a spasm of pain from his wounded shoulder and splintered collarbone. He glared at Wager out of eyes that were bloodshot with pain and which made the pale hairs of his eyebrows seem even blonder. Wager looked back at him.

"Feel good?"

The voice croaked, "You son of a bitch."

"Makes me feel good. After what you and Nichols and Gregory did."

"We should've buried you." He panted. "Give me some more water."

Wager handed the man the canteen. Water had been the price of Litvak's earlier confession about beating Wager senseless—Wager sloshing the water loudly as the truck lurched, splashing some over his face and chest in the broiling heat of the slowly moving cab, spitting a mouthful out of the window. All while Litvak slowly seeped more blood and his tongue swelled and ran more and more often across his crisping lips.

He smiled at the man who grunted and winced to lift the canteen to his dry mouth. "Want to tell me about Larry Kershaw, too?"

Litvak stopped swallowing, face taut beneath the dust and dried blood. "What about him?"

"I figure you killed him. Was it with or without the help of Nichols and Gregory?"

"You don't know crap." He choked back a cough and grunted at the spasm. "You're full of crap!"

"It was to throw us off the reason for the other murders, wasn't it? The FBI, Sheriff Spurlock, the people on the reservation who might raise hell if they found out what you and Ramey were planning. Kill a BLM man, set off a few bombs, make people think it was the Posse . . ."

Litvak closed his eyes.

"We've got you for attempted murder." Wager glanced back at the silent figure cramped behind his seat. "Looks like first-degree murder, now. That's the death sentence, Litvak. But maybe your lawyer can work a deal with the DA if you clear up the Kershaw killing, too. Maybe you get life instead of execution—you know, guilty plea and full confession as a sign to the court of your sincere and heartfelt remorse."

"Go to hell!" But the heat had gone out of Litvak's words and he was thinking over what Wager had said.

Ray had finally reached someone and he nodded to a voice on the radio. Then he leaned toward the truck window from his saddle, glancing once at the backseat and then keeping his eyes on Wager. "Helicopter should be here in half an hour, forty-five minutes."

SPURLOCK WAS WAITING for Wager when, on its second trip, the orange rescue helicopter settled in a cloud of dust blown up from a dirt runway just outside La Sal.

"Luther Del Ponte's dead." The heavyset man held his Stetson against the rotor wash of the clattering machine that began to lift away.

Wager, face turned against the flying dust, nodded. "Looked that way in the truck." The man's death might be a shame and it had upset Ray, but Wager didn't feel much of anything about it. He really thought Luther got what he wanted, and it also saved the taxpayers the cost of a trial and of housing one more lifer. "I'm filing charges against Louis Gregory and Bradley Nichols—assault on an officer."

"They the ones beat you up?"

"That's what Litvak said. They helped him."

Spurlock watched the helicopter move swiftly away, toward the south and the hospital in Montezuma County, an orange dot whose straining engine popped as it struggled for the altitude to clear the distant mountains. "Stan told me he and Bradley Nichols set off those bombs. Said he killed Larry Kershaw, too. Did it so people wouldn't start thinking the other deaths were related to the Flying W project." The sheriff spat and watched the white dot land on the earth. "Scraped up every penny he had for that investment. Borrowed against his ranch, everything."

"Did he tell you that Nichols and Gregory helped with Kershaw's murder, too?"

"No. Said it was just him. Used the same rifle he used on Luther. I reckon ballistics will verify it. Said he did it alone—was very clear about that, in fact."

Wager heard what Spurlock was really saying. "I intend to file charges, Sheriff."

"Any citizen's got a right to do that. And I guess I couldn't really blame you if you did." His wide chest rose and fell with a deep sigh. "But you know Nichols is already in custody. Durkin and his lawyer worked out a deal: lesser charges for a guilty plea on two of the bombings."

"So what's he get, six months?"

"No less than two years. Plus a pretty hefty fine."

"When he finishes that, he can move into state prison for assault on an officer."

"I wish you wouldn't, Wager. Nichols had a lot of money in that Flying W deal, too, and now it's all gone. There's a good chance he'll lose that ranch of his if he spends more time in prison. And Louis Gregory was just dumb, that's all: he just went along with Litvak and Nichols because he was drunk. All this," he shook his head, "all these killings, a lot of people in the county are hurting now. Litvak has relatives who didn't have anything to do with this—that new wife. And a daughter by his first wife. They're going to suffer this for the rest of their lives. Rubin had a family, too. And so did the other Indians. Now Durkin's gone and thank God he's not stirring up any more folks,

but there's a lot of healing needed around here." Another sigh.
"So I wish we could just say it's all over now."

Wager gazed across the expanse of piñon and brush-dotted
earth that lay as level as a pond out to the western horizon. Here
and there beyond the rim of earth peeked the snowcap of a
mountain range. With the fading noise of the helicopter, the
silence returned, deepened by the rustle of stiff grass in the
wind. "Nichols and Gregory, they're friends of yours?"

"No. And I don't know if they voted for me, either. Don't
much care, Wager, tell you the truth. But Nichols's got a wife
and children. They all got wives and children, and those people
are my neighbors. A lot of people who don't have anything to do
with any of this are caught up in it even if they don't want to be.
And they live here, Wager. In this county. My county."

As it was, both Ramey Many Coats and Ronald Pyne would
get off. There was no evidence to connect either of them to the
murders, nothing a lawyer couldn't suppress, anyway. The only
penalty they would pay for making so much bad medicine would
be the crash of their plans for their little Las Vegas. Ray had
told Wager this would also be the end of the Many Coats's
ownership of the tribal council. When the people on the reservation learned what Ramey had tried to do, the man and his
influence would be finished.

Wager studied the pale blue of the horizon and the meandering lip of a nearby gully. The bright green of new leaves
covered the once wintry branches of cottonwoods. What Spurlock was talking about was community—the sense of what one
person ought to owe another just because they shared the same
land and breathed the same air. It was a fragile thing, Wager
knew, that sense of community. "Yeah. Well. What the hell,
forget it then." It was a thing that needed all the help it could
get.